Cal's eyes sauntered back to her body, only this time she felt...worshiped.

So much so, that Dawn didn't even object when he took a step closer, then closer still, to lay one large, gentle hand on her still-flat belly.

She swallowed. Twice. Once from a plain old-fashioned rush of awareness, the second time from something achy and weird that she couldn't even define.

"Tell you what," he said. "Let me stay for your checkup, then we'll spend a couple of hours together, just for us. How about it?"

For a moment she was sorely tempted, then her senses returned. "There is no 'us,' Cal. There's never been an 'us.'"

And quit standing there making this so damn hard. Quit making me long for things that can't be.

Dear Reader,

What better way to start off a new year than with six terrific new Silhouette Intimate Moments novels? We've got miniseries galore, starting with Karen Templeton's *Staking His Claim*, part of THE MEN OF MAYES COUNTY. These three brothers are destined to find love, and in this story, hero Cal Logan is also destined to be a father—but first he has to convince heroine Dawn Gardner that in his arms is where she wants to stay.

For a taste of royal romance, check out Valerie Parv's *Operation: Monarch*, part of THE CARRAMER TRUST, crossing over from Silhouette Romance. Policemen more your style? Then check out Maggie Price's *Hidden Agenda*, the latest in her LINE OF DUTY miniseries, set in the Oklahoma City Police Department. Prefer military stories? Don't even try to resist *Irresistible Forces,* Candace Irvin's newest SISTERS IN ARMS novel. We've got a couple of great stand-alone books for you, too. Lauren Nichols returns with a single mom and her protective hero, in *Run to Me*. Finally, Australian sensation Melissa James asks *Can You Forget?* Trust me, this undercover marriage of convenience will stick in your memory long after you've turned the final page.

Enjoy them all—and come back next month for more of the best and most exciting romance reading around, only in Silhouette Intimate Moments.

Yours,

Leslie J. Wainger
Executive Editor

Please address questions and book requests to:
Silhouette Reader Service
U.S.: 3010 Walden Ave., P.O. Box 1325, Buffalo, NY 14269
Canadian: P.O. Box 609, Fort Erie, Ont. L2A 5X3

Staking His
Claim
KAREN TEMPLETON

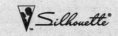
Silhouette®

INTIMATE MOMENTS™

Published by Silhouette Books

America's Publisher of Contemporary Romance

 SILHOUETTE BOOKS

ISBN 0-373-27337-1

STAKING HIS CLAIM

This edition published by arrangement with Harlequin Books S.A.

® and TM are trademarks of Harlequin Books S.A., used under license.
Trademarks indicated with ® are registered in the United States Patent
and Trademark Office, the Canadian Trade Marks Office and in other
countries.

Visit Silhouette at www.eHarlequin.com

Printed in U.S.A.

Books by Karen Templeton

Silhouette Intimate Moments

Silhouette Yours Truly

†How To Marry a Monarch
*Weddings, Inc.
**The Men of Mayes County

KAREN TEMPLETON,

a Waldenbooks bestselling author and RITA® Award nominee, is the mother of five sons and living proof that romance and dirty diapers are not mutually exclusive terms. An Easterner transplanted to Albuquerque, New Mexico, she spends far too much time trying to coax her garden to yield roses and produce something resembling a lawn, all the while fantasizing about a weekend alone with her husband. Or at least an uninterrupted conversation.

She loves to hear from readers, who may reach her by writing c/o Silhouette Books, 233 Broadway, Suite 1001 New York, NY 10279, or online at www.karentempleton.com.

Acknowledgments

Without the following people's willingness
to answer what must have, at times,
seemed like the dumbest questions on earth,
this book would not have been possible:

To Nicole Burnham and Douglas Onsi
for help with Dawn's career path

To Wendy Wade Morton, DVM, of Golden Gait Farms,
who's always there to answer my horse-related questions

and to
Mike Jackson from the OK Dept. of Human Services
for his assistance with child welfare issues

Chapter 1

None of this had been her choice.

Not the car, a leprous, pumpkin-orange GTO with one front fender painted, inexplicably, baby blue. Not the trip itself—as if she had time to schlep back to Oklahoma with all those pending cases sitting on her desk nearly two thousand miles away. And God knows—she waited out a wave of nausea—not the reason for the trip.

Well, that wasn't exactly true. The outcome might not have been her choice, but the events leading up to it definitely had been.

So much for living for the moment.

"No shame, no blame," Dawn Gardner muttered as she drove up in front of the single-story, sprawling farmhouse, still cinnamon brown with white-and-dark-green trim as it had always been. Edging a lawn faded from the early September heat, the same deep-pink roses bloomed, as they always had, only now against a backdrop of tangled deadwood. Cottonwoods stirred listlessly in the breeze, as if worn-out from the effort of shading the house for a whole summer, their lazy susurration no competition for the late-afternoon drone of a bumper crop of cicadas. The mingled scents weighting the humid air—of horse and fresh cut hay, the sweet, heady tang of overripe fruit—assaulted both her reluctant memory and her hypersensitive nose, making her stomach pitch. Making her feel... untethered, like a soul in limbo.

A retriever mix, whose name she'd forgotten, his coat flashing gold in the late-day sun, sauntered over to the car with a halfhearted *woof.* She smiled, patting the door so he'd come close enough for her to pet. As she did, her gaze meandered to the front porch step, only one riser up from the yard. Memory nudged into view a pair of children, a boy and a girl, sitting there as they had hundreds of times. They might have been six or seven, the boy—much younger than his two older brothers, who were already in high school—boasting features that foretold of the handsome man he would eventually become, with heavy-lashed eyes, green as new grass, and thick blond hair that refused to be tamed. A little spoiled, perhaps, being the baby, but not a whiner. And not a tease.

About the same height as the boy then, with long strawberry-blond hair her mother refused to cut, the girl liked that about the boy, that he never put her down. While their mothers chatted in the kitchen, the boy would often take the girl with him while he did his chores around the farm, mostly feeding the animals—pigs, goats, chickens, rabbits. The horses. Since they were too young to be around the huge animals by themselves, sometimes his daddy would be with them, a tall man with a white crewcut, dark eyes and an easy smile who always had Tootsie Rolls in his overall pockets and called the girl "young lady," but not the way people did when you did something wrong.

Sometimes she envied the boy his daddy, although she never let on.

Dawn's inner ear perked up at fragments of a conversation she hardly knew she remembered, drifting over from the porch.

"Maybe Ryan and Hank don't want to stick around, but I'm never gonna leave here," the boy said, crunching into an apple from one of the trees off to the side of the house. Totally at ease with himself, in himself, he leaned back on his elbow, an expression on his dust-smudged face the girl would later peg as *serene*.

Even at that age she thought it was peculiar, not wanting to see what else was out there in the world, and she told him so. Her mama had taken her into Tulsa once when she was five, and all she could think about was getting to go back someday. Except Mama was always busy helping ladies have babies and couldn't afford the time away very often, she said, in case one of the babies decided to come while she was gone.

The boy shrugged and took another bite of his apple. "Whaddya wanna do now?" he said. "Play with my trucks or somethin'?"

"Trucks are dumb."

"Not as dumb as stupid old dolls."

"Well, I don't play with dolls, do I?"

The boy gave her a funny look. "But you're a girl."

"So? That doesn't mean I hafta play with dolls. Besides, that's sexist."

"Ooooh, I'm gonna tell! You said 'sex.'"

"I did not. I said *sexist.* That's when somebody thinks you oughta like or do something because you're a girl or a boy. Mama told me. An' she said nobody should hafta act a certain way just 'cause people expect 'em to."

The boy threw his half-eaten apple off into the yard. One of the farm dogs trotted over to investigate, but since it wasn't meat, he let it be. "You're weird, you know that?" the boy said. "And anyway, so why *don't* you play with dolls?"

"I dunno. Maybe because I see so many babies and little kids when Mama takes me with her on her 'pointments? Babies cry a lot, you know. And make real stinky messes in their diapers. And their hands get tangled in my hair." The girl sank her chin into the palm of her hand, waiting out the peculiar feeling she got sometimes, like an itchiness on the inside that you couldn't scratch. It wasn't fair, having to get up in the middle of the night to go with Mama when one of her ladies had her baby. But thinking about that made the itchiness worse, so she pushed the thoughts away and said instead, ''We could read, maybe.''

''Reading's boring,'' the boy said, but the girl had a pretty good idea he said that because he didn't read as well as she did. ''I got a new puzzle. Wanna do that?''

''I don't like working puzzles with you, you never do 'em right.''

The boy thought for a minute, then said, ''We could go dig in the backyard if you want.''

''S'too hot.'' They sat there for a long time, listening to their own thoughts—well, the girl was, anyway, she was never sure what the boy thought about, if anything—until she suddenly said, if for no other reason than the silence was beginning to hurt her head, ''Brenda Sue Mosely called me a bad word today.''

The boy looked like this could be interesting. ''What kinda bad word?''

''I can't say it.''

''Sure you can. I mean, I won't tell.'' When she slanted her eyes at him, he crossed his heart. ''Promise.''

So she leaned over and whispered the word in his ear, thinking she liked how he smelled, like earth and animals and apple, and how it made her feel safe for some reason. She'd heard the word several times before, but she wasn't exactly sure what it meant. She just knew it was meant to hurt her.

''Brenda Sue Mosely is stupid,'' was all the boy said, giving the girl the impression he didn't know what the word meant, either. ''If she was a boy, I'd beat her up for you.''

''I don't want you beatin' anybody up for me, Cal Logan, you hear me? I can stick up for myself….''

''Dawn? What the hell?''

She jumped a foot, her memories scattering like the roaches in her apartment when she turned on the light in the middle of the night. Panic sliced through her, knotting her stomach. His long, denimed legs wading through an entourage of dogs of all shapes, sizes and parentages, a very much grown-up Cal Logan approached the car, his face creased with concern. A cool breeze ruffled that same unkempt hair, now darker than it had been as a child, and *bam!* Just like that, even though the thought of sex with anybody right now made her green around the gills, every nerve ending she had screamed, *"Remember?"*

Not fair.

All her life, Cal had been just Cal. Well, mostly. There'd been the odd tickle of fantasy from time to time, but then, what else was there to do in this town besides fantasize? Their single sexual encounter had been an aberration, a momentary detour off the Road of Reason. She knew that, he knew that, they'd discussed it like rational adults the morning after and she had put the whole episode behind her, chalking it up to One of Those Things. Thought she had, anyway. Her current, totally unexpected condition didn't change the aberration aspect of this. His "just Cal-ness."

Except, now, as her gaze slithered over the body that was no longer a mystery underneath his workshirt and jeans, she silently dubbed herself six kinds of fool. What on earth had she been thinking? That she could simply forget how good the man was in bed? How good he made *her?* That within twenty minutes he'd changed her mind about sex from *whatever* to *whoa?*

That she'd start salivating at the sight of him?

Be that as it may. Salivating didn't change anything, other than perhaps raising her standards for future encounters. If there were any future encounters, which at the moment looked highly doubtful. One minute they'd been old, albeit lapsed, friends, the next they were lovers. Unfortunately, it was about this gaping hole in between. A hole they'd never, ever, be able to fill in a million years.

Except for this child they'd made that would now bridge that gap, in some ways, forever.

Just as Cal had bridged the gap between his house and her car. Dawn's swallow wedged in her throat, mere inches above her heart. Then she noticed he seemed far more interested in the car than her. She couldn't decide whether to be relieved or offended.

"This Scooter Johnson's old GTO?"

"Uh-huh."

Cal chuckled. With good reason. Her mother had taken the ghastly vehicle in trade for delivering the Johnsons' second baby, but Scooter had definitely gotten the better end of that deal.

"Honey, even with you in it, that is one butt-ugly car." His light mood abruptly departed, however, when he once again focused on her face. The man wasn't stupid. And by the time she'd forced herself to open the car door, untangle herself from her long broomstick skirt and haul herself to her feet, she could tell from his expression that he'd jumped to the only conclusion he could have.

Hope struggled for purchase in worried green eyes. "Dawn? Why are you here?"

Dogs milled about them, panting and wriggling; birds chirped; yellowing leaves danced against a peaceful blue sky in a place as far away from the life she'd made for herself as the moon. And Dawn, who still had no idea what to think about any of this herself, hauled in a huge breath and said, "Remember the condom that broke?"

Then her knees gave way.

A few choice epithets flashed through Cal's brain as he carted Dawn into the family room, that long, crinkly skirt of hers clinging to him like plastic wrap, her soft white blouse smelling of flowers. With a grunt he clumsily laid her on the old tan leather sofa that had stood in the center of the scuffed, slanted wooden floor ever since he could remember. Ethel, the Logans' housekeeper for even longer, came streaking in from the kitchen, a glass of water trembling at the end of a spotted, chicken-skinned arm.

"I saw it all from the kitchen window. She sick or something? Oh! She's comin' 'round!"

Cal felt set apart, like he was watching one of those reality shows on TV, as Dawn stirred and grimaced and finally opened her eyes. Talk about your life changing in an instant. He had thought—hoped—when he hadn't heard after a month, that they'd been lucky. Not that the idea of making babies with Dawn Gardner hadn't crossed his mind a time or six over the past decade or so. He just didn't figure the fantasy was reciprocated, was all. Actually, judging from the edge to her voice when she mentioned the busted condom, he was sure of it.

"Here, sugar," Ethel was saying, simultaneously offering Dawn the water and wriggling her ample butt, stuffed as usual into a pair of jeans made for a woman a good size or two smaller, onto the edge of the sofa beside her. Cal noticed her peach-colored hair could do with a touch-up. "Drink this."

Dawn obeyed, her waist-length braid slipping back over her shoulder as she struggled to sit up so she could take the glass. It was always easier to just do what Ethel asked.

"You look absolutely terrible, child," Ethel said. "The heat got to you?"

Now fully upright, if still wobbly, Dawn glanced at Cal, then smiled for Ethel. "That must be it," she said, taking a sip of the water.

Ethel crossed her arms over the sleeveless blouse crammed into those too-tight jeans and said, "Uh-huh," which prompted Cal to ask if she didn't have something she needed to be tending to in the kitchen, because he was not about to discuss this very private matter with anybody—not even Ethel—before he'd have five seconds to come to terms with it himself. News'd get out soon enough.

Still, he was hard-pressed not to wither under Ethel's glare before she popped to her feet, spun around hard enough to make her tennis shoe squeak against the floor, and marched back to the kitchen. The silence left in her wake was so heavy, Cal half expected the room to tilt.

Dawn noiselessly set the glass down on the end table, then fingered the lace table topper, yellow with age. "I can't believe this is still here." She glanced around the room, frowning slightly at the collection of Early American furniture, the worn fake oriental rugs, the card table set up by the window with a half-finished jigsaw puzzle spread out on it. It occurred to him she hadn't seen the living room the last time she was here, neither of them being much interested in a house tour just then. "Incredible. Everything's exactly the same. From when we were kids, I mean. Even the piano," she added with a nod toward the baby grand taking up the far corner of the room.

Cal linked his arms across his chest. "I like it like this."

Her deep-brown eyes met his, her fingers curled around the edge of the sofa. That slightly pitying expression women got when faced with home-decor issues flickered across her features before she said, on a sigh, "I'm sorry. I didn't mean to scare you, showing up out of the blue like this."

Worry settled into the pit of his stomach like it planned on staying for a while. She looked like death warmed over, too pale, too thin, no makeup, bits of her tea-colored hair—still long, even after all those years of living back East—hanging like tipsy snakes around her face. And yet, even motionless, she seemed to vibrate with the same restless energy that had marked her as different from everyone he knew—especially himself—from the time they were kids.

"No problem. You feelin' better?"

"As opposed to being dead? Yeah, I suppose."

They needed to talk, he knew that, but he didn't have a clue what to say. Or think, even. He kept trying to drive the words *I'm gonna be a daddy* through his skull, but they wouldn't go. To be truthful, Cal had worked his way through a fair number of condoms in his time—he wasn't much into torch-carrying—but this was the first time one had let him down. That it should do so at the precise moment somebody's egg was moseying on down the pike was just not fair.

Panic raced through him like a brushfire.

He glanced outside, toward the barn and the pasture beyond. Toward that part of his life that was still what it had been ten minutes ago. It was selfish, yeah, but right now he needed to be somewhere where he felt like he knew what the hell he was doing. He looked back at Dawn, met her questioning gaze.

"I don't suppose you'd be up to takin' a short walk? Just to the pasture?"

Her answer was to take another sip of water, nod and get to her feet, that multicolored skirt floating around her ankles as she wordlessly followed Cal outside into the molten early-evening sunshine. The dogs massed around them, tongues lolling, butts wagging; Dawn spoke to each one, softly, her words still tinged with an Oklahoman tang, even after all this time. He also noticed, when he looked over, that her hair flamed.

And so did he.

No point denying either his memory of their encounter two months ago or his body's reaction to her, he realized as they made their way to the pasture where several of his mares still grazed, yet to be brought in for the night. He knew she'd always felt uneasy in her own body, her legs too long, her breasts too large for her frame. So he'd been sure to show her that night—Cal had always been one to take advantage of an opportunity—the truth of the matter in as many ways as he could think of. Not that the size of her breasts mattered one whit to him, but he had to admit God had outdone Himself this time.

And maybe it wasn't right, his thinking about her breasts at this moment, but it wasn't like he could forget them, for one thing. And for another, he'd always thought of sex as kind of a mental comfort food. It was hardly all he thought about, but when things got tough, he found letting his mind wander down that path brought him a certain measure of peace.

"Cal? Wait a sec…"

He turned. Dawn was leaning against the trunk of a cottonwood, her hands cupped over her nose and mouth. "The odor," she mumbled from behind her hands. At his probably perplexed expression—it was just a little fresh dung, for heaven's sake, and the wind was blowing away from them at that—she added, "Everything smells…stronger right now."

So much for peaceful thoughts. Not even thinking about Dawn's breasts was going to do it this time.

"Oh. Uh…you wanna go back…?"

But she shook her head, pushing away from the tree and plastering on a fake smile. "Nope. All better. Let's go."

Never mind that she looked like she was gonna hurl for sure.

In the pasture, most of the mares, all pregnant, as well as the ten or so foals he was still hoping to sell before winter set in, stood in sociable clumps of twos and threes, like folks at a barbecue. Cinnamon, a sleek and sassy bay, pregnant with her ninth foal, ambled over to the fence, begging as usual. In this light, the mare's coat and Dawn's hair were nearly the same color.

Cal patted the mare's glistening neck, chuckling when she nibbled at his hair. The mare whuffled, nodding toward Dawn, then back to him.

"Cindy, meet Dawn. She's gonna have a baby, too."

He saw Dawn's attention snap to him, but by then Cindy had cantilevered her massive head over the fence for some loving. Dawn was smart enough, or needy enough, not to turn down the horse's offer. She linked the fingers of one hand in the horse's bridle, stroking the mare's white stripe with the other, an expression on her face like she wanted to somehow sink into the mare's calmness and never come out. One of the barn cats, out for his evening hunt, rubbed up against her leg, marking her.

"She's gorgeous," Dawn said of the mare. "They all are. What are they?"

"Horses."

That got a laugh. Well, what you could hear around the snort. "No, doofus. I mean what…kinds. Breeds, whatever."

He smiled. "Quarter horses, mostly. But I've got a couple of mutts, too—the chestnut back by the fence is part Tennessee walker. And we think Josie, there—the dapple gray—might have some Arabian in her."

"How large is the herd?"

"On the permanent roster? Fifteen mares and a stallion I put out to stud. Plus the youngsters. All retired prizewinners or offspring of prizewinners. Good listeners with easygoing dispositions. And they all produce some real pretty foals."

"And you're doing okay?" The concern in her voice made him turn to meet her equally concerned eyes. "It can't be easy," she said gently, "making something like this work."

"I won't lie and say it is. Especially with foal prices taking a hit the way they've done the past couple of years. But the stud fees I get for Twister keep me afloat. In fact, I've almost finished buying out my brothers. By this time next year, this'll be all mine."

He watched her scan the new up-to-date barn replacing the old barns and outbuildings she would've remembered from when they were kids. "You've really found your niche in life, haven't you?"

"I guess I have," he said, trying to peg whatever he thought he'd heard in her voice, even though figuring out what went on inside women's heads was definitely not his strong suit. "There's something, I don't know, honest and basic about working with horses. You treat 'em right, they'll return the favor and do their best for you. I get up in the morning, and even when there's a boatload of work to do, or even when I'm worried about one of my gals for one reason or another, I look forward to the day. How many people can say that? And really mean it?… Dawn? You okay?"

Her forehead lowered to the mare's muzzle, she muttered, "I'm sorry," although almost more to the horse than to him.

"For what?"

She gave him a doleful expression.

"Not for being pregnant?" he said.

"Maybe," she said on a rush of air. "I just keep feeling I should be apologizing for something. For falling into bed with you, if nothing else."

"Hey. Unless I missed something, that was a mutual decision. One I sure as hell didn't regret." She canted a look at him. "No, not even now."

"Never mind how stupid it was."

"Is that what you're thinking? That it was stupid?"

"Uh, yeah?"

"Well, that's just nuts."

"And now you're pissed."

"Hell, yes, if I'm readin' you correctly. Just because neither one of us expected more'n that one night doesn't mean it was stupid. Or meaningless." He leaned his forearms on the top of the fence, trying to tamp down his irritation. Trying even harder to understand it. Cindy, realizing she was no longer the focus of the conversation, clopped off, her black tail swishing. "Okay, so we got more out of it than we'd bargained. And yeah, I suppose I'm gonna be in shock for a while about that. But that doesn't mean anybody has anything to be sorry for. Actually, if you're lookin' to blame somebody, it wasn't you who forgot to check the date on those condoms, was it?"

A pained smile crossed her face. "Should I be flattered it had been that long?"

Cal hesitated, then said, "To tell you the truth…I grabbed one out of the wrong box. The one I should've thrown out when I bought the new one the month before."

"You know, I could have lived without knowing that."

"Thought women wanted men to be honest with them."

"Not *that* honest."

He glanced over. She was leaning against the fence much like he was, but everything about her was tight—her set mouth, her hands, knotted together in front of her, her shoulders, rising and falling in tandem with her shallow, hurried breaths.

Cal gazed back over the pasture, over what had been his life for more than ten years. Building up his breeding business had given him something to focus on after his parents died, something he could count on to bring him satisfaction and pleasure even when his personal life sucked. He would be lying if he didn't admit, at least to himself, that he didn't need this distraction, this monkey wrench in the orderly, safe, relatively painless life he'd made for himself. At the same time excitement tingled in his veins with the realization that the one thing that had eluded him so far—the promise of family—was suddenly within his grasp.

He stole a quick look at the side of Dawn's face, her expression resolute. Well, the promise of part of a family, anyway. Where he saw hope, however, his guess was that she saw catastrophe. Where he saw opportunity, she clearly saw entrapment.

And her fears were doing a damn good job of kicking his wide awake.

"How come you waited so long to say something?" he asked softly.

"Denial," came out on an exhaled breath. "I'd had a bad cold, thought maybe that screwed up my cycle." She gave a dry, humorless laugh. "Okay, I couldn't believe it. Didn't want to believe it."

The sun nestled a little closer to the horizon as they stood there, not looking at each other, not saying anything. One of the dogs sat down to scratch, jangling his tags; a couple of mares decided to get up a game of tag, their pounding hooves raising a cloud of dust. Cal kept thinking he was supposed to say something, to come up with some sort of solution. Instead, he could practically hear the wind whistling through the cavity where his brain was supposed to be.

"I guess you're sure—"

"Oh, yeah. I'm sure. And yes, I'm having the baby. And keeping it."

Her eyes darted to his, then away, as his stomach screeched to a halt a breath away from *splat!* "So you never considered—"

"I didn't say that." At what must have been his horrified expression, she pushed out a breath. "To be honest, my first thought was this can't be happening. And my second thought was how can I make it *un*happen? So I went for a walk. A long walk. A walk that took me past a family planning clinic. On purpose. And I stood there, staring at the door, visualizing walking up the steps, making an appointment…" Her eyes went wide, the words shooting from her mouth like a flock of freaked birds. "I'd never even thought about having a baby, Cal! Let alone like this! Who knows what kind of mother I'll make? For all I know, this could be a major disaster in the making—"

She let out a little yelp when Cal grabbed her by the shoulders. "And you can stop that kind of talk right now! You're gonna make a dynamite mother. Maybe not a normal one, but a damned good one."

She rolled her eyes, then said, "And you know this how?"

"Because I know you. Or at least, I did. And the Dawn I remember never did anything half-assed." Purely from reflex, his thumbs started massaging her shoulders. Purely from reflex—he assumed—she shivered slightly. "I'd be real surprised to find out you'd changed."

"Yeah, well, raising a kid isn't the same as acing a course. Or even winning a case. Which I don't always do, by the way."

"But—" He actually caught the thought before it sailed out of his big mouth, but only long enough to examine it and let it go, anyway. "But you were all set to get married."

"Oh." She sighed. "That. As it happens, Andrew wasn't all that hot on parenthood. And to be honest, I was ambivalent. About having kids, I mean."

"You got any idea why?"

That got a shrug. "Maybe because so much of my work revolves around children. I don't know." At his frown, she said, "I do a fair amount of pro bono work for the firm, most of it involving family issues. Many of the kids I see have been knocked around pretty badly. By life, by The Man, by—all too often—their own parents. And the looks on their faces…" The expression on hers twisted him inside out. "Oh, God, Cal, they'd break your heart. The way they want to trust so badly, and are so afraid to…"

Tears shone in her eyes. "Everybody says, don't get involved, don't let it become personal. Except that's the reason I became a lawyer to begin with, to try to make a difference. Lame as that might sound," she added with a wry smile. "But having a kid of my own…" She let loose another sigh, this one long and ragged. "I've never been one of those women who gets all mushy when they see someone else's baby or feel a pang of envy at seeing a pregnant woman, okay? I've never felt that having a child would complete me, because I never felt anything was missing to begin with. But here I am, pregnant. Pregnant and confused, and sick half the day, and scared. That's about all I know. And that I had to tell you. Beyond that, it's a blank. A very screwed-up, messy blank.''

Their gazes danced around each other for a second or two, then she took off for her car, leaving Cal so tangled up in his emotions, he had no idea which one prompted him to yell out, ''We could get married.''

She spun around, her mouth open. Then she burst out laughing.

''It wasn't that dumb a suggestion,'' he muttered, closing the space between them.

She crossed her arms when he reached her, that pitying look in her eyes again. ''Who'd you vote for in the last election?''

He told her, and she laughed again. The car door groaned when she opened it. ''We'd never survive the next presidential campaign. Besides, even if I was sticking around, you know as well as I do shotgun marriages rarely work out.''

He couldn't argue with her there. Of the three couples they'd gone to high school with who'd ''had'' to get married, only one was still together.

''Hold on.'' He clamped hold of the top of the door. ''What do you mean you're not sticking around?''

Her brows shot up. ''You honestly don't expect me to move back here just because I'm pregnant?''

''I didn't *expect* anything. But I sure as hell didn't think you'd drop a bombshell like this and just take off again!''

''I'm not. I'll be here until the end of the week.''

''Oh, well then. That's different.''

''Dammit, Cal…'' She smacked a loose hair out of her face. ''I know your life is here. But mine isn't. And hasn't been for a long time. I've invested far too much in my career, and Mama sacrificed too much to help me get there, to just drop it because I'm—we're—going to have a baby.''

Her words only added to the debris-laden whirlwind swirling around inside his head. Yes, he'd always accepted, even if he hadn't fully understood, that Haven could never provide Dawn with whatever it was that fed her soul, something he assumed she'd found in New York. And an hour ago he didn't even know about this baby. Yet he already knew not being able to see this child grow up, day by day, minute by minute, would kill him.

"And if you think I'm gonna settle for being an e-mail daddy," he said sharply, "you're more off your nut than I thought. You can be a lawyer anywhere. Even here."

"Right. As if there's room for more than one attorney in a town with a population of nine hundred."

"Hey, we're up to nine hundred and nine now. At least three people had babies last year, nobody died and a new family with four kids bought Ned MacAllister's property and are building on it. And besides, I hear Sherman Mosely's thinking of retiring. That heart attack he had last year put the fear of God in him. So maybe there would be—"

"And what kind of work would I do here? Help people make out their wills? Write up contracts? My life isn't something out of *Ally McBeal*. I don't spend my days handling frivolous cases and my nights boogying in some bar."

"I didn't figure you did."

"Then you should understand that I need to be someplace where I can make a real difference in people's lives. Those kids I told you about? They need me, Cal. And if I make partner, I can help them even more."

"In other words, Podunkville's petty little problems don't matter."

"I didn't say that! And I didn't mean that. It's just that…oh, hell—how can I possibly make you understand this without sounding like a snob? I'd feel stifled and useless here, can't you understand that?"

Cal slammed his palm against the car's roof. "And how the *hell* do you expect to raise a child together if we don't live in the same place?"

"I don't know! But I can't just give up my life!"

"Your work comes before your child, in other words."

"No!" Anguish swam in her eyes. "Oh, God, Cal—I may

be totally clueless, and I'm still in shock, too, and I may not know what kind of mother I'll make, but there's a reason I never got beyond looking at the front door of that clinic! It takes my breath, how much I already love this kid. And I'm prepared to give it anything it needs. But is it so wrong to not want to lose myself in the process?''

He felt his eyes blaze into hers. ''Is it so wrong for me to want to be a real part of my child's life?''

''Of course not, but—''

''A kid shouldn't have to grow up without its father, Dawn! And I'd think you'd be the last person to want to see that happen to your kid!''

Her face went rigid. Then she threw up her hands, shaking her head. ''I'm sorry. I'm too tired to talk about this anymore right now.'' He didn't hinder her when she climbed into the car. ''Maybe tomorrow?''

His chest all knotted up, Cal propped his now-stinging hand on the roof. ''You plannin' on changing your mind overnight?''

After a moment, she shook her head again.

''Well, honey—'' he let go and stood up straight ''—neither am I. So I'd say we're at an impasse, wouldn't you?''

He watched her peel out of the drive, wondering if it would have made things better or worse to admit he was every bit as scared as she was.

If not more.

Chapter 2

After he'd put up the horses for the night and returned to the house, all he did was prowl from room to room. An activity which finally drove Ethel, who was crocheting something or other in the living room because the TV reception was better in here, she said, over the edge.

"For pity's sake, boy! Either sit your backside down and talk to me or take it someplace else! And I already figured out she's pregnant, so there's one decision out of your hands."

He stared at the top of her pin-curled head—she was already "in for the night," as she put it. "How'd you know that?"

"Because it's true what they say. About pregnant women glowing. Even if her particular glow looks more like it's due to radioactive waste. Besides, why else would she be here?"

Cal sighed. Ethel clicked her tongue against the roof of her mouth, her crochet hook a blur. Whatever it was she was making, it was frilly and the most godawful shade of pink Cal had ever seen. Suddenly she plopped the whatever-it-was in her lap and peered at him over her reading glasses, with as much concern in those button eyes of hers as if she'd been his real mother. Which, considering she'd pretty much filled that gap in his life from the time he was nine, wasn't surprising. "Why don't you go see your brother?"

"Which one?"

"Does it matter?"

He almost cracked a smile at that. "And what good would that do?"

"Other than getting you out of my hair? I have no idea." She picked up her work again, weaving the hook in and out of all those little holes so fast it made him dizzy to watch. "But that's what big brothers are for—to talk things over with. Now that the two of them's finally figured out a thing or two about women, maybe they can share their wisdom. Besides, you'll be tellin' 'em the truth soon enough. Might as well get a jump on it."

Well, maybe she had a point at that. Not that he relished the thought of being around either just-married Ryan or about-to-be-married Hank, but since he was fresh out of bright ideas, what did he have to lose?

"Don't wait up," he said, heading out the door.

"I don't intend to," she said, adding a row of lime green to the godawful pink.

He'd stopped by Ryan's place first, but Maddie, his new wife—who, judging from the scent of warm fruit and fresh-baked pie crust rushing out the kitchen door from behind her, was busy making her next batch of pies to sell to Ruby's Café—had said he was on duty at the clinic tonight until ten and was there anything she could help him with? But Cal said, no, he didn't think so, and went on to Hank's.

His oldest brother, an ex-cop, ran the Double Arrow Motel and Guest Lodge on the outskirts of town, a fixer-upper he bought as a sort of therapy after his first fiancée's death a few years back. Not only had Hank made the dump into someplace respectable, but he even had a developer seriously interested in turning the place into a bona fide resort. And a few months back, damned if a second chance at love hadn't come along and crashed his pity-party.

And then stayed until every last guest was good and gone.

Now living in a modest two-story house at the edge of the motel property, Hank seemed understandably surprised at Cal's showing up unannounced, especially since the three brothers had grown apart after their father's death when Cal was fourteen. Ryan's and Hank's trials and tribulations on the road to true love during the past year, however, had driven the three brothers to talk to each other more than they had in the fifteen years before that.

Now it was Cal's turn.

Hank led Cal through the living room—painted some orange color that only Ethel could love—to the kitchen where he offered him a beer, which Cal gratefully accepted. Hank's teenaged daughter, Blair, sat at the kitchen table, her coppery hair gleaming under the lamp as she pored over what looked like an album.

"Wedding invitations," Hank said by way of explanation. He took a long swallow of his own beer and swept a hand through his short black hair. Falling in love with Jenna Stanton had worked miracles on a mug few people would ever have called good-looking, with its craggy features and twice-broken nose. Hank hadn't even known about his daughter until a few months ago, when Jenna, a widow herself, had come looking for him after her sister's—Blair's mother's—death and her subsequent discovery that Hank was Blair's father. The romance had just been a real nice, and totally unexpected, bonus.

"Lord help us," Hank said, "but I think we've got a wedding planner on our hands."

"Da-ad," the freckled teenager said, rolling her blue eyes and flashing her braces. "You think Jenna'll like this one?" She turned the album around. Both men stared at the prissy invitation she was pointing to, trying to figure out what set it apart from the eight other equally prissy invitations on the same page.

"I suppose you'll have to ask her when she gets back,"

Hank said, clearly already well-versed in how to take the easy way out.

"Where is Jenna, by the way?" Cal asked.

"Back in D.C., taking care of loose ends before moving here for good."

"Y'all decided on a date, yet?"

"Sunday after Thanksgiving, after Jen turns in her next book."

Leaving Blair to her search, they wandered out onto the back porch. As one, both men sank into twin wooden rocking chairs Hank said Jenna'd ordered from some catalogue or other. Hank's half-grown puppy, Mutt—the consensus was half black Lab, half German Shepherd—came bounding up the steps to them, planting his big black feet on Cal's knee.

"I hear Dawn's back," Hank said nonchalantly. Cal might've laughed if his gut hadn't felt like somebody'd filled it with a bucket of broken glass.

"You know, I'm beginning to think this entire town's clairvoyant."

"Nope. Luralene just happened to be standing in the doorway to the Hair We Are about the time Ivy and Dawn drove past this afternoon. I imagine the news has gotten clear to Claremore by now. Far as Pryor, at the very least." Hank glanced over, his expression unreadable in the dim light coming from the screen door, then took another swallow of beer. "What's got everyone speculatin', though, is *why* she's back. Especially since she was just here in July."

Cal stuck one booted foot up on the porch railing, pushing back the chair on its rockers as far as he dared. "Let's put it this way—looks like you and Ryan aren't the only ones to have fatherhood sprung on 'em this year."

Hank had the beer can halfway to his mouth; now he lowered it, glancing back to make sure they wouldn't be heard. "You got Dawn *pregnant?*"

"Yep."

Hank sat back in his chair, taking this in. Rocked some more. Then he said, "Remember that night you cheated me out of twenty bucks when we were playing pool? And I asked you whether anything happened between you and Dawn when she was here on the Fourth, and you wouldn't answer?''

"Well, now you know why I wouldn't answer. And I did not *cheat* you out of twenty dollars. Not my fault you can't play worth spit."

Several seconds passed before Hank said, "So…what's this mean? You two gettin' married?''

"Nope."

"She at least moving back here?''

"Nope."

"And I take it you're not sellin' up and moving back east with her?''

"Hell, no."

"Then what in tarnation—?''

"The way I see it," Cal said, "is what we've got here is a baby on the way, a pair of parents who probably shouldn't be having this baby together, and a whole bunch of questions without answers." He took a swallow of beer and said, "Make for one helluva crappy night, let me tell you. Well, except for the baby part. I mean, I wasn't exactly plannin' on it right now, but it could be worse."

Another several seconds passed before Hank said, "Yeah. It could be. She might've decided not to tell you at all. Then twelve or thirteen years down the road, you suddenly discover you have a kid."

At that moment the kid in question banged through the screen door to say good-night, bending over to give her father a hug and a kiss before going back inside. Both men sat and rocked for a moment, the rockers' creaking competing with a lone cicada buzzing its butt off.

"So what're you gonna do?''

Cal sighed. "Damned if I know. Our goin' to bed together was a fluke. Our havin' a baby an even bigger fluke—''

"And you've been sweet on her your whole life."

"You know, I've never given anybody cause to think that, so why—''

Hank just laughed. Cal rocked some more, thinking about that look on Dawn's face when she was talking about those kids she worked with. "Her life's back east. And there's nothing Haven, or I, can give her that could even begin to replace what she'd be giving up."

"Must've been some reason she got cozy with you."

"Yeah. Boredom."

"You know that for sure?"

Cal wiggled his bottle on his knee, frowning. "No. But maybe I've got better things to do than set myself up for a fall. There's a reason I didn't pursue her when we were in high school, you know. Even when we were kids, she practically buzzed with all the things she wanted to do, places she wanted to go. Causes she needed to champion. As we got older, it became crystal clear that Haven would never be enough for her. That *I'd* never be enough for her."

"So you think she's better than you?"

"No," he said, irritation dragging out the word. "Just different. Life here suits me. It never did Dawn. And it never would. Especially now."

"I see." The floorboards squawked when Hank leaned forward. "So answer me one thing."

"What's that?"

"All those gals you've dated over the years…how come you never settled down with any of 'em?"

"How the hell should I know? None of 'em…felt right, is all. Not for the long haul, anyway."

"Uh-huh. As in, none of 'em were…enough for you?"

"You're not hearing what I'm saying," Cal said wearily. "Dawn's a helluva lot more—" he banged the beer on the arm of the chair, fighting for the right word "—complex than I am."

Hank laughed. "All women are more complex than men, bozo brain."

"And who the hell are you to give me advice, anyway?"

Heavy dark brows shot up. "Hey. Nobody told you to come over here. All I'm saying is, don't sell yourself short. So the

two of you are different. Big deal. So're Jenna and me. And
look at our parents, for the love of Mike. A farmer and a classical pianist? Look—at least you've got a fighting chance to
see your kid grow up. That's more than I had. And if you don't
try…what's the alternative?''

From inside, the phone rang. Hank bounded out of the chair,
dog scrambling and screen door banging shut as he grabbed
the portable off the hall table. ''Well, hey there, yourself,
honey,'' Cal heard his brother say, and his heart did this stupid
thumping thing in his chest. He stood, as well, waving so long
through the door before heading back to his truck. Once back
out on the road, though, Hank's words hit Cal like a well-aimed
spit wad.

Why *had* Dawn ended up in his bed that night?

And, more important, why had he let her?

The answer whalloped him so hard, he nearly drove off the
road: because he figured nothing *would* come of it, that's why.

Because he thought he'd be safe. That since there was no
danger of her falling in love with him, the opposite was also
true.

If he hadn't've been driving, he would've banged his head
on the steering wheel. God knows his brain could use a little
loosening up, anyway. Because now, thanks to the most pitiful
excuse for doing something since Adam's blaming Eve about
the whole apple business, he'd fathered a child. If he wanted
any chance at all of being part of this child's life, he'd have
to convince the child's mother to stay in Haven. And if the
child's mother—a woman he'd never allowed himself to work
up strong feelings about for any number of reasons—did stay
in Haven, what were the odds that Cal's heart would mind its
own business and stay out of trouble?

And maybe he should stop thinking about the *what ifs*—
which was only depressing him—and start thinking about the
what nows, a regrettably long list headed up by Figuring Out
the Female Mind, with *Dawn* right there under subheading 1A.
Knowing what needed to happen and how to make that happen
were two different things. For this he needed an ally.

Preferably a female ally.

Preferably a female ally who knew Dawn pretty well.

Preferably a female ally who was probably no more thrilled than Cal with the idea of having this child—her first grand-child—live nearly two thousand miles away.

As for the rest of it... He supposed his poor heart would just have to muddle through as best it could.

Dawn was still sacked out when Ivy got back from seeing Faith Andrews, who was expecting her and Darryl's fifth child around Christmas. In one way, Ivy was just as glad, since Dawn needed her rest. But it didn't take a rocket scientist to figure out it wasn't only the pregnancy that had rendered her daughter virtually comatose for the better part of three days. Uh-uh—this was definitely the old "Oh, God—why me?" syndrome at work here.

With which Ivy was only too familiar.

After hanging the tote bag with all her work paraphernalia on the hook by the back door, she peeked in on Miss Sleepy-head, totally oblivious to the late-morning sun shining smack in her face, then tromped back down the short hall to the kitchen, her Birkenstocks slapping against her bare feet. Ivy's little bungalow in the center of town wasn't much to speak of—two small bedrooms, the living room, one bath and an eat-in kitchen—and for sure she was in no danger from being set upon by the *House Beautiful* people, but it was all hers, and there was a lot to be said for that.

She poured herself a cup of leftover coffee and stuck it in the microwave, smoothing strands of graying hair off her fore-head. It killed her, seeing the pain her daughter was in, hearing the hopefulness in Cal's voice when he'd called, knowing there wasn't a blessed thing she could do to help either one of them. They'd gotten into this fix by themselves, and they'd have to figure their way out of it on their own, as well. That history should repeat itself with her daughter...well. But then, Dawn had been given to doing things the hard way ever since she was little. Wasn't like her stubborn daughter would let Ivy take the burden from her shoulders, anyway, even if she could.

And the idea that Ivy could somehow run interference for Cal was downright laughable.

She jumped slightly when the microwave beeped, then retrieved her warmed-over coffee and plopped down at the kitchen table, flipping her long braid over her shoulder and yanking her bunched-up denim skirt out from underneath her whopper of a butt. Maybe things'd be different now for Dawn than they'd been for Ivy thirty years ago, but not a day went by that Ivy didn't question if her having to sometimes drag Dawn out of bed in the middle of the night, or leaving her to her own devices in a strange house while Ivy saw a client through a protracted labor, hadn't warped the child in some ways. And then there was that business with Charley when Dawn was eight.... Ivy sighed. Not that the child had ever complained, and she'd seemed remarkably adaptable to most every situation, but still—Ivy took a sip of her coffee—it was cause for worry.

"Whatcha thinking so hard about?"

Ivy's gaze jerked to Dawn's at the sound of her daughter's sleep-graveled voice. And wasn't she a sorry sight? Her hair was a holy mess, her right cheek was creased, and that nightgown wouldn't pass muster as a dust rag.

"Wondering if I screwed you up," Ivy said, flat out.

Dawn grimaced, gingerly lowering herself into the opposite chair. "No, I managed that all by myself. And if you go any further down this road, I may have to shoot you."

Ivy took another sip of coffee. "Want some breakfast?"

"You must be kidding."

"I hate to say this, but you look like you've been on a bender."

"If only." Dawn let her head fall forward onto her folded arms. "At least then I'd have some idea when everything would stop spinning."

"You know, morning sickness is a good sign. Means the hormones are strong."

Her head still down, Dawn made a "whoop-de-do" circle with her right forefinger in the air above her head, then slapped her arm back down on the table.

"How about some tea?"

"Trust me. Anything I try to put into this stomach right now is only going to bounce right back out." One eye squinted open. "Were you this sick with me?"

"'Fraid not."

"Figures."

"Cal called," Ivy said casually. "Again."

That got a groan, then Dawn shifted to lay her cheek on her arms, staring up at Ivy with her hound-dog eyes. "This is going to sound terrible, but I almost wish I hadn't told him."

"No, you don't."

"I said 'almost.'"

"You did the right thing. That's gotta be some comfort, doesn't it?"

"No."

Ivy decided a different approach was in order. "You never told me, how'd your first prenatal appointment go?"

"It didn't. I haven't seen anyone yet."

"You're not serious?"

That got a very teenage-sounding sigh. "Mama, I just found out a week ago. I was up to my butt at work and was doing well to wrangle the time off to come out here. And finding the 'right' OB in New York is second only to finding an apartment."

"What happened to the doctor you were going to?"

"Dead. No, it's okay," she said at Ivy's gasp. "The woman was like 110. And she'd stopped doing deliveries twenty years ago. So I'll have to start over when I get back."

"I could do your initial workup," Ivy said, running her finger over the rim of her mug. "Or Ryan, if you'd rather. Or you could find somebody in Claremore…"

"Fine. You can do it." At what must have been the surprised look on Ivy's face, Dawn said, "I do not have the energy for either a protracted argument or a trek to Claremore, and there's no way I'm letting Cal's brother give me an internal exam. I don't care if he is the only doctor around.''

''Actually, he and a couple other doctors from nearby towns got a clinic going about twenty miles away, so you wouldn't have to go as far as Claremore—''

Dawn gave her a black look.

''Well…'' Ivy fought to keep a straight face. And to keep from asking her if she was sure. ''Okay, then. Why don't you go ahead and get a shower, then we can do it right after.''

''Whatever.'' She dragged herself out of the chair and over to the refrigerator, which launched into a deafening, whiny hum when she opened it.

''Thought you weren't hungry?'' Ivy said as Dawn pulled out a carton of orange juice.

''That was five minutes ago. Things change.'' She glowered at the avocado-green monster as the door slammed shut. ''And you seriously need a new refrigerator. Wasn't this one here when you bought the place?''

''Thought maybe I'd hang on to it long enough to be buried in it, save myself a few bucks.''

''And wouldn't *that* frost a few folks,'' Dawn said on a chuckle. She poured herself a glass of juice and sat back down at the table. ''Why didn't you ever tell me who my father was?''

Ivy nearly spilled her coffee. ''What?''

''My father. I don't even know his name, or if he's in town, or if he's even alive or not.''

Ivy carefully set down her cup, then said, even more carefully, ''Would it make any difference if you did know?''

After a swallow of juice and a shrug, Dawn said, ''Probably not.''

''Then why now?''

''I don't know. I mean, why should I give a flying fig about a man who never wanted anything to do with me? But now, with the baby coming, I just got to thinking about it.'' Her eyes narrowed. ''You know where he is, don't you?''

After a moment Ivy nodded, her heart knocking painfully against her ribs.

"But you're not going to tell me."

"I can't." She met her daughter's gaze. "I made a promise."

"Which means you can't tell me his name, either."

"No."

"Well. *That* was elucidating. Did he even know you were pregnant?"

"Dawn, please—"

"Did he leave you when he found out?"

"Honey, there's really no point to this. Your father and I...it was a mistake, okay? Not you," she added at the raised brows in front of her. "Us."

"Because...?"

Well, at least she could be honest about this part. "Because we...got together for all the wrong reasons. There never was a future it."

"Like Cal and me, you mean?"

Ivy got up from the table to rinse out her cup. "No, not like Cal and you. And there's no point comparin' the situations, so don't even try."

"You mean, because Cal wouldn't walk out on *his* child."

"Seems to me it's not *Cal* walkin' out that's the issue here."

"For God's sake, Mama!" Ivy turned to see tears cresting in her daughter's eyes. "I do want to do what's right, I swear! What's right for everyone—the baby, Cal, me...dammit! Why can't I get through a simple conversation without crying?" A tear streaked down her cheek. "I just don't know what that is, okay? I mean, Cal and I have talked, what? Three times since I've been here? And we never reach any conclusion beyond the 'fact' that I'm being muleheaded. And don't think I haven't figured out the two of you are in cahoots!"

Ivy crossed her arms and took the offensive. "Okay, fine. I think he would make a damn fine son-in-law. So sue me."

"Too bad you'll have to find another daughter for that to happen."

"He's sure as hell better than that creep you were going to marry!"

Dawn's laugh surprised her. "No arguments there. But this isn't about Cal's qualifications for husbandhood. He'd be a terrific husband. Just not for me."

"Why not?"

"Lord, you're as bad as he is! Have you not heard a single thing I've been saying since I got here?" She shot up from the table, forking her fingers through her matted hair. "I think I'll go get that shower now, if you don't mind—"

"Knock, knock…anybody home?"

Dawn shrieked and grabbed a kitchen towel to hold in front of her as Cal waltzed in through the back door as if he owned the place. She lobbed her mother what was supposed to be a searing look, which, combined with her campground-for-demented-squirrels coiffure, probably didn't have quite the impact she'd hoped for. And, since she'd been 30,000 feet over Cincinnati when she remembered she'd never actually put her pajamas in her suitcase, was this the high school vintage nightgown with the holes in it? She wasn't sure. She was sure, however, that she had a lot going on underneath that soft, clingy, might-as-well-be-Saran-Wrap fabric. More than usual. Another whole cup size more than usual, in fact.

Cal's gaze raked lazily from toes to towel, at which point that damned dimpled smile of his—the number one cause of female hormonal meltdown in high school—slid across his just-shaved face. To add insult to injury, his eyes twinkled like new grass after a spring shower. And, yep, her nipples perked right up. Damn things had been betraying her around Cal Logan ever since her blossoming boobs had pushed them front and center when she was thirteen. It was as if he had this psychic connection with them or something.

And if Cal and she could somehow forge a relationship on that point—or points—alone, they might have something. Since they couldn't, it was all moot.

"Why are you here, Cal?" And when had her mother vanished?

"Oh, no special reason." More grinning, more tingling. He set a wrapped parcel on the counter. "I had to come into town, anyway, so Ethel figured y'all might like some of her apple cake...."

Food and gossip. The life blood of a small town.

"Then I figured I'd take you out for a while, since it's finally cooled down some, give you a chance to see what the town's like these days. And you can let go of the towel, honey, since I already know what it's covering."

Dawn clutched the towel more tightly, nausea momentarily distracting her from her duplicitous knockers. For the first time in weeks she was almost grateful she felt like crud.

"The last thing I want to do right now is go anywhere. Besides, I don't imagine the town's changed all that much since the last time I saw it."

Cal's hands slid into his back pockets. Like most guys out here, his belt buckle was shiny and silver and only marginally smaller than Texas. And Dawn noticed the bottom didn't lie exactly flat against his belly. She jerked her eyes to his face— dimples and lazy grins were a lot safer than angled belt buckles—in time to hear him say, "And when was the last time you saw Haven?"

Cheeks burned. "Two months ago."

"I didn't say the last time you were here. I said the last time you saw it. As in, paid attention to what it's like now. Not what you remember."

She shut her eyes. Let's see...she looked like hell, felt worse, and was standing in a socially unacceptable nightie arguing semantics with a man who made her hot just by breathing. And not even on her. Yep, she was officially having a sucky day.

"It doesn't matter," she finally said. "Mama's giving me my first prenatal checkup after I get cleaned up."

Immediately Cal's expression changed, as something that looked close to awe obliterated every bit of the smartaleckiness…and walloped her emotions right out of the ball park. Again his eyes sauntered back to her body, only this time, she felt…worshipped. So much so, she didn't even object when he took a step closer, then closer still, finally tugging the dish towel from her hands to lay one large, gentle hand on her still flat belly.

She swallowed. Twice. One from a plain old-fashioned rush of awareness, the second time from something achy and weird she couldn't even define.

"Tell you what," he said, bending slightly to look in her eyes, and she saw not the man who rattled her hormones clear into the next county, but the boy with the courage to cry in front of her when his mama was dying. "Let me stay for your appointment, then I'll take you over to Ruby's for lunch and we'll see how it goes from there. How's about it? A couple of hours, just for us."

Senses returned. She removed his hand—managing not to sigh—and crossed her arms. Under her braless breasts. Wrong. So she lowered her arms, feeling them bounce back into place. Terrific.

"There is no 'us,' Cal. There's never been an 'us.' And there's never going to be an 'us.'"

And quit standing there making this so damn hard, with those damn sweet eyes of yours and that damn, double-damn, stupid, infuriating, unflappable grin.

Quit making me long for things that can't be.

"But there is a baby," he said. "*Our* baby. So I'm sticking around."

"God. I'd forgotten how stubborn you are."

"One of my more endearing qualities."

She sighed. "There's really no point, Cal. It's not as if you can see or hear anything yet."

He crossed his arms, the smile gone. "I don't suppose I can stop you from going back to New York if that's what you're determined to do. But let me tell you something—when you are here, there is no way you're keeping me from being part of your life as far as it concerns our child. So you might as well get used to it, right now, and save yourself a lot of head-aches down the road.''

Hoo-boy. Major-deer-in-headlights time. If only…

If only what?

She had no idea.

Dawn blinked until the fog cleared and Cal's calm, set-to-simmer gaze swam into focus. She blew out yet another sigh, her hands flipping up on either side of her head.

"Fine. Stay. But I'm not going anywhere afterward."

Then Cal grinned, Dawn's nipples went *tra-la-la* and she took off down the hall for that shower, in as dignified a manner as she could manage in a nightgown a breath away from dis-integration.

"You might want to bring a sweater or something," he called after her. "It's kinda chilly out today."

Chapter 3

"Just remember," Dawn said as Cal held open the door to Ruby's two hour later. "I'm only letting you do this because I'm starving. Got that?"

Her shampoo scent distracted him for a second, but he caught himself fast enough to both say, "Yes, ma'am," and swallow his smile. She narrowed her eyes slightly, then turned to head inside. Only she wheeled back around so fast her hand whapped him in the stomach.

"And not one word about…you know."

She'd been right, that there really hadn't been much point to his sticking around for the exam, especially since Ivy threw him out before they got to the fun stuff, anyway. Except that being there helped make the whole thing feel more real, somehow. Dawn would probably have kittens if she knew, but he'd already been up in the attic and found the cradle he and his brothers had used as babies, the one his daddy had made the instant he found out he was gonna be a daddy, after nearly fifteen years of marriage. And when Cal thought about his own baby lying in it, looking up at him with a big, goony grin, he got all choked up.

When he thought about Dawn having the baby in New York…well, it just made him sick, is what. But he also had enough sense to know when to back off.

"I'm not stupid, Dawn," he said, nudging her from behind before they attracted any more attention than they already were. As it was, the noise level in the diner—which at lunchtime generally hovered somewhere between deafening and mind numbing—dropped considerably at their entrance. Cal was tempted to call everybody on it, only he knew that would only make it worse. Besides, Dawn had gone still as a statue, one arm pressing against her stomach.

Damn. He'd forgotten what she'd said about strong smells. And the grease-to-air-molecule ratio in here was running, at a conservative guess, a good fifty-to-one.

"You okay?" he said quietly, taking her elbow whether she liked it or not. The look she gave him pretty much indicated she didn't.

"What?"

"The smell," he whispered. "Is it getting to you?"

Except for a couple of clips, her hair was hanging loose down the back of her light blue sweater, which was the same color as the flowers in another of those long, floppy skirts that looked like something her mother would wear. Just like the ugly, clunky shoes. The ends of her hair teased the top of his hand, sending memories racing around inside his skull for a second until he silenced them by focusing on the present.

"Lord, yes," she whispered back. "I want every single thing on the menu. Oh, there's a booth! Grab it!"

As the noise level gradually worked its way back up, Charmaine Chambers, Ruby's newest waitress and the same age as Cal and Dawn, leaned over to wipe down their table, her initial—and customary—smile for Cal vanishing the instant she caught sight of Dawn.

"Special today's a boneless barbecue rib sandwich," she announced in a monotone, her breasts shifting restlessly underneath a baggy uniform that was so bright pink it hurt Cal's eyes to look at it. She straightened, then poured them both water from a dripping plastic pitcher she'd grabbed from the nearby station. "You need a menu?" she asked Dawn, her words all tight.

Dawn flicked a glance at Cal, then pressed one hand to her chest. "Hey, Char! It's me, Dawn."

The brunette's slate-blue gaze bounced off Dawn. "I know." Her mouth twitched, but calling it a smile was pushing it. "Thought you were in New York."

"I'm…here visiting my mother. How're those gorgeous boys of yours?"

"They're fine. You know what you want yet?"

Dawn shoved a hank of hair behind her ear, obviously wrestling to keep her thoughts to herself. "The rib sandwich sounds great. That come with fries?"

"And slaw, yeah. Soup's extra, though."

"What kind?"

"Split pea."

"Really?" she said, her whole face lighting up. "Lord, I can't remember the last time I had split pea soup. Could I get a double bowl?"

Wordlessly, Charmaine scribbled the order down on her pad, then took Cal's, yelling them out to Jordy, Ruby's husband, before stomping off to tend to the next customer.

Dawn sighed. Cal leaned over. "Don't let her get to you—"

"It's okay. We weren't exactly best buddies when we were kids, you know."

"Maybe not, but the thing is…she's been having a hard time of it lately. Brody walked out about a year ago, leaving her with the kids. Ruby gave her a job 'cause she felt bad for her, but I don't think waitressin's exactly her thing."

Dawn's dark brows dipped. "Brody left her?"

The split had surprised Cal, too, especially since Charmaine and Brody had been tight as ticks since the seventh grade. That they'd managed to wait until after high school to get married had been a miracle in itself, although Cal knew for a fact they hadn't waited about anything else.

"Yeah. Kids took it real hard, too."

"I bet they did. Oh, God, Cal," she said on a sigh, "how awful for her." Her eyes following the waitress's moves, Cal supposed, she asked, "Is she at least getting child support?"

"I seriously doubt it—"

"Dawn Gardner!" Ruby Kennedy said next to them, hands the color of bittersweet chocolate parked on seriously wide hips. "What on earth you doin' back here so soon, honey?"

"Giving you a hug, that's what," Dawn said with a laugh as she clambered out of the booth and did just that.

After they'd hugged themselves out and Dawn was settled back in the booth, Ruby asked, "You order the rib sandwich, baby?"

"Like I was gonna pass up Jordy's ribs," she said with a grin. "Or the fries or the slaw or the soup."

Ruby *mm-mm-mm'd* and said, "Why is it the skinny one's're always the ones who can pack it away? Me, all I have to do is look at one of Jordy's ribs and my butt starts expandin'. Oh, and Maddie brought over a peach cobbler this morning that's so pretty it'll make you cry. You want me to save you some?"

"Whoa, whoa—" Cal raised his hand. "I don't hear you offering to save me any!"

"That's because, Mr. Me-Too," Ruby said, "being's Maddie's your sister-in-law, I suppose you can taste her cobbler anytime you like—"

"Hey!" Charmaine yelled over by the display of gum and candy bars and stuff underneath the cash register. "You have to pay for that—come back here!" Cal looked over just in time to see a blond kid just this side of puberty tear out the door, nearly knocking over Homer Ferguson in the process.

Seconds later Cal was hot on the kid's tail, his much longer legs catching up to the boy before he'd even reached the Hair We Are two doors down. He grabbed the skinny thing around the waist and plucked him right up off the ground, getting a barrage of elbows and fists and rubber-soled feet for his efforts.

"Lemme go! I didn't do nuthin'!"

"You gonna run?" Cal said softly in the kid's ear.

"What do you think?"

Cal let go, but not before getting a good handful of too-big T-shirt just in case the boy had any ideas about booking it. The kid took a swing at him, but he didn't really put his heart in it. Besides, Cal ducked.

"I said, let me *go!*"

Still hanging on with one hand, Cal held out the other one, palm up. "Give me what you took."

"I didn't—"

"Now."

The boy glared at him for several seconds, his breath coming in sharp bursts. He didn't exactly look like he'd had a bath any too recently, but then, how many boys his age did? Finally the boy rammed his hand into his pocket and yanked out a slightly smashed candy bar.

"That it?" Cal asked.

"Yeah."

"You sure?"

"You don't believe me, you can look for yourself."

"Okay, you can ditch the attitude. Unless you like lookin' ugly." When the kid only scowled harder, it suddenly struck Cal where he knew him from. "You're Jacob Burke's boy, aren't you?"

"I don't have to tell you nothin'."

Cal was sorely tempted to cuff the kid upside the head. Or feed him, one. "What's your name?" he said gently.

More scowling.

"You can tell me now, or I can call your daddy—"

"Elijah."

"That what they call you, or you got a nickname?" At the shake of the shaggy head, Cal grimaced at the Three Musketeers in his hand. "You mean to tell me you caused all this ruckus for one lousy candy bar? How dumb is that?"

"Yeah, well, it's none of your business, is it?"

''You stole something from a friend of mine. That makes it my business—''

''Is he okay?''

Cal turned at the sound of Dawn's voice, noticing a small crowd had gathered to watch the proceedings. For Haven, this qualified as excitement.

''Yeah, he's fine.'' He handed her the flattened candy bar. ''This, however, isn't. Come on,'' he said, tugging the boy in the direction of the diner.

''I ain't goin' back there.''

''Yes, you are. And when we get there, the first thing you're gonna do is apologize for your momentary lapse of good sense. Then we're gonna see what you can do for Ruby to make up for it.''

''Like what?''

''I don't know. Some kind of job, I'm thinking.''

''A job? No way! For one candy bar?''

''I'm a firm believer in nipping things in the bud, bud.'' The small crowd dispersed when Cal dragged Elijah through the door, Dawn on their heels. ''We're back, Ruby,'' he hollered from the doorway. ''Where you want him?''

''Kitchen's good,'' she called from the back of the diner.

They all trooped back into Ruby's gleaming kitchen, Elijah a trifle more subdued than he had been five minutes before. Especially when he caught sight of Jordy, Ruby's bald, bad, six-foot-three, 280-pound husband. After a brief discussion, it was decided Elijah could mop the floor after the lunch rush.

''I don't know how.''

''Well, I suppose you can learn, can't you?'' Ruby said, after which four people chorused, ''You hungry?''

After Dawn and Elijah had packed enough away between them for a church potluck, Cal and Dawn took the boy and his bicycle, which he'd left in front of the hardware store, back out to the small farm he lived on with his widowed father. Who, as best they could figure out from Elijah's grudging explanation, had been on disability for some time. He also told them he was home schooled, since his father needed him around to "help." Help with what, was the question, since neither the small, drab house with its peeling paint and missing shutters, nor the bare dirt yard littered with junk and a couple of old pickups, indicated that any attention had been given to either for a very long time. Granted, Cal had seen worse, but the bleakness of the place turned his stomach. No kid should ever have to live like this.

"Mind if we come in for a minute?" Dawn asked, but the kid said no before the words were all the way out of her mouth.

"We won't say anything about the candy bar," Cal added.

"It ain't that," Elijah said, pushing open the back door of Cal's extended cab truck. "It's just…uh, Daddy's usually asleep this time of day. An' he don't like bein' disturbed."

With that, he bolted out of the truck and across the yard, stopping for a second to pet a large mongrel dog tied up to the lone tree in front of the house before bounding onto the porch and on through the screen door.

Dawn kept her eyes on the house as they drove back down the dirt road leading to the highway. "I hate seeing kids left to their own devices like that."

"Oh, I imagine he's all right," Cal said, briefly meeting her gaze when she finally brought it around. She blew out a sigh, then faced front, her brow knit, as the truck meandered over the gently rolling, lush green hills that Cal couldn't imagine giving up for skyscrapers and concrete and rush hour traffic.

"Still," she said, holding her hair with one hand so it wouldn't blow to kingdom come. "Somebody should check up on him. From the county, I mean."

"There's no real cause, far as I can tell. I didn't get the feeling he'd been abused. And he has to take tests or something if he's being home schooled. If he doesn't pass, they'd catch it."

"But he's so thin! A stiff breeze would blow the poor kid away!"

A smile inched across Cal's face. "You're obviously forgettin' how skinny I was as a kid then. Just because he's all bones doesn't mean he's not eating.''

"He *stole,* Cal.''

"A candy bar. Because he's twelve and it was there and he saw what looked like a golden opportunity." He glanced over. "Didn't you ever take something just to see if you could?''

"No! Never!''

"You were never even tempted?''

"Well…maybe. But I didn't *act* on it." She sucked in a breath. "Did you?''

"Yeah, once.''

"Oh, God.''

"Oh, unknot your panties. I was nine, for cryin' out loud. It was maybe a few months after my mother died. I snitched a pack of gum from the supermarket checkout, pretty much like what Elijah did.''

"What happened?''

"Well, at first I felt like hot stuff because I pulled it off without Ethel catching me. But somehow the gum didn't taste near as good as I figured it would. And I couldn't sleep that night. So I finally confessed to Daddy.''

"Ouch. I can imagine how well that went over.''

"All he did was look at me. Like I'd let him down. Well, and march me back to the store to 'fess up to the manager, which was humiliating as hell. I was never even tempted to filch anything after that.''

"Never?" He heard the smile in her voice.

"Almost never, anyway.''

She laughed, but it didn't last long. "Still," she said, "it worries me. About Elijah." He could feel her gaze on the side of his face. "I'd call Family Services myself, but I wouldn't be around to follow up….''

He didn't know which irked him more, her leaving or her pushing him to do something he didn't think needed doing.

"Dawn, I hear what you're saying, I really do. But I'm not gonna embarrass that kid, or his father, by calling the authorities on 'em when I don't see any reason to. Looks to me like they've got enough to deal with without people sticking their noses in where they don't belong.''

She pushed herself back against the truck door, as if needing to distance herself from him. ''Problems aren't always obvious, you know—''

''And living in the city for so long has made you see spooks lurking in every shadow. This isn't New York—''

''Neglect is neglect, Cal. No matter where it happens.''

''You know what? If you're so hot about this, why don't you stick around and take care of it yourself?''

''Because I can't, which you know. And how dare you try to blackmail me!''

Cal let out a nice, ripe cussword, to which Dawn spit back, ''My sentiments exactly.''

Nobody said anything for another mile or two. Then she said, ''I suppose I can at least make the initial call before I go back.''

Cal sighed. ''You really feel that strongly about this?''

She turned to him, and he could hear her voice shake. ''If you'd heard what I have, seen the effects of people looking the other way, you would, too. Working with these women and children hasn't made me delusional, it's made me think twice about taking things at face value. And I couldn't live with myself if something happened that could've been prevented by a single phone call.''

He glanced over to see her mouth all set like it used to get when she was a kid. Aw, hell. ''Tell you what. If I promise to personally check up on the boy, and his father, would that be enough to keep you from making that call?''

''Are you serious?''

''Are you out to see just how far you can try my patience before I lose what's left of my mind? I wouldn't've said it if I didn't mean it…hey!''

She'd flown across the seat to hug him, nearly sending the truck off the road. ''Thank you,'' she murmured into his neck, her breath far too soft and far too warm for anybody's good right now.

"Honey? Not that I'm not enjoying this, but I think that's Didi Meyerhauser's Bronco closing in on us, so you might want to—"

She was instantly on the other side of the seat like nothing had happened.

Not that anything *had* happened.

Exactly.

The preacher's wife passed, waving. Cal and Dawn waved back, Cal suddenly remembering that Dawn used to be friends with Didi's daughter.

"You seen Faith yet?" he said.

"Faith? No. Not sure there'd be any point. It's been years since we've talked or written or anything."

"Then I guess you didn't know she and Darryl are having another baby?"

"Mama might've said something about it. Their third?"

"Fifth." He grinned. "Now there's one shotgun wedding that took."

No response.

They drove past the turnoff that led back to the farm. For a second, he'd thought about asking if she wanted to come back, to see the cradle. But only for a second.

"So…Ryan and Maddie are doing okay, I take it?" Dawn asked.

Now, Cal knew it had not been her intention to hike up the temperature inside the truck several degrees. Except the last time Dawn would've seen them all was on July Fourth. The day he and Dawn made the baby. Which naturally provoked some real vivid memories of just *how* they'd made the baby, although to the casual listener—as in Dawn—his thoughts, like his words, were totally focused on Maddie's youngest taking her first steps a few weeks ago, how his new sister-in-law had worked wonders to bring his reclusive workaholic brother out of his shell.

"And Hank and Jenna?" she said. "Mama told me they were getting married?"

He glanced over at her, his brain jumping its tracks as his

gaze landed on her mouth. Which, when it wasn't yapping a mile a minute and making him crazy, was soft and warm and—

He looked back, mentally flogging himself. This sex-as-mental-comfort-food business was fine to a certain extent, but at some point, a man's gotta grow up and eat his vegetables.

"Right after Thanksgiving, yep."

"I liked Jenna a lot," she said, crossing her arms. "Her books are good, too. And I don't usually read mysteries."

"Her next one's coming out in hardcover," he said, thinking about that mouth. About how he'd kissed a fair number of women in his time, but Dawn…well, she was what you'd call a natural talent. "You know," he said, because thinking about her mouth was making him feel reckless, "even though Jenna's lived all her life in D.C., she doesn't seem to have any reservations about moving out here."

No response. Again.

One more little hill before they reached Haven proper. "I bet if you had a chance to know Jenna better, you'd really like her."

Dawn laughed. Not what he was expecting. And she was hard enough to figure when she did something he *was* expecting.

"What?" he asked.

She said, "Nothing," which would've ticked him off if she hadn't immediately followed up with, "You're going to make an amazing father," which simply threw him.

To Nebraska.

"What makes you say that?"

"Deductive reasoning is kind of my stock in trade," she said with a smile. "Watching how you handled Elijah, the way you related to him…" Out of the corner of his eye, he caught her breasts lifting with the force of her sigh. First time in his life he'd ever thought of his peripheral vision as a liability. "At least I won't have to worry about leaving our child alone with you. Me, on the other hand…"

The insecurity flickered in her voice for barely a second, just long enough to bring back another memory, this one of a eight-year-old girl, her chin defiantly tilted up underneath a quivering mouth, who'd refused to come right out and say how much it hurt when that man Ivy was supposed to marry suddenly moved away. Charley...Beeman, that was his name.

"What do I need a daddy for, anyway? And besides, Mama says a man just gets in the way of what a woman wants to do...."

Cal frowned, bringing himself back to the present. "Well, sweetheart, if things go the way I hope, you won't have to worry about leaving him or her *alone* with me at all."

Several beats passed. Then: "Stop the truck."

"You gonna be sick?"

"Possibly. But not because of the baby."

He pulled onto the shoulder; she jumped out and took off down the road. Cal stuck his head out the window. "What the hell are you doing?"

"Walking the rest of the way!"

Grumbling to himself, Cal got out and went after her.

"You know—" the words came in little puffs as he trotted along behind her "—the one thing I used to admire about you was that you never pulled this female crap."

"Yeah, well," she puffed back, "I've never felt this much like a female before."

Along about this time, Cal happened to notice her behind had filled out some with the pregnancy, too. Not a lot, and not so's anybody but him would notice, probably, but there it was, jiggling away in front of him as she strode, and while one part of him was pretty ticked at her behavior—he liked kids, but not ones his own age—she looked so damned silly and cute and sexy, hoofing it away like this, that, well, something crazy just bubbled up inside him and made him want to kiss her.

So he did.

After he caught her, that is.

She was too shocked to protest. At least, that's what he was working with. Oh, there was a little *mmphh* on her part when their lips met, but he chalked that up to the surprise element.

Oh, yeah, she was a natural talent, all right. And she tasted like barbecue sauce and fresh peach cobbler, which Cal decided right then and there pretty much summed up his definition of heaven. Except he could have done without the *mmphhs,* which were definitely increasing in their intensity.

The fists beating on his shoulders weren't doing much for the mood, either.

He let her go, grinning down at her.

She was not grinning back.

"And you did that why?" she said.

No way was he telling her about the bigger-butt revelation.

"Because I felt like it. And I had fun. Well, I would have had fun if you'd cooperated more—"

She burst into tears and sank onto the ground.

Cal squatted beside her. "I didn't think it was *that* bad."

That got the head-shaking, air-batting routine, then a series of sobbed syllables not even remotely related to the English language. Figuring she probably wasn't going anywhere in the next few seconds, Cal went back to the truck and retrieved two or three tissues from the smashed box in the glove department, then returned to where she was still sitting and handed them to her. When she was drier and—he presumed—more coherent, he said, "You wanna run that one by me again?"

A few rattly sighs, a few more eye wipes, and at last she said, "You are such an idiot."

At that he figured he might as well join her in the dirt and weeds.

"You mean that in general?" he said as his backside touched down. "Or you got something specific in mind?"

"At the risk of this going straight to your head, if not elsewhere—" she looked pointedly at the *elsewhere* in question "—my being hot for you isn't the issue here."

"It's...not."

She smacked him in the arm, honked into one of the tissues, then gave one of those oh-God-deliver-me-from-the-clueless sighs. "You didn't exactly have to talk me into your bed a couple months ago. If you recall."

He squelched the laugh just in time. "Yeah, I seem to remember a certain…eagerness on your part. But I figured that was…''

''What? You figured that was what?''

''That you were still hurtin' after that guy dumped you, is all,'' he said gently, refusing to look at her. ''And maybe you were looking for someone to boost your self-confidence back up a notch or two.''

Silence. Then: ''I was a little…bruised, it's true. But more because I was duped than dumped. Andrew and I broke up because our visions of marriage—or rather, his vision of what he expected of a wife—didn't mesh. What pissed me off was that he didn't bother to tell me this until after we were engaged. And I felt, I don't know…betrayed as much as anything, I guess.''

''About what?''

She yanked a poor defenseless weed out of the ground, then shifted to sit cross-legged, making lines in the dust with the weed as they talked. ''We were really compatible on so many levels. Similar tastes, similar viewpoints, similar personalities.'' Her shoulders hitched. ''He was…comfortable. After some of the so-called men I'd gone out with, it was a pleasure being with someone I never had to second-guess. Or so I thought.'' Her mouth hitched up into a rueful smile. ''When he proposed, my first thought was, No more stupid dates! No more worrying about making an impression!''

Cal frowned. ''Oh, yeah, that sounds like a real good reason to marry somebody.''

''Trust me, after what I'd been through, it was a damn good reason. Anyway, I figured our lives wouldn't change all that much after we got married, that we'd just be a typical professional New York couple. But it turned out…''

The weed snapped in two; she tossed it away and squinted into the sun. ''He didn't love me, I know he didn't, but he still wanted more from me than I could possibly give. Looking back, I think he didn't want kids because the competition would've made him crazy, because Andrew wanted to be my world. For me to love him in a way I knew I never could. In a way I know I'll never be able to love anybody.''

Cal waited out the stab of pain before he asked, "Why?"

"I don't know." She sounded surprised, like she hadn't expected him to challenge her. "Just the way I'm wired, I guess."

"I see." His insides churning, he focused on a clump of late-season wildflowers shivering in the breeze. "So…you'd rather be alone?"

She seemed to think about this for a second. "I've been on my own for a long time and I've learned to enjoy my own company. But I'm not a recluse. I wouldn't have agreed to marry Andrew otherwise. I have nothing against male companionship. Or sex," she said with a tilted smile. "I can even love, in my own way. Just not the way the rest of the population loves. Or wants to be loved."

Cal wondered if she heard the sadness in her voice. Oh, she undoubtedly thought she was being…well, whatever people who came to conclusions like that were. Upfront? Resigned? Something. Frankly, Cal thought she was several sandwiches short of a picnic.

The thing was, though, it didn't matter what he thought, did it? Because it was what she believed that mattered. It was like what Ryan said about attitude affecting a person's health—people who expected to get sick generally did far more often than people who didn't think about it too hard. So Cal could sit here and tell Dawn she was full of it until the cows came home, but as long as she was convinced she couldn't love like a normal person, he'd be wasting his breath.

"So," she was saying, "about that night. You were flirting, and I'll admit I was still feeling a little off balance, and from everything I'd heard, I figured I probably wouldn't regret going to bed with you."

His eyes snapped to hers. *"From everything you'd heard?"*

"Hey. Women talk, too. And unlike men, *we* don't embellish. Granted, my information was a little out-of-date, but…"

She shrugged. Cal looked back out across the road. A couple

of trucks passed. Everybody waved. Cal figured Ruby's would be buzzing to beat the band by tomorrow.

"In any case, I wasn't pushing you away just now because I didn't want to be kissed, but because kissing you is like opening a can of Pringles. Sour cream and onion. Or nacho cheese, in a pinch. If I start, I can't stop until I've eaten the whole damn can."

"So…what you're saying is, all those rumors you heard about me…?"

"Weren't rumors. Which is one of those good-news/bad-news kinds of things. Wanting to have sex with you isn't the issue. But it would totally ball things up. And I think things are plenty balled up enough already, don't you? And dammit, I'd kill for a can of Pringles right now."

After a couple of tense seconds, during which Cal mentally beat back enough testosterone to fuel the sex drive of every man in the state, he stood, then extended his hand to pull Dawn to her feet. "C'mon. Here's one problem I can solve."

Fifteen minutes later, having bought, not one, but three cans of Pringles from the Git-n-Go and used the bathroom—both of which would have raised Angel Clearwater's penciled brows if her tightly pulled-back hair hadn't already made them an inch higher than normal—Dawn sat with her legs dangling off the lowered gate of Cal's truck, having a scarffest. Without her saying anything, Cal'd pulled off the road to park underneath the whacky old cottonwood where they used to go when they were kids. Split by lightning long before they'd been born, it looked like a huge gray hand, its fingers bent toward the sky. It still put out more leaves than any other tree for miles around, though, the sunlight lancing through the sharp green, casting quivering shadows over the two of them, reminding her of other times. Happy times. Times she wasn't sure she wanted to remember right now.

She hadn't meant to blab about Andrew, especially considering she wasn't exactly proud of her naiveté at having taken the man at face value. And God knows, if Cal hadn't kissed her, she would never have brought up her, um, interest in him. But since he had, she figured she might as well disabuse him of the notion that he could seduce her into coming back to Haven.

"I was really that good, huh?" he said beside her.

She nearly choked. And nodded, since her mouth was full of chips. Just her luck to find the only man in the universe who *could* read a woman's mind.

"So tell me…" Cal leaned back on one elbow, his hands folded across his hard, flat, definitely yummy tummy. "What is it about New York that would make you sacrifice this—" he swept one hand over his torso "—for that?"

There he went, being just Cal. Charming. Goofy. Making light of things.

Feeling suddenly and unaccountably tetchy, Dawn crammed more chips into her mouth and mumbled something about being sick and tired of everybody equating city dwelling to devil worship.

Chips flew six ways to Sunday when Cal grabbed her wrist. She jerked her head around to see his brows slammed together.

"Maybe I don't understand why anybody'd want to live where you can't go outside without a hundred people shoved up against your butt, but that doesn't mean I think there's anything wrong with people who do. All I did was ask you a simple question." He released her. "Don't go reading things into it that aren't there."

"Sorry," she said softly, wiping her salty fingers on a tissue. "Bad habit."

"Preemptive strikes?" he said behind her.

She skootched around to rest her back against the truck-bed wall, flipping her skirt out over her legs. "I guess." She sighed. "I can't even explain it."

Cal looked at her steadily for a long moment, then said, "I'm not looking to judge you. I'm only trying to understand."

"I know that. It's just…"

"Honey? Why don't you try just answering the question?"

His refusal, when they were younger, to let anything get to

him used to irritate the life out of her. Now, however, even though his cocksure attitude only reinforced her conviction about how different they were, her battered psyche yearned to inhale his unflappability, like she'd done the Pringles a few minutes ago. Those cool green eyes said, *I've got you, it's okay, I won't let you fall. You've got nothing to be afraid of.*

If only.

Those eyes, and his goodness, were treacherous. And it finally whapped her over the head that this was possibly her only chance to convince him, once and for all, to let her go.

Not only for her sake, but for his.

"To be truthful," she said, "I didn't know what to expect when I first got there. An eighteen-year-old hick in the big city?" She smiled. "I thought I'd be eaten alive. My first place was a shared room in a cramped apartment with five other roommates, and it took me twenty-four hours to get up the nerve to go out by myself. But within a week I was hooked."

"Why?"

"It's hard to explain if you haven't been there. I mean, in many ways New York is just like any other place, mostly filled with ordinary people going about their ordinary lives, cooking and shopping and doing laundry and eating out."

"There's just a lot more of them."

"Okay, yeah. It's crowded. But there's this…energy that pulses through the city, you know? This sense of possibility, that any second, every second, something exciting could happen."

His mouth curved just enough to show off the dimples. "Even when you're doing your laundry?"

"I didn't say it made sense. And it's not easy living there, don't get me wrong. It's expensive and competitive and, yes, crowded. But God—I can go straight to a major museum from work, or get a half-price ticket to a Broadway show on the spur of the moment. And the music…" She leaned forward, her eyes shining. "The Metropolitan Opera, Cal. Think of that."

He made a face. "That's Hank. Opera's not my thing."

"Okay, fine. The Mostly Mozart Festival, then. The freaking

New York Philharmonic. Live. In person. Free concerts in Central Park—''

''You're still not makin' any points here, sweetheart. Although Ryan would be in hog heaven.''

''And then there's shopping. Bergdorf's. Barney's. Bloomingdale's.''

He just stared at her.

''So maybe that's not working for you, either. But just think—our child would be able to go to some of the world's greatest museums on a regular basis, see shows and go to the ballet and…'' She paused. ''Wouldn't your mother have been thrilled to know her grandchild would get to hear one of the greatest orchestras in the world on a regular basis?''

Cal pulled himself up to sit across from her, stretching out his legs so she could feel his sun-warmed jeans against her calves. ''Did you know she spent a year studying at the Manhattan School of Music?''

''No! Wow. No wonder she was so good.''

He got this funny look on his face then, one that made her insides pitch, made her ache to put her arms around him and lay her head on his shoulder and comfort him, somehow. But comforting was what got them into this predicament to begin with. So instead she nudged his hip with her foot. Which was bad enough.

''I know this isn't an ideal situation,'' she said, talking through, over, around another kind of ache, ''but once I make partner, I'll be making pretty good money. And I can work from home at least a couple days a week, if I need to, so I'll be there for our baby. And we'll come back a lot, I promise.''

He sat there, silent, staring straight ahead, then suddenly scrambled out of the truck bed, reaching out to help her down, as well.

''Guess I'd better get you back to Ivy's,'' he said. ''Gotta lot of work to do this afternoon.''

He said nothing else until he'd deposited her a few minutes

later in front of her mother's house, and then only to ask when she was leaving.

"Saturday. Cal—"

"Don't make it worse, okay?" he said, then took off, leaving her standing on the sidewalk feeling like sludge.

Chapter 4

"I can't believe you just let her go."

From the passenger side of Ryan's truck, Cal squinted over at his next oldest brother. Ostensibly, they were out spreading the word about the new clinic. In reality, Cal was using Ryan as a means to finally check up on Elijah, like he'd promised Dawn.

"It's been a week since she left, Ry. This a delayed reaction or what?"

"I've been busy," Ryan said, his dark blond hair sticking up every which way when he removed his cowboy hat and tossed it on the dash. "Besides, I kept thinking you'd come up with some sort of rational explanation on your own without me having to do the big brother routine, which we both know you hate."

"You got that right."

"So?"

"What was I supposed to do? Tie her up?"

Ryan's smile vanished underneath his mustache. "In other

words she's the only woman on earth immune to Cal Logan's powers of persuasion.''

"More like she's the only woman I've ever known with enough backbone to stick to her guns about what she needs." Cal squirmed in his seat. Letting somebody else drive bugged the life out of him. "Let me ask you something—you think Mama ever regretted giving up her career?"

Clear-blue eyes flicked in his direction. "She never had a career, remember? She and Dad got married when she was twenty."

"Okay then, a chance at one."

"Okay then. No, I don't. Where are you going with this?"

"I'm not sure. Except listening to Dawn talk about New York got me to wondering about Mama. I used to see her standing at the window, like there was something out there she wanted but couldn't reach. I'm not saying she was unhappy, but…hell, how could she stand it, day after day, listening to some kid murder Mozart or Beethoven, when maybe she could've been famous, you know?"

"And maybe she didn't want to be famous. You ever consider that?"

"Yeah. But I also know her folks couldn't afford to give her more than the one year away. So she came home and became a two-bit farmer's wife instead."

"Because she fell in love, dimwit. And if she'd really wanted to stay in New York, she could have. Leastwise, that's what she told me when I asked one time."

"And what if she was only saying that? Because she didn't want you to feel guilty or something?"

Ryan sighed. "At the risk of pulling rank, I did spend more time with Mama than you did. And I never once got the feeling she wasn't right where she wanted to be, doing what she wanted to do." He paused. "She and Dad had fifteen years together before Hank came along, remember. Seems to me if she thought she'd made a mistake, she had plenty of opportunity to get out. But she didn't, did she? This the turnoff to get to the house?"

"What? Oh. Yeah."

The truck shuddered as the paved surface gave way to pock-marked dirt. "And anyway," Ryan shouted over the truck's bumping and squeaking, "since Dawn's pregnant, which Mom wasn't, seems to me we're talking apples and oranges."

"Maybe so. But baby or no baby, I still can't force her to move back here." He remembered the look on her face when she talked about her work, the city she now called home, and blew out a stream of air. "And to be honest, Dawn can give the kid more than I can right now. From a financial standpoint at least. But only if she stays in New York. If she comes out here, we'd barely have a pot to pee in between the two of us."

Cal caught the frown Ryan tossed his way. "What the hell are you talking about? I thought you were doing okay."

Too late, Cal realized his mistake. "Just a temporary glitch. You know, because of the economy and all. I'm still getting by, though, even if only by the skin of my teeth. But not too many folks're buying pleasure horses right now, so prices have tanked. And I'm still in debt to you and Hank, they raised the damn taxes on me, and…well, let's just say the timing couldn't be worse."

"For crying out loud, Cal—why didn't you say something sooner?"

"Because it's my problem and not yours?"

"Look, if you need help—"

"Which I don't. In case you missed it, Ry, I'm close to thirty years old. I do know what I'm doing, believe it or not. And market fluctuations are part of the business." He fiddled with the radio until he found his favorite R&B station, knowing it would annoy the life out of Ryan. "'Course, I hadn't counted on becoming a father, it's true. That doesn't mean I can't han-dle…whatever the hell it is I have to handle. Once I figure out what that is."

Ryan was quiet for a second, then said, "Can I make a suggestion, or you gonna jump down my throat?"

"That's a chance you'll just have to take, won't you?"

He chuckled, then said, "You thought about maybe selling

up and moving back east, then? I mean, if Dawn won't come here, maybe you could go there.'' He held up a hand to ward off Cal's protest. ''You don't need to finish buying me out. And I'm sure Hank'll feel the same way.''

''And while I appreciate that, even if I did, what I'd get for the place wouldn't buy me a vegetable garden there, let alone a stead big enough to start over.'' At his brother's arched brows, he said, ''Hank asked me the same thing, and I said no without a second thought. But then I got to thinking it over, did a little research…but it wouldn't work. So that means I'm stuck. Right here. If I can hang on until the economy gets off its butt, I might be able to salvage the business yet. But there's no way I can start over, let alone anywhere within a hundred-mile radius of Manhattan.''

''So back to Plan A.''

''Hell, there never was a Plan A. Or a Plan anything. And I was a dumbass to think there ever would be.''

They bumped along for another several seconds. ''Why not?''

''Why not? Because I've known from the time we were little that Dawn's goals never included staying here. I might have been a convenient buddy to hang out with when we were little, but I was never a part of her long-range plans.'' He removed his hat, shoved his hand through his hair, screwed the hat back on his head. ''Or even her short range, for that matter.''

''Well, the two of you sure as hell are part of each other's long-range plans now.''

''Only as regards this baby. Nothing more.''

After a long moment Ryan said softly, ''Maddie was telling me the other night about a conversation the two of you had before she and I were married. About how y'all got to talking about dreams, and she said there was no point in wishing for things that weren't gonna happen. And *you* said that without dreams, you may as well lay down and die.'' He paused, then said, ''According to her, what you said made her go after me. So if it hadn't've been for you, I'd still be the miserable bastard

I was before Maddie showed up in my life… That's the house, right?''

His head buzzing from Ryan's comments, it took Cal a second to realign his thoughts. ''Yeah, that's it.''

''Doesn't look so bad from here. Nothing fancy, but no law against that.''

Ryan pulled up next to the newer of the two pickups, which wasn't saying much. Place looked pretty much the same, except maybe one or two pieces of junk had been moved around. Barking its head off, the dog was still tied to the tree, too, which didn't sit well. Dogs were supposed to be free to explore, go where their noses led. Not giving this one a chance to do that seemed mean.

''You do realize there's not a whole lot I can do,'' Ryan said over the dog's excited yapping as they got out of the truck. ''Unless there's real signs of abuse or neglect.''

''I know that. But honestly? I don't expect to find any. I'm only doing this for Dawn.''

Nobody answered the bell at first, but they could hear a TV on inside. On the third try, Elijah finally came to the door, breathing a little hard. He offered a tentative smile for Cal, an even more tentative one for Ryan.

''Hey, Elijah,'' Cal said. ''You know my brother, Dr. Logan?''

The kid warily eyed Ryan. ''Yeah…I've seen him around.''

Ryan stuck his hands in his back pockets. ''We were just in the neighborhood, y'know, getting the word out about the new clinic. You and your daddy know about that?''

''I…I'm not sure he does.''

''You mind if we come in, then,'' Ryan said, ''so I can tell your daddy about it in person?''

''He's…he's asleep.''

''He sure does sleep a lot, doesn't he?'' Cal asked.

Elijah's eyes zinged to his. ''It's the medicine he has to take. It makes him real sleepy.''

''You know what kind of medication he's on?'' Ryan asked.

"No, sir. He keeps the bottle where I can't get it. Like I'm a kid or something—"

"What's goin' on out there, Eli? Who's that at the door?"

The boy jerked, then yelled, "Nobody, Daddy—go on back to sleep." A second later he stepped outside, shutting the door behind him. "Why don't you just go on? Like I said, he's asleep—"

"Does your father drink, son?" Ryan said quietly.

"No!" Wide, mud-colored eyes darted from one to the other. "I told you, it's his medicine! You just came at a bad time, is all—"

Cal caught the boy by the shoulder. "We're not here to stir up trouble, I swear. But you shouldn't have to deal with a sick father on your own. Let Dr. Logan see for himself that the two of you are okay. If you are, we'll be on our way and we won't bother you again."

A bony chin shot out. "And what if I say no?"

"Elijah," Ryan said, "I have a legal duty to report any suspicion of neglect or abuse. For your own protection. Now, if you let us come in, there's at least a chance I won't have to report this. If you don't…"

The boy's eyes got all shiny. "All we got is each other. And he never beats me or nothin', I swear. But if you take me away…what's gonna happen to him?"

"Nobody's sayin' anything about taking you away," Cal said. "I promise."

After a good five seconds or so, Elijah nodded, then opened the door and led them inside.

The last voice Dawn expected to hear when she picked up her office phone was Cal's. And the last thing she expected was her reaction to that voice. Like that first lick of an ice cream cone on a blistering hot day.

Or spilling that ice cream down the neckline of your low-cut tank top.

"Ivy gave me your office number," he said. "You busy?"

The obvious smile behind the words, a flash of dimples and

gold-flecked irises and perpetually rumpled hair provoked an immediate and visceral response right where their combined cells were dividing and multiplying their little nuclei out. Wonderful.

"Depends on your definition of busy," she said mildly over something that sure sounded like a teensy, tinsy voice yelling, *It's Daddy! It's Daddy!* "I don't have to walk out the door in the next five minutes, but I do need to have this brief filed within the next—" Damn, how had it gotten that late? She sighed. "—half hour. What's up?"

"Just thought you'd like to know…Ryan and I went out to Elijah's."

She clamped the phone to her ear, even as it slowly registered that he was being all business. No flirting, no teasing, not a trace of his usual couldn't-you-just-eat-me-up? attitude. Which was good. Right? "And?"

"And…it's borderline. The place was clean enough, although we both wondered if the kid'd straightened up after we got there, since it took him a while to come to the door. There was plenty of food in the house, from what we could tell, and all the utilities were in working order. Eli showed us his home schooling materials, too, so that much seems true, as well. And Ryan said there were no signs of abuse that he could tell."

"And his father?"

"Hard to say. Kid's real protective of him, that's for sure. And Ryan talked to him, told me the meds he found were mostly painkillers, apparently for a bad back. Jacob's younger than I had at first thought, maybe in his late forties? Elijah swore his father didn't drink, and I'm inclined to believe him. The back keeps him in a lot of pain, but he's not in any danger of dyin' anytime too soon."

"Any chance of his getting better?"

"Have no idea. Jacob said his regular doctor's over in Claremore, he goes to him for his disability checkups and his prescriptions, but since he's otherwise uninsured, apparently that's about all anyone can do."

Dawn's killer instincts came roaring to the surface. "Do you know if he got hurt on the job?"

"He didn't say. Why?"

"Then workman's comp should cover it. Sounds to me as though somebody's trying to cheat him out of the care that's due him. You tell Jacob to get some legal advice, find out what his options are…why are you laughing?"

"Because I sure wouldn't want to be on the wrong side of a case you were arguin'. Whoo-ee—I can practically see your eyes glow from here."

So much for his not teasing. She felt a dumb smile stretch across her cheeks— *Oops.* Teasing: not good. Liking it: let's not go anywhere *near* there.

"That poor man, though," she said, bringing her thoughts to heel. "And poor Elijah, having to deal with that on his own. What happened to his mother…?"

"You okay?"

"Me? I'm fine. Why?"

"Your voice got all funny, that's all."

"Oh." She cleared her throat. "Dust. Or something. So. About Elijah's mother?"

"Died when Eli was real little. No grandparents or other relatives that the boy knew of. Or that Jacob would admit to, at least. So it's just the two of them. But, honey, from what we could tell, there really doesn't seem to be any cause to involve the authorities. Might cause more problems than solve them, you know?"

"You're sure?"

"Trust me—if I thought the boy was in any real danger, don't you think I'd do something about it? Or Ryan would?"

She let out a sigh. "I suppose. But…you'll keep an eye on him, anyway?"

His laugh filtered down the line. "You know, that mushy side of you kinda takes the edge off the scariness."

"Was that supposed to be a compliment?"

"Nope. Just an observation." He paused. "Well. At the risk

of venturing into dangerous territory…how're you feeling?
Still gettin' sick?''

''What? Oh. No. Well, just a little in the mornings sometimes. But I'm otherwise fine.''

''You eatin' okay? Gettin' plenty of rest?''

''Yes, Cal. I really can take care of myself,'' she said at the
same time she heard him say, ''I would've checked up on you
sooner—''

''You don't have to 'check up on me'!''

''—but I didn't want you to think I was getting in your face.
But you know what? It occurs to me, what with this being my
baby you're carrying and all, I don't give a damn whether you
think I'm getting in your face or not. So you find a doctor
yet?''

After she peeled herself off the wall from where his tirade
had plastered her, she said, ''I'm still looking.''

''Dammit, Dawn! You're nearly four months along!''

''I know how—'' she lowered her voice ''—far along I am,
okay? Which happens to be ten weeks, if you're keeping track.
Oh, Lord…does this mean you're gonna call every day from
now on?''

''Maybe. You gonna screen my calls?''

''Of course not. That would be…'' *Tempting.* ''…childish.''

''That would be my take on it, but you never know with
women.''

''And that, buster, is a sexist remark.''

''Only kind I know how to make, darlin'. And don't you go
getting all pissy on me—you know I'm just messing with
you.''

She decided against pointing out that ''messing with her''
was how they got into this particular *mess* to begin with. Fiddling with a paper clip on her desk, she asked, ''How's things
with the farm?''

''Fine,'' he said in that clipped, don't-wanna-talk-about-it
tone endemic to macho country boys. Then he said, ''You
know, I barely recognized you when you answered, but now
you sound like yourself again.''

"You really know how to make a girl's day, don't you?"

He laughed. Her toes curled. She could have stayed on the phone with him forever, she realized, which prompted both a reality check and a glance at the clock. And a mild coronary. "I hate to do this, but I'm really pressed for time—"

"Just one more thing and then I'll let you go—you thinking about coming home for Christmas?"

"What? Oh, geez, I don't know, I hadn't really thought about it. Depends on how much work I have to do—"

"Because I'm thinking of coming there."

Her breath left her lungs. "What?"

"I've always wanted to see New York, after hearing Mama talking about it so much. You could show me around. And we can start discussing names. Damn, Frank's bellowing about something out by the barn, I'd better go see what's up. Anyway, I'll talk to you later, okay?"

And he was gone before she had a chance to decide whether it was okay or not. Although at the moment, "not" was winning, hands down.

Cal in New York? The idea was as preposterous as…as his putting one of his horses on a plane and sending it here. The thought of him striding down the streets she walked every day, seeing for himself what she took for granted…sitting on her Macy's sofa in her tiny Upper Westside apartment, his long legs stretched out half way across her Turkish rug…

Wait. *Names?*

Well, yes, when a couple has a child, the couple usually names it.

She made a face. She'd be six months pregnant by then. *Really* pregnant.

Pregnant enough that—if she could believe some of her colleagues who'd already been this route—she might not mind a reenactment of The Night We Made Baby.

Oh, man. Was she screwed or what?

Cal leaned back in his office chair, one foot propped up on the edge of the sorry old desk that still smelled of his father's pipe tobacco whenever he opened the middle drawer. Talking to Dawn had sent a thousand memories skedaddling through his brain, memories from way before last summer. When they were kids, little kids, her presence in his life had simply been a fact, like the earth being round and that two plus two would always be four, no matter what. That they never saw eye-to-eye on anything, that she seemed to think it was her mission in life to piss him off on a regular basis, was beside the point. Her existence alone was enough. When she was around, things were just…good. Right. The way they were supposed to be.

When had that changed? When had she stopped being simply there, like air or sky or the smoky blue Ozarks in the distance? And why had it changed? Even after his mother's death, when Ivy no longer had as much reason to bring Dawn out to the farm to visit, they were still in school together, in the same classes, even, until high school, when Dawn took extra classes so she could graduate early.

Had she pulled away?

Or had he let her go?

"Lunch is on the table," Ethel said from the doorway, her tightly curled hair the color of a brand-new penny today. "If you can drag yourself away from your daydreaming long enough to eat."

Cal's boot clomped to the wooden floor. "I'm not daydreaming."

"No, you're plotting to go to New York City to see Dawn."

"How the hell'd you know that? You been standing at the door?"

"I was passin' by on my way to the john, and your voice carries." She crossed her arms over a red sweatshirt with beads and junk stuck all over it. "Don't tell me you're thinking of dragging her back here like some caveman."

"Ethel, believe me…" Cal stood, stretching out his back to make the vertebrae pop between his shoulderblades. "Even if I was dumb enough to entertain that idea, I'm sure not dumb enough to think it'd work."

A minute or so later, seated in front of his sandwich and

potato salad, he said, "You were around when Ivy was carrying Dawn, right?"

"Honey, some days I feel like I was around when Eve was carrying Cain and Abel. Why?"

"You got any idea who her father is? Or was?"

Pouring his tea, she shook her head. "None at all. Ivy never so much as dropped a hint. My guess is, he wasn't local. Or maybe he was married. Or both."

"How'd people feel about that? Ivy being an unwed mother, I mean."

Ethel came over and sat down across from him, peeling the shell off a hardboiled egg. "What do you think? Some took it as a personal insult, especially those predisposed to thinking Ivy was a little on the strange side to begin with. Bad enough when word got out she was a registered Democrat. Others, like your mama, didn't take it one way or the other." She dispatched the top half of the egg and said around it, "What brought this on?"

"I'm not sure. Just playing around with the puzzle pieces, I guess, seeing which way they go. I always thought Dawn left because she had bigger plans for her life than she'd ever be able to realize around here, but now… Hell, I don't even know why I'm thinking about any of this. It's not like it changes anything."

Ethel finished her egg—which she would undoubtedly call "lunch," only to polish off a slab of cake or something later in the name of not letting it go to waste—her brows dipped behind her glasses as if she had something to say but had decided not to. For the moment. Then she waved her hand. "Oh—I almost forgot—Sherman Mosely called, said to tell you that paperwork's all ready to go. It's gonna be a real pain when he retires, and that's a fact. Who the heck wants to trek all the way to Claremore just to make out a will or something? I mean…" She got up to carry her plate to the sink, dumping the eggshell into the garbage. "Might be just the ticket, you know, for a bright young thing who's looking for something part-time after she has a baby? Or something."

"Excuse me? What was that about not dragging her back here like some caveman?"

"There's a difference between forcing someone back against her will and dangling a little bait in front of her."

"The bait's been dangled, Ethel. The she-wolf isn't interested. She left Haven for a reason, you know."

"Oh, I have no doubt she left Haven for a reason. I'm just wondering if she really knows what that reason is. Or if you do, for that matter. You finished with that plate yet?"

"You can see I'm not and what the hell's that supposed to mean?"

"I mean, I don't think that gal left because of her ambitions, or because of what some narrow-minded people might have said or done to her because her mama wasn't married. I think she left because of you, I think she's staying away because of you, and I think if there's any chance at all of the two of you raising this baby together, you're gonna have to figure out what that is."

Cal let the glass of iced tea thunk back onto the table. "I didn't drive her away, Ethel."

"Didn't say that. Although her seeing you cozy up to everything with curves and a willing smile all through high school probably didn't help matters any."

"You think Dawn was *jealous*?"

"Didn't say that, either. But I saw the way she used to look at you when you two were little. Like Donna Reed gawking at Jimmy Stewart in *It's a Wonderful Life,* only in the early part when they were kids, so it was different actors playing Donna Reed and Jimmy Stewart."

Cal knew better than to even try to straighten that one out. Besides, he was having enough trouble straightening out his own thoughts at the moment. "I did ask her out, once," he said. "She turned me down."

"When was this?"

"I don't know. Ninth grade, maybe?"

"And you mean to tell me you actually think she meant that no?"

"Well, let's see…I said, 'Wanna go to the movies with me on Saturday?' and she said, 'Why would I want to do that?' If there's any other way to interpret that, I'd sure like to know."

"How about you probably took her by surprise and those were the first words to come out of her mouth? For the love of Pete, Cal—how many foals've you raised that took to the bridle right off, either?"

Cal frowned. "So you're saying I should've tried again?"

"Boy, you have just set a new record in the 'better late than never' category."

"So where the hell were you sixteen years ago, when your advice might have done some good?"

They both fell silent, remembering exactly what they'd been doing—watching Henry Logan, Sr., fade away after Cal's mother's death, five years earlier. Not two weeks after Cal's ill-fated attempt at taking his and Dawn's relationship into new territory, his father died in his sleep of an apparent heart attack.

"All the Logan men love real hard," Ethel said quietly. "In some cases, like your daddy's, maybe too hard. When they hurt, they hurt deep. So deep, sometimes, they find it easier to give up than to try again. Ryan and Hank, both, nearly let the pain of losing, of *living,* stop them from finding the happiness that was theirs by rights. And your father…" She sighed. "Lord knows I thought the world of that man, but grieving's a process. Not a destiny."

"I'm not grieving, Ethel, if that's your point. You can't mourn something you never had. Or never would've had. What if I had asked her again, and she'd said yes? What would've come of it? Seems to me our getting close back then would've only made things worse when it came time for her to leave. Because she would've still left, Ethel, no matter what she and I might've had going."

The old woman shrugged. "If that's what you wanna believe, nothin' I can do to stop you."

Confused and agitated and just plum annoyed with life in general, Cal pushed himself up from the table. "Okay—since you're so all-fired smart about all this, I don't suppose you have any suggestions about Dawn's and my *current* situation?''

"Me? Hell, no. Far be it from me to stick my nose in where it doesn't belong."

"I've got work to do," Cal muttered, slamming his hat on his head and heading for the back door.

"You can say that again," she yelled behind him.

Chapter 5

The woman sitting across from Dawn's desk in the no-frills storefront legal clinic in East Harlem was just like dozens of others Dawn had helped over the past four years. Oh, their skin colors varied, and some were so overweight they barely fit on the seat of the thirty-year-old molded plastic chair while others were thin to the point of emaciation, but the how-did-this-happen-to-me? look in their blue or black or brown eyes was always the same.

At twenty-two, Valerie Abernathy already had four kids. The last one's father had walked out three months ago. She was there because some collection agency was calling her ten times a day about a bill she didn't know anything about, she said.

"I don't get it," Valerie said, jiggling the fussy six-month-old in her arms while her other kids ransacked the toy bin on the other side of Dawn's cubicle. "Things was good between him and me for a *long* time. I mean, he'd talk so pretty, and bring me all kinds of little treats and stuff, swearin' up one side and down the other ain't nobody for him but me. Then he goes and pulls this crap."

Their stories were all the same, too, each recital scraping off another piece of Dawn's heart. She thought of the divorce clients in her eastside firm who'd practically come to blows over who got *which* house, the Miro and/or the Peugeot. Did any of them even have a clue what it might be like to have to fight for a few dollars a week so your kids didn't go hungry? Still, rich or destitute or hovering somewhere in the infinite middle, the upshot was the same:

I thought I could trust him.

I thought I'd made the right choice.

Trust me, honey, no matter how good the sex is…it's not enough.

Nope, class or society or whatever you wanted to call it knew no distinction between women who'd hooked up with men for the wrong reasons—or even, sometimes, for what sure looked like the right ones. In the end, they all came looking for help to straighten out the mess love had left them in.

"Miss Gardner—you okay?"

Dawn jerked herself back to the present. Latesha, a round-cheeked three-year-old with a dozen chubby braids sprouting from her head, lifted her arms to crawl into Dawn's lap. Hauling the toddler up and giving her a pencil and piece of scrap paper to scribble on, Dawn said, "Yeah, sorry. Now, look— next time one of these turkeys calls, you tell him in no uncertain terms that it is illegal to harass you like this, and that furthermore you are *not* responsible for your boyfriend's debts in any way, shape or form, whether he put your name down or not. *And* if they call again, they will be hearing from your lawyer."

Valerie's eyes got so big, her pale-blue eyeshadow was obliterated. "Couldn't you just call 'em for me?"

The fear in the young woman's voice nearly toppled Dawn's resolve, but she shook her head. "They know what they're doing is against the law. But they hear a young woman on the other end of the line, and they figure, what does she know? This really isn't something you need a lawyer for," she said gently. Along with dispensing cut-rate—or, more often, free—

legal advice, the lawyers who worked here often found themselves acting as social workers and mentors to these women, many of whom lacked both self-confidence and basic coping skills. "Besides, remember what we talked about before—" this wasn't the first time the young mother had come to them for help "—that you can do more for yourself than you think you can, right?"

The young woman made a face, then sighed. "I s'pose. But I sure am tired of cleaning up after this dude." Then she beamed. "You see where we all signed that petition to get Crown Management to finally fix up that dump we livin' in?"

"I did. And I think you've got an excellent case. Now see, there's where you need a lawyer to act as the heavy."

"You know nobody been able to win against 'em yet?"

"There's always a first time," Dawn said with a grin.

The young woman stood and called her brood, then cocked her head at Dawn. "You somethin' else, Miss Gardner, you know that?" she said as Latesha slid off Dawn's lap and went to her mama. "You don't take no crap off nobody, do you?"

"Not if I can help it."

The young woman laughed, then said, "There's a lot of folks gonna be real sorry to see you go."

"Go? I'm not going anywhere."

"Oh, I don't mean right this minute, but none of you stick around forever, you hear what I'm saying? Well, except Miss Menendez, but she's different. The others, though, they all leave sooner or later. But that's okay. That's just the way life is. Anyway, you have a good night, and I'll be sure and let you know how everything turns out."

The minute the woman and her chicks left, every last ounce of energy drained from Dawn's body. It was past eight—theoretically, and according to the people who paid her salary and whose names she hoped would soon be joined by hers, she wasn't supposed to spend more than ten percent of her time working pro bono cases, which meant sneaking in what she thought of as her "real" work after regular hours—and she

knew she needed food. But right now she was too damned tired
to do anything about it.

She let her head fall forward onto her folded arms, feeling
a hairpin slither out of the Gibson girl hairdo she wore for
work. Brother—if she felt like this now, what on earth was she
going to feel like at eight months?

"Should I just throw a blanket over you and turn out the
lights?"

Dawn smiled at the sound of Gloria Menendez's voice, forcing herself to look up at the still-beautiful fifty-something face
surrounded by a mane of thick brown curls. "You have no
idea how tempting that is."

"I got something better to tempt you with," her boss said.
"Chinese food."

"You're on." Dawn unlocked the bottom drawer to her desk
and dragged out her purse. "Except I gotta pee first."

"Didn't you just go a half hour ago?"

"Too much tea," Dawn lobbed back as, suddenly energized
by her full bladder, she scurried across the floor.

A few minutes later, shivering in the damp October breeze,
the two women walked up Lexington Avenue toward the
cheapo Chinese restaurant Dawn saw more than she saw her
own apartment. Gloria tucked her hand into the crook of
Dawn's jacketed arm. "So," she said, swiping a curl off her
forehead. "When were you planning on telling me?"

"Telling you what?" As they neared the restaurant, the scent
of egg rolls and fried rice revived Dawn enough to pick up her
pace.

"Baby, you're starting to show."

Eggs rolls forgotten—for the moment—Dawn froze, then
shifted her gaze to Gloria's. "Busted?"

"Uh-huh. You might still be wearing your regular clothes,
but your face is fuller, your boobs are bigger, and you're in
the bathroom every five minutes. So when are you due?"

Dawn pressed her lips together for a second, then said, "First
week of April."

"And the father is…?"

"Nobody you'd know. And if I don't get an egg roll in this stomach within the next five minutes I refuse to be held accountable for my actions."

"Fine. But don't even think that's a ploy to make me drop the subject."

And, since Gloria was nothing if not true to her word, they'd no sooner been seated at their regular booth when she said, "So talk."

So Dawn talked. About everything except Cal's calling almost every night because…well, because no matter how she worded it, someone—in this case, old eagle ears on the other side of the booth—might get the wrong impression. About their relationship. Or something.

"And you honestly believe this is gonna work?" Gloria said. Salivating in anticipation of that first, soy-sauce-laden bite, Dawn watched in reverential silence as several silver-lidded dishes clunked on the Formica table in front of them. The instant their server left, both women attacked their meals with the zeal of a horny teenage couple finding themselves alone for the first time. Gesturing with a half-eaten eggroll, Gloria said, "How on earth do you think the two of you are gonna raise this kid with roughly a hundred states between you?"

"People do it all the time," Dawn muttered around a mouthful of pork fried rice.

"Not well, they don't. And would you listen to yourself? All the time you spend trying to get fathers to do right by their kids, and here you'd keep your own from his or her father."

"But I'm not," she said, chewing. "Not forever, anyway." At Gloria's snort, she added, "I never said it was ideal. And at least I told him."

"You want a medal for that?"

"No. But a little support wouldn't hurt. That's not my home anymore. This is. Even Cal understands that."

"Home's not a place, honey. It's where family is."

"And which *Chicken Soup* book did you get that out of?"

Gloria jabbed her chopsticks in Dawn's direction. "Watch it. Cynicism gives you gas. Besides, just because something's corny doesn't mean it's not true." She narrowed her eyes. "This…Cal. You say he's an old friend?"

"When we were kids, yeah."

"But not later?"

"Not the same way, no."

"Yet you slept with him."

"What's your point, Glory?"

"I'm not sure. But then, I don't think you are, either."

"It was a fling, okay? A crazy, dumb, impulsive one-time thing. Combined with a friendship that more or less fell apart once we hit puberty, I'm not exactly seeing a terrific foundation for marriage, are you?"

Gloria's eyebrows lifted. "Who said anything about marriage?"

"Well…you did. Didn't you?"

"Not me, honey. First time I heard that word was when it came out of your mouth two seconds ago."

Dawn shoveled in a piece of steamed broccoli. "Well, pretend you didn't hear it, because it's not an option."

They ate in silence for a good minute or two. Then: "What's he like?"

"Glory, I really don't want—"

"I'm only gonna keep bugging you until you tell me, so you might as well give in now."

"Okay, fine. He's…I don't know. Your typical guy. Six-something, light-brown hair, green eyes, great smile, dimples—"

"Dimples?"

"Yeah, you know, those creasy things some men get in their cheeks when they smile—"

"You want this egg roll in your lap, smartass? I mean, what's he like? As a person?"

Dawn decided the only way to get through this was to pretend this was somebody else talking. As if she were an actress playing the role of a pregnant woman sitting in a Chinese restaurant, describing the guy who'd knocked her up. "Calm. Dependable. Honest. Good with kids. No—great with kids. And animals. He raises horses, did I mention that?''

"As in, faded jeans? Cowboy boots? Bob Redford in *The Horse Whisperer*?''

"Well, kinda. But without the soft focusing.''

Gloria blinked. "And…he's not right for you why?''

"Oh, oh!'' Dawn's hand shot up over her head. "I know this one! Because, if you saw the girls he dated in high school—and there were many of them—''

"Thought you said you lived in some tiny town?''

"Oh, trust me, they sniffed him out from all over northeast Oklahoma. Anyway, if you saw these girls, and then compared them with what you see here—'' she pointed to herself "—you would understand. In no way, shape, form or fashion am I what Cal Logan wants in a mate.''

"He tell you that?''

"He doesn't have to. That's just been a given from the time we were twelve. Now can we please drop the subject?''

"Suit yourself.'' More face stuffing, more chewing, then: "So. When do you think you'll hear whether or not you make partner?''

Dawn sucked in a breath and nearly choked on a piece of pork. "Friday,'' she got out around her coughing.

"You think you've got a good shot?''

"Considering the amount of blood they've gotten from me over the past several years, I should hope so. My billable hours were down a bit last year, but so were everybody's.'' She leaned forward. "I overheard two of the divorce attorneys talking about how their workload's slacked off because nobody can afford to get divorced anymore.''

Gloria chuckled, then frowned. "You've been spending a lot of time up here, though. Bet that doesn't sit well.''

Dawn waved away her friend's concern. "It's never interfered with my work for the firm. Besides, if I make partner, I'll have more clout with some of these class-action cases we've got coming up.'' Grinning, she doused her next helping of fried rice with soy sauce. "I feel really good about this,

Glory. Like I'm right on the cusp of a major turning point in my life.''

Dark eyebrows lifted. ''And if that turning point doesn't take you in the direction you'd planned on?''

''It has to, Glory,'' she said over the chill zipping up her spine. ''I've worked too damn hard…'' With a shrug, she popped a shrimp into her mouth. ''It just has to.''

What Crawford Reynolds, the firm's senior partner, lacked in stature he more than made up for in an intimidating preciseness, from the cut of his megabucks charcoal-gray suit to the styling of his megabucks haircut to the tasteful gold signet ring on his megabucks manicured pinkie.

That is, until he opened his mouth and channeled Robert De Niro.

''So…'' He tented his fingers in front of a barely smiling mouth. Behind his black leather chair, a massive, Technicolor Southwest landscape vibrated against a charcoal-gray wall. ''Dawn—'' *Dooawn.* ''—I suppose you know why I've called you in.''

Seated on a charcoal-gray upholstered chair across from Crawford's über-contemporary teak desk, her taupe Naturalizers firmly planted in the plush, charcoal-gray carpeting, Dawn willed her stomach still and her accent to die.

''You've made your decision, then?''

Dark-brown eyes bored into hers for three or four seconds longer than necessary before the man got up and walked around to lean one hip onto the edge of his desk in front of her.

''You're a hard worker, no doubt about it. And I've noticed you don't get all caught up in office shenanigans.'' He pointed one finger at her. ''I like that. Shows you put your work ahead of personality.''

His hand dropped to his lap to link with the other one, which was when she knew, with a sickening thud, where the conversation was going. ''Unfortunately,'' the senior continued, ''some of the other partners questioned whether you were as dedicated to what we do here as you are to your pro-bono clients. Don't get me wrong, we all commend your selflessness, but we're still running a business here. And we can't help but feel, well, that perhaps your focus is more divided than it should be.''

"I see.'' Despite the blood rushing in her ears, not to mention the futility of her argument, she felt compelled to say, "The vast majority of what I do for the clinic is on my own time. I've never let it interfere with my work for the firm, or been late on any project—''

"Which is exactly what I told the others. But I think some of my colleagues detect a certain…lack of enthusiasm on your part, as evidenced by your billable hours, which unfortunately fall somewhat short of the mark.''

"But everyone's hours are down!''

"True. Then again, I think it's safe to say that some people are just more naturally suited to rainmaking than others? And, I hate to say this, because I'm sure you never did this intentionally, we've had a…complaint here and there from a client, that perhaps you weren't giving them quite as much attention as they thought our hourly fees entitled them to.''

To her horror, Dawn felt her cheeks get hot. But damned if she was going to let her voice waver. "I've never neglected a client. I swear.''

"I'm sure you didn't think you did. But part of being successful in a firm like ours is being able to know which clients need a little more hand holding, if you know what I mean. And the consensus seems to be that maybe your other duties…distract you from being able to give a hundred percent here.''

She swallowed down the hot, hard lump at the back of her throat before saying, "I honestly wasn't aware… I mean, these are areas I could certainly work on improving…''

"I'm sorry, Dawn,'' Crawford said gently. "The other partners simply don't feel you're a team player.'' He glanced at his hands, then back at her. "We really think you'd be happier working in another environment.''

"You're…*firing* me?''

"Things are tough all over, Dawn. You know that. You're smart as a whip, and conscientious, but your qualities aren't commensurate with what we need at the moment." He got up and held out his hand, her signal to stand. Even in the low-heeled shoes she'd thought a more prudent choice today, she still stood eye-to-eye with him. "Is three weeks enough time for you to tie up any loose ends?"

"I'll be out of here in two," she said, wishing like hell she'd worn the four-inch Manolos anyway.

In her sweats, sitting cross-legged on her sofa, Dawn hugged a pillow to her middle, tuning out her neighbors' muffled laughter filtering through the living room wall. Since moving to the city, she'd come to define *quiet* as any noise that had nothing to do with her. Usually she savored the aloneness, letting it cocoon her from the demands and pressures of her day, her life. The life she'd chosen. Tonight, though, it seemed to slap her upside the head, taunting her about the one thing she'd sworn she would never do:

Fail.

She felt hollowed out. Numb. Swallowing back tears, she glanced around the apartment she loved so much, even if she could only fit her double bed into the tiny bedroom by pushing it up against one wall. But the place was a bargain, by Manhattan standards, and even after three years she still felt a tingle of victory every time she opened the door and knew there were no roommates lurking on the other side of it. Tonight, however, the events of the day had barged through the door with her, fighting for space in what was supposed to be her sanctuary, like passengers scrambling for seats on a crowded subway train.

For nearly a month she'd used work as a barrier against reality. But tonight, faced with this new reality, she realized she'd been so busy helping others piece together the shards of their shattered lives she hadn't even noticed the bleeding wounds from stumbling around in her own.

Twelve years she'd spent studying and working and toadying, mindlessly pursuing a goal she couldn't even define any-more. Twelve years spent driving herself to that next level, never stopping, never breathing, never giving whoever might be on her tail a chance to plow her down and get "there" before her.

But…what was "there"? And who, exactly, were these phantoms she'd been so determined to keep one step—if not two or three—in front of?

Dawn keeled over onto her side, more weary and confused than she could ever remember being, just as her portable phone chirped. She fumbled for it, even though she knew it was Cal. Or maybe because it was Cal. She no longer knew. Or cared.

"'Lo?"

"Dawn? What is it?" She could hear the apprehension in his voice, thought it was sweet in a distant, fuzzy kind of way. "Is something wrong with the baby?"

She shook her head, then remembered he couldn't see her. "No, no…the baby's fine. But…" She hauled in a breath, hugging the pillow more tightly. "But I didn't make partner," she said in a tiny voice. "In fact, I was canned."

"Are those people idiots or what?" blasted through the line. "You worked your tail off for them. And I thought you said you thought your chances were better than good?"

"They were. Just…not good enough, I guess." She filled him in, her recitation frequently interrupted by Cal's repeated "That's B.S. and you know it!" When she'd finished, though, he said, "You know what? He's right about one thing, honey—you don't belong there. If they can't appreciate you, they don't deserve you! You'll find another job, Dawn. A better one. You hear?"

Despite the heaviness inside her, she had to smile. "You're remarkably confident for someone who basically knows nothing about what I do."

"Yeah, well, I've known you since you were a snotty little know-it-all—"

"Hey!"

"—and now you're a less snotty, though equally aggravating, big know-it-all. You have always known what you wanted, and for the most part, you've gotten it. So you're not real used to setbacks. Which is all this is, honey. A setback.''

She blinked, then said, ''You're not going to tell me this is a sign I'm supposed to move back to Haven?''

Silence. Then, in a genuinely surprised tone, ''Why would I do that? I mean, is your work there finished?''

''Well, no. But—''

''Then why the hell would you come back here?'' Before she could wrap her head around this about-face, he added, ''What about that free clinic?''

''What about it?''

''If you don't find another job with a bigger firm, maybe they could hire you full-time.''

Her heart pounding, she pushed herself back upright. ''Oh my God, Cal—you're brilliant! I mean, it would mean a huge cut in pay, but I've been very careful with my money, I've got enough put away to get me through if I can't find something right away, which is very likely with the way things have been—''

''And that's the kind of work you really want to be doing, anyway, right?''

She felt as though a dark, ugly cloud had been lifted from her brain. ''Yes. Yes, it is. Oh, Cal…thank you. Thank you, thank you, thank you…for calling right now, for being a pain in the butt, for—'' she clutched the phone ''—being there.''

After a long moment he said, ''You're welcome, honey.''

Then he hung up before things got any sappier than they already were.

Cal stared at the phone on his desk for probably a full minute before dragging his carcass outside. It was getting on time to bring in the herd for the night, and he still had a couple of stalls to muck out, what with having to mend that fence on the north side of the pasture today, since Frank, his only hand at the moment, couldn't do it. The older man had never missed a day's work, going back as far as Cal could remember, but his arthritis was beginning to slow him down more that he wanted to admit. Meaning Cal could really use another pair of hands to at least help out with the routine stuff. However, not only did unsold horses mean more work, they also meant smaller profits. Cal couldn't afford to hire somebody else as well as keep Frank on. And there was no way he'd ever let him go.

Just as there'd been no way he wouldn't've given Dawn that pep talk. Hell, the devastation in her voice had nearly done him in. The kicker, though, was that he'd meant every word of it. Of course, that made the loss of his sanity official, but that had been all over but the shouting for some time, anyway. Thing was, though, nobody believed hard work deserved a payoff more than Cal did. And nobody'd worked harder toward something than Dawn. In fact, if it hadn't been for the baby, he probably wouldn't even be all twisted up inside like he was now.

Of course, if it hadn't been for the baby, he wouldn't have been calling her in the first place, would he?

And because he was obviously in major masochistic mode, instead of going straight to the barn, he made a detour to the freestanding workshop Hank, Sr., had built before Cal was born. His father had been a mean woodworker in his time. Taught all his boys the basics, too. Not that it had ever taken with Ryan, who could set a bone so you couldn't tell it had ever been broken but whose only use for a saw was to remove the cast later. And while Hank had more or less single-handedly replaced every shingle and rotten porch floorboard at the Double Arrow, the finer points of carpentry were lost on him, too. Cal, however, got a kick out of building the occasional table or cabinet, of fitting the pieces together, of taking pride in every detail, right down to the hand-rubbed finish.

Or, in this case, *re*finishing.

Breathing in the comforting tang of raw wood and oil stain, he crouched in the sawdust by the solid maple cradle, which he'd stripped last week and was just waiting for a spare hour or so to restain it. He skimmed one hand over the smooth edge, trying without much luck to banish either the tightness in his chest or the image of the toothless baby smile that came to mind every time he looked at the piece. However, the cradle belonged to the baby, not to Cal. And it wouldn't do the baby any good if the baby wasn't here.

And it didn't do Cal any good wishing for things that simply weren't going to happen.

Mooner came up beside him, sticking his snout into the cradle, then nosing Cal's arm to get petted.

"You should've heard her, boy," he said, roughly scratching the mutt between his shoulder blades. "The way she suddenly perked up when I suggested a way she could stay there…" He frowned at the cradle. "Wonder how much it'd cost to ship this to New York?"

The dog's only reply was to wriggle around so Cal would scratch his rump.

"Okay," Dawn announced the next morning when she walked into Gloria's office fifteen minutes before the clinic opened. "I've got good news and bad news. Good news first." She removed her swing coat and flopped it over the back of an extra chair. "If you still want me, there's no longer any impediment to my working here full-time."

The folder in Gloria's hand smacked onto her desk. "Damn. You didn't make partner?"

"Okay, that was the bad news. But you wanna know *why* I didn't make partner? Because, according to the man who signed my checks for four years, my loyalties were divided. And you know what? He was right. That's not what I want to do. *This* is. Only it took Cal's smacking me in the face with that fact to realize it."

Eyebrows lifted. "Cal?"

Damn. "He…kinda gave me a pep talk. When he called." Eyebrows went higher. "About how my work here wasn't done yet and how I couldn't give up, and had I thought about a full-time job at the clinic. Anyway…" Before the woman's eyebrows flew clean off her head, Dawn hooked one foot around the leg of the chair in front of Gloria's desk and yanked it underneath her so she could sit, leaning on the edge of the desk. "So whaddya think? Remember how you said you might even be able to swing a grant or something for my salary? I mean, I certainly don't expect anything near what I was making at Reynolds. I know that. But it's not as if I'm making payments on a Beemer or anything. I can manage on a lot less—"

"That's not it, baby."

Dawn sat back in her chair, not liking the pained expression on Gloria's face. At all. "Don't tell me you were just blowing up my skirt all this time."

"And if you think that," Gloria snapped, "you need to have your head examined! I'd kill to have you full-time, you know I would."

"Then what's the problem?"

"The problem is…" Brows drawn, she blew out a harsh sigh. "The problem is, they're closing this office down at the end of the month."

"*What?* Why?"

"Because they can. And because, as you well know, money's tight. They figure they can save a few bucks by consolidating this office with the one up on 135th Street. I'd known this was in the works for a month, but I didn't hear definitely until yesterday. And I didn't say anything because…oh, hell. I figured you'd get that partnership and working here would be a moot point. That you'd go on to bigger and better—and far more lucrative—things."

"Oh. Well. I didn't. Go on to bigger and better things."

"I'm so sorry, baby."

Dawn sucked in a breath. "Oh, God, Glory—you're not losing *your* job, are you?"

Gloria tapped her long, red fingernails on her blotter for a moment, then shook her head. "Actually, they want me to run the 135th Street office, since that manager's retiring, anyway. But…I can't take anybody from here."

In a daze, Dawn somehow got to her feet and made her way back to her own office, still piled high with case folders. She looked at them, shaking her head. Gloria came up and slipped an arm around her shoulders.

"You have any idea what you're going to do?"

"Set up a little cardboard booth in Penn Station? You know, like Lucy in *A Charlie Brown Christmas?* 'Legal advice, five cents.'"

"Hey, with inflation, you could probably charge a whole buck."

"I doubt it, considering the competition I'd have from the roughly five million other recently jettisoned attorneys who'll be right there with me." She picked up Valerie Abernathy's folder, picturing the earnest young woman and her four children. "How can I leave here, Glory? Leave these people?"

"Baby, I don't mean to sound callous...but these people were here before you came, and for damn sure they'll be here after you leave. And don't take this the wrong way, but you aren't exactly a unique species, either. As long as there are PR-conscious law firms in this town, there's no danger of the supply drying up of bright-eyed pups determined to make a difference."

"I jeopardized my career for this, Glory," Dawn said quietly. "Not that I realized it at the time, but still. That hardly puts me in the same league as some junior who can't wait for her six-month pro-bono stint to be up."

"I know that. But I also get a real strong feeling you drown yourself in work to avoid facing reality."

Hearing her own revelation bounced back at her brought a wry smile to her lips. But she said, "Oh, yeah? Then what does that say about you?"

"All right. Let's look at that. Or better yet, look around you. This is my life, baby. Has been for nearly twenty-five years. I make bupkes, have lost two husbands because of it, and frankly, I'm not even sure how much good I've done."

"Then why are you still here?"

"Because I can't think of a single other thing I'd rather be doing."

"Then why should I be any different?"

''Because you *are* different. Because you're pregnant by some guy who actually wants the kid—a guy, by the way, who obviously cares enough about you to help you figure out how to salvage your life here—and because, dammit, you owe it to yourself, and to him, and to this child, to try to make things work. *Together.* Not with him one place and you another.''

''Hold on—how'd this get to be about me and Cal and the baby?''

''Because like it or not, that's what your life is about right now. I know wanting to help people comes as naturally to you as breathing. And our clients know it, too. But God knows, New York isn't the only place on earth where you can do that, you know? You really want to make a difference, you go back home, and you make your peace with this child's father, and with being a mother, and with whatever drove you here to begin with. And you let your light shine every bit as bright as it has here. But hiding out halfway across the country, instead of facing whatever it is you need to face, makes you just as much of a victim as any one of those people who walk through our door.''

''I am not a victim!''

''Then quit acting like one. Look—if this office weren't closing, you'd better believe I'd've done everything short of selling my soul to the devil to have gotten you on full-time. But that would have been selfish. So God, in His infinite wisdom and mercy, decided to remove the temptation, okay? For both of us.''

Dawn looked down at her desk again, fingering the Abernathy file. ''It wasn't supposed to happen like this.''

''And maybe it was, *chica.*'' She gave her another hug. ''Maybe it was.''

A month to the day after he'd last seen Dawn, Cal stood with his arms crossed over his denim jacket, watching the stream of passengers come through the security checkpoint. She'd be expecting Ivy, but the midwife had called him an hour ago to tell him one of her mothers had gone into labor, she might not make it back in time to meet Dawn's evening flight so did he mind picking her up at the airport?

Did he mind? No. What Dawn's reaction might be was something else again.

Then he saw her, her face drawn, no makeup, her braided hair coiled around her head.

Her belly, pushing slightly against a plain gray sweatshirt.

She spotted him. Shifted her carry-on higher onto her shoulder as he walked toward her, unsmiling, unsure. His breath left his lungs as it hit him just how badly he'd wanted her to come home.

But not like this. Not because she'd had no choice.

He was close enough now to see the exhausted defeat in her eyes, as unfamiliar and out of place as snow in August. And he realized he would give anything, do anything, to be able to restore to her what she'd lost.

Cal opened his arms…and with a sad smile, the woman he could no longer deny he loved walked into them.

Chapter 6

"When'd you get this?" Cal said to Ivy, skimming a hand down the handle of the sparkling white, brand-spanking-new, double-door refrigerator in Ivy's kitchen. Dawn had gone to her room to freshen up and unpack; they'd all gotten to Ivy's at the same time, the delivery having gone without a hitch, Ivy said, although she needed to go back to check up on mama and baby in a little bit.

"Isn't it pretty? Dawn apparently ordered it off the Internet and had it delivered as a surprise a couple of weeks ago. Sure is quieter, for one thing. Not to mention it's nice not to have half-frozen cucumbers when I go to make a salad." The midwife glanced toward the door, then whispered, "How'd she seem?"

"Resigned," Cal said, sitting at the table and leaning back in the kitchen chair, scowling at his glass of iced tea. "It's like an alien took over her body."

"Huh," was all Ivy said, bringing her own tea to the table. "She say anything, though? About her plans?"

"Not much. Just that she decided she didn't want to put

herself through the stress of job hunting right now, so she may as well stay here until after the baby comes. She sublet her apartment for the time being, but the rest of her clothes and what-all should be here next week sometime, she said.''

"Well, at least we know the baby'll be born here now." At his shrug, she added, "I would've thought you'd be happy about that."

His gaze shot to Ivy's. "Why would I be happy about something that makes Dawn miserable?"

Ivy looked at him steadily for a moment, then said, "I know she's down, and it's killin' me to see her like this, feeling like her dreams've gone up in smoke. But I also know moping's not her style. She'll land on her feet, you'll see."

"I don't doubt it for a minute. But I'm not so much of a fool as to think she'll stick around, either—"

"The subject of the conversation is now entering the official eavesdropping zone," Dawn announced as she entered the kitchen, now wearing a pair of jeans and a baggy, dark-green sweater with one of those big floppy collars that never stayed in one place. "And to avoid rampant speculation—" she poured herself a glass of milk from the fridge, slamming shut the door with her hip "—I guess I might as well let you in on what I'm thinking."

She sat at the table between them, dispatched half the glass of milk, then took her mother's hand. "First off, I decided I want you to deliver the baby."

Ivy gasped. Then beamed. "You sure?"

"Wouldn't have it any other way. And secondly…" She studied her glass for a good long time, then said, "At some point, the economy's bound to turn. I've got enough saved up to live on for probably a year or so, especially if I stay here. So I thought maybe I'd start sending out résumés around my eighth month or so, and we'll see what happens."

Cal and Ivy exchanged a lightning-fast glance. "You think you'll go back to New York?" she said.

"Maybe." Cal watched Dawn's slender fingers worry the corners of the cloth placemat. "And even if I'm not…

aggressive enough for Manhattan, God knows there are plenty of other firms, in plenty of other towns. Until then, I guess I get to sit around and wait for my belly button to pop like a turkey timer.''

"Speaking of turkey timers," Ivy said, "Maddie invited us for Thanksgiving. So you can fit it into your social calendar."

"Already? Isn't it like six weeks away?"

"Five. It's early this year. And with Hank and Jenna's wedding coming up right after, Maddie wanted to get everything squared away early... Oh, for heaven's sake," she said as her pager buzzed. "Who could that be?" She checked the number, then got up to go to the phone in the living room, muttering something about first-time mothers thinking every twinge meant they were going into labor.

After Ivy left, Dawn kept up her infernal twiddling with the damn place mat until Cal grabbed her hand. Her eyes flashed to his. "That's making me nuts," he said.

She mumbled, "Sorry," and tucked both hands under her arms.

"I'm really sorry it didn't work out," he said. "You getting to stay in New York, I mean."

That got an amused glance. "You are such a bad liar."

Cal was quiet for a couple seconds, then said, "I don't lie, Dawn. You being here when you don't want to be isn't likely to be much fun for anybody."

She started messing with the place mat again. "But that's just it. I do want to be here."

"Now who's lying?"

"No, I mean it. There're some things I need to settle in my head. And this is the only place I can do that." Her forehead crinkled. "For one thing, I want to find out who my father is. And...I was wondering if you'd help me."

"Me? Wouldn't it make more sense to ask Ivy?"

"I have. She says she can't tell me."

"Then maybe there's a reason for that."

"What? That he's a despotic dictator? A drug lord? A midget with the circus? Since I'm nearly five-eight, I doubt the third one's a possibility. And one doesn't tend to run into too many drug lords or despotic dictators in northeastern Oklahoma.''

"True," Cal said with a smile. "But why? And why now?"

Her shoulders bumped. "Just something I need to do, a gap I need to fill in. I mean, haven't you ever felt you had to do something that didn't even make sense, but you know you'd go nuts if you didn't at least try?"

He looked at her for a good long time. "Yeah. And sometimes the results are disastrous.''

It took her a moment before the blush raced up her throat and stained her cheeks. "Point taken," she said.

"And anyway," Cal said, "why do you think I'd be any help?"

"Because people talk to you. Trust you." She paused. "Whereas a lot of folks probably aren't real inclined to talk to me."

"That's nuts—"

"There's a reason Charmaine acted like I was a disease carrier, Cal. I was a snot in high school. I didn't mean to be, but that's the way I came off, I know it. Except to you and Faith and maybe a couple others. But I was so convinced I didn't have anything in common with most of the kids my age, I didn't bother finding out if maybe I did.''

His arms still crossed, Cal tipped the chair on its back legs. "You think you've got something to atone for?"

"I think I need to make peace with this town. For our baby's sake, if nothing else. And I need—" her breath left her lungs in a sharp burst "—and I need to make peace with you."

The chair legs slammed back to the floor. "Come again?"

Her mouth pulled up to one side. "I didn't have time to make many friends in New York. Or to keep up with the ones I made in college. And I was basically okay with that. Then you started calling me every day, and…I suddenly realized how much I looked forward to those calls." She smiled, and Cal thought his heart was going to pound clean out of his chest. "You're the only person I know who's not afraid to tick me off, who refuses to let me take myself too seriously. Who can make me laugh when that's the last thing I feel like doing. Then when you called that night after I lost the partnership…''

Her expression earnest, she leaned forward, wrapping her hand around his and sending his hormones into a tizwaz. ''That's when I realized how much I missed what we had as kids. And how much I want us to be friends, real friends, again—''

''Well,'' Ivy said, bursting back into the room in a flurry of agitation, ''looks like this isn't a false alarm after all, seeing's how her water just broke. So I guess I'm off again.'' She stopped just long enough to take in Dawn's hand still linked with Cal's, then skedaddled out the back door.

Cal dropped Dawn's hand and stood, agitation simmering in his gut. ''I need to get going, too,'' he said, grabbing his hat from the rack by the back door. ''Need to check on the mares one last time for the night.'' But before he let himself out, he turned back to Dawn and said, ''You really mean that? About wanting us to be friends again?''

She looked puzzled. ''Of course I do.''

''Well, darlin'—'' he rammed his hat on his head and yanked open Ivy's back door ''—if you want my friendship, it's all yours. Hell, it always was, even if you didn't always seem to want it. But if you think I'm gonna settle for *just* friendship, you are seriously barking up the wrong tree. For twenty-five years, I've been watching you push and pull and tug things to make everything go your way. So I'm thinking maybe it's time things started going *mine*.''

He pulled the door shut behind him and stomped around the house to his truck, feeling better about things than he had in a long, long time.

Oh, dear. That hadn't gone exactly the way she'd planned, had it?

Huddled inside one of her mother's ponchos, Dawn stood at the edge of the bungalow's small front porch, shivering in the firesmoke-tainted October night air, but not only from the cold.

Stars twinkled calmly against the black sky; dried leaves scurried down the street, much the same way as Cal's parting words did through her brain.

The instant she'd caught sight of him in the airport, she'd known she was in trouble. Big trouble. With all the fixings. That look on his face, the compassion and tenderness and understanding in his eyes…

Damn him.

Her vulnerability last summer was nothing compared with her vulnerability now. Oh, she'd rally, she knew that. She'd figure out this whole mess and land on her feet, just as her mother said. But to be honest, right now the only place she wanted to land was in Cal's arms.

Which is exactly what she'd done in the airport, inhaling that scent that both stirred and soothed, cherishing, for those few moments, his genuineness. But the thing was, see, she knew all that lovely compassion and understanding was just part of who Cal was. Not that there was anything wrong with that, unless one started thinking in terms of More.

Because thinking in terms of More with Cal was just plain silly. Whatever affection there might be between them, she was still who she was, he was still who he was. If anything, they were less alike now than ever, simply because they'd led very different lives for so long. Which was the part he didn't get. Not that his ''if you think I'm gonna settle for just friendship'' rant wasn't a nice ego boost, but for heaven's sake…it wasn't as if she could take that seriously.

She didn't dare.

Dear God—making a baby was nothing to what would happen if she gave even a smidgen of credence to this…fantasy, that they could ever be a real couple. The nice thing about fantasies, though, was that you could control the outcome. As opposed to reality, which you couldn't.

So. They could be friends. Buddies. Like they used to be before hormones upset the apple cart.

And if it killed her, things would stay that way. Because if they didn't, she might start believing in the fantasy herself.

Which wouldn't be fair to anybody.

Counting on the unlikelihood of Delia McNally's baby making an appearance anytime too soon, Ivy pulled into the Git-n-Go parking lot, right next to the pay phone outside the door. A second later she'd plunked in her quarter and dialed the number she'd known by heart for nearly thirty years, even though she could count on the fingers of one hand the number of times she'd actually used it.

He answered on the first ring. Ivy identified herself, then said, "Just thought you'd like to know…she's asking about you. And I think it's high time we all move on, don't you?"

"Ohmigod, is it really *you?*"

At the familiar voice, Dawn whirled around, letting out a whoop of joy for the tiny, very pregnant blonde with a headful of wild curls and a grocery cart filled with more kids than food. "Ohmigod, is right! Faith Andrews! Get your fanny over here and give me a hug!" Faith had been her only real girlfriend in Haven, the only classmate other than Cal who, if she'd thought Dawn was weird for wanting to go off to New York, at least had had the decency to keep her opinion to herself.

A week after her return—a week during which Cal had been blessedly too busy to pester her—Dawn's mood, while not exactly bubbly, had at least leveled off to *okay*. Or she would be, at any rate. Now, as the Saturday-morning Homeland crowd looked on, her old girlfriend engulfed Dawn in the same Vanilla-Fields-scented hug she remembered from high school.

"Your mama told me you were back in town!" Faith said with a laugh as she let Dawn go. She parked one hand on her hip underneath an oversize sweater to accommodate her swollen middle, the other one hanging on to a towheaded toddler determined to climb out of the cart. "Something about takin' a break between jobs?"

Dawn's eyes zinged to her friend's as she realized she'd been gawking at the bulge and the kids, trying to wrap her head around somehow connecting *that* with *her.* It hit her that nobody could tell yet she was pregnant, especially since she favored loose clothes, anyway. If she wanted to, she could probably keep her condition a secret for a good two months yet. But what would be the point? "Yes, something like that. My God," she said with a too-bright smile, "look at you with all these little *people!*"

"Mama!" a girl-child shrieked from the cart. Six, maybe. Yellow curls, blue eyes like her mother's. "Jake won't stop hittin' on me!"

"That's *hittin'* you, sugar. Hittin' *on* you's something else. Jake, quit messin' with your sister."

"She stole my Tootsie Roll pop!" This from the only boy in the group, light-brown buzzcut, freckles, maybe four or so, making short work of a box of vanilla wafers, which Faith took from him only to realize she had no place to put it except back in the cart.

"Crystal, did you take Jake's Tootsie Roll pop?"

"Only 'cause he licked mine! Yuck!"

"But it's not yucky if you eat the one he was licking anyway?"

That seemed to stump the child for a second. Dawn stood there, half fascinated, half horrified, while Faith sorted it all out by giving Jake Crystal's pop—the one he'd contaminated—hauled a container of Wet Wipes from her purse to clean the littlest one's hands, all the while keeping one ear out for the story the boy suddenly decided he needed to tell, *right now.* When the child paused to take a breath—which Dawn had begun to think would never happen—Faith's gaze bounced back to hers.

"Now. You were saying?"

Dawn cleared her throat and just spit it out. "You're not the only one who's having a baby."

Faith's jaw dropped. The littlest one let out a howl, making her mother jump a foot before hauling the little overalled body out of the cart and up into her arms, arranging assorted wriggling limbs around her unborn child.

"Ohmigod...are you serious?"

Dawn pushed back her open jacket and smoothed out her sweater over her tummy. Faith shook her head, then said, "I thought I'd heard you were engaged—"

"We broke up. It's not his."

"Oh." Faith smoothed the baby's flyaway hair off her forehead. "Do I say 'congratulations' or 'oh, dear'?"

Dawn looked pointedly at her friend's burgeoning belly. "How about…these things happen?"

Faith made a face. "To some of us, over and over again." Her expression turned serious. "But not to you. You were always so…I don't know. *Together*—"

"Ma-*ma!*"

"Listen," the blonde said on a sigh, "I figure I've got maybe ten minutes before these twerps spontaneously combust, so I better get a move on. But how about you come over for lunch one day next week when most of 'em are in school? And since I'm obviously due before you are, I can probably pass on some of the newborn sleepers and stuff, since they outgrow those so fast—"

A shriek only marginally softer than a car alarm sounded from the cart.

"Okay, okay…I'm gone," Faith said, whirling the cart around. "But I'll call you, okay?"

Dawn watched cart and kids and friend vanish in a blur, then turned back to her own shopping. Ivy'd given her a list a mile long, full of fruits and veggies and whole-grain thises and thats, which Dawn dutifully piled into the cart along with a few items of her own choosing. As she rounded the corner into the canned goods, though, movement out of the corner of her eye caught her attention—Elijah Burke, looking over the car magazines in the display at the end of the aisle, a hand basket at his feet filled with microwave dinners and soft drinks. Dawn watched as he fingered the magazines, then lifted one out to flip through it. A second later he casually rolled it up and slipped it into the pouch on his hooded sweatshirt, then picked up the basket, heading in her direction.

"Elijah, hi!" she said, equally casually, as she pushed her

cart in front of him. At his startled expression, she said, "You don't remember me, do you? Dawn Gardner? Cal Logan and I gave you a ride back to your place, oh, about a month ago or so. How're you doing?"

"Uh, fine. I'm sorry, I gotta get back—"

He tried to push around her cart, but she angled it so he couldn't. "How'd you get here? It's a long way from your house to here."

"My bike." He swallowed; twin dots of color bloomed in his pale cheeks. "And I really gotta go—"

"If you can wait until I check out, I could give you a ride. I brought my mother's truck, so we could chuck your bike in the bed—"

"Uh, thanks, but that's okay…"

Dawn slipped one arm around his shoulders and whispered, "You know, if you're planning on making stealing a career, I strongly suggest you rethink your goals. Because—" she reached over and tugged the magazine out of his sweatshirt pouch "—you really suck at it. And don't you dare try to run away," she added, tightening her grip on his shoulders, "or I'll tell."

She could see his pulse hammering at the base of his throat, his eyes wide and dark and not nearly as mutinous as he probably thought they were.

"What makes you think I wasn't gonna pay for it?"

"What makes you think I'm stupid? Come on," she said, letting go of him to push her cart again. "And put the magazine in with my things."

"What're you doing?" he said, trotting along beside her, probably too stunned by her actions to question his own.

She glanced over at the food in his basket. "You got milk at home? Fruit? Juices?"

"I just got what Daddy told me to. I don't have money for anything else."

"That why you took the magazine, too? Because you didn't have the money?"

"I said—"

"I know what you said. Well?"

Out of the corner of her eye, she saw the skinny shoulders hitch.

"How about we make a deal?" she said.

"What kind of deal?"

"I'll buy you the magazine, and a few things to round out what you've got in that basket, then I'll give you a ride home. In return, you can maybe come over later today or tomorrow and help us with some yard work. We've got more leaves to rake than you can shake a stick at."

Dawn suddenly realized she was talking to herself. Thinking the kid had bolted after all, she turned to see him standing in the middle of the aisle, looking at her as if she'd sprouted wings. "What?" she said.

"How come you're bein' so nice to me?"

"Because I like challenges. So did you hear what I said?"

"Yeah, I heard."

"Well?"

He seemed to mull things over for a minute, then said, "You think maybe we could get some of that string cheese, too?"

"Only if you promise me your sticky fingers days are over."

Elijah grinned. "Cross my heart."

Dawn turned her head so he wouldn't see her roll her eyes.

Ivy's battle-ax of a truck was missing when Cal pulled up in front of her house on Sunday afternoon, but that godawful GTO wasn't. From the side of the house he heard voices—Dawn's and what sounded like a kid's.

His boots crunched through a thick layer of sweet-smelling fallen mulberry leaves as he walked around the house. He found Dawn and Elijah in the backyard, both in gray hooded sweatshirts and jeans and covered with bits of leaves. Her hair pulled back in a single braid, her cheeks flushed, Dawn was holding open one big black plastic bag, gently fussing at the boy as he scooped great mounds of leaves into it. She seemed to be having a pretty good time; Elijah most certainly did not.

Not exactly the kind of image one usually associated with a kick to the libido, but there it was.

"You can't tell me all these leaves come off that one puny old tree!" the kid said, glowering up at the fifty-foot tree looming over the house.

"Haven't you ever noticed how the mulberries drop all their leaves at once," she said, "soon as we have a frost?"

"No," the boy said, clearly unimpressed, as he dumped the next batch of leaves into the bag. She laughed, the sound as rich and warm as fresh-brewed coffee, and Cal simply stood there, taking it in, taking *her* in, trying to imagine her with her own kid a few years down the road—

"Cal! What on earth are you doing here?"

He snapped out of the Land of What Might Be and grinned. "I brought you something," he said, which got a raised eyebrow as he added, "Hey, Eli. She got you working?"

"Slave labor, more like," the boy said, his mouth turned down at the corners. "I've been here for like hours—"

"He's been here since one," Dawn said to Cal, her eyes bright. "And half that time was spent eating."

"Was not!"

"Was, too. Now why don't you go around back and finish getting those leaves into piles?"

"C'n I get a drink of water first?"

"Yes. And I know exactly how much money I've got in my purse, so don't go getting any bright ideas about making an unauthorized withdrawal."

The kid looked more annoyed than stricken, but he dumped the rake with a clatter and tromped around to the back door.

"I caught him trying to shoplift again," she said softly after he left. "At the Homeland this time."

"Damn. He get caught?"

"Only by me."

"So what is this?" Cal said, gently tugging her braid because he was gonna pop if he didn't touch her. "Blackmail?"

She laughed. "Not exactly. More like a tradeoff. I bought him the magazine he was trying to snitch, as well as some decent food—Lord, Cal, you should've seen what he had in his basket, it was pitiful—in exchange for his help around the house. Of course, once the yard's clean, there won't be anything else I can have him do. But it's a start.''

"I don't know, Dawn…aiding and abetting a criminal…''

"He's a little kid,'' she said, suddenly serious. ''A kid who I get the feeling isn't having much of a childhood—''

"Hey, hey…I was just yanking your chain, honey. Relax.'' When she grunted, he said, ''I hate to tell you this, but you are dangerous when you're not gainfully employed. I still think you need to go talk to Sherman Mosely, I bet he'd be only too happy to have you come work for him.''

But she was shaking her head, her mouth set in that stubborn line he'd dreaded since they were kids. ''After what I just went through, I'm in no hurry to see the inside of another law office anytime too soon. Oh, don't give me that look, I'll figure something out, okay? In the meantime—'' she nodded toward the house, indicating Elijah ''—I've got a pet project that's keeping me occupied just fine. And why're you grinning like that?''

"Just thinking how easily you got your accent back.''

"You got a death wish or what?'' she said over his laughter. But she was smiling at least, one of those smiles that makes a man feel real good. ''So. What'd you bring me?''

Against his better judgment, he reached for her hand. ''Come on.''

She let him lead her back to the truck, where he flipped down the tailgate with a clatter. ''I just refinished it a few days ago, so it might still be a little tacky to the touch. I hope you like it.'' Realizing she hadn't made a single sound, he turned to her. ''Dawn?''

She looked like she was in shock. Good shock or bad shock, though, he couldn't tell. Her arms had been folded tightly across her middle; now she stretched one hand out to stroke trembling fingers across the cradle's hood.

"Oh, Cal,'' she said on a long, soft breath, and his heart turned over in his chest. ''It's beautiful. You made this?''

"No. Daddy made it for us. Well, for Hank. But we all used

it. We have to get a new mattress for it, the old one's pretty
well shot…honey?'' She'd brought her hand up to her mouth
and was just standing there, shaking her head. "Hey…what is
it?'' he asked, slipping his arm around her shoulders, fully
expecting her to pull away. Instead, she melted against his side,
as if giving over her burden to him, even if only for a few
seconds.

"This…just makes it so *real*,'' she finally said, her temple
barely an inch from his mouth, her scent igniting a pleasant
little glow in his belly. "In less than six months, there's going
to be a baby lying in there…oh, God. I need to sit down.''

He led her over to what passed for a porch on Ivy's little
house, where she sank cross-legged on the single step. "You
want me to get you some water or something?''

"No, no…I'm okay. Well, not *okay,* but…''

She wouldn't look at him, wouldn't let him into whatever
was going on inside that confounded brain of hers. And it irked
him, frankly, since, dammit, she wasn't the only one staring
unexpected parenthood in the face, here.

"How about I bring the cradle into the house?'' he said
stiffly, then stomped off to do just that.

She was on her feet again when he came back up the walk
with the cradle, wordlessly holding open the door so he could
get it inside.

"Where do you want it?''

"Cal? Are you okay?''

"I'm fine. Well?''

He caught her look of concern and confusion before she said,
"Um…I don't know yet—'' The back door slammed closed.
Elijah going back outside, he guessed. "How about right here
for the moment?'' She pointed at the bound beige carpet rem-
nant in the middle of the living room floor. Once he'd set it
down, they both stood there, staring at the thing like it might
blow up on them or something. Since the tension was likely to
kill him, he decided to change the subject.

"Ivy around?'' he asked,

"What? Oh, no. She's over at Ryan's and Maddie's. Why?''

"I started asking around a little. About your father."

"Oh. Who?"

"Frank, for one. He said he didn't know anything. But he acted kinda peculiar, like maybe he knew more than he was telling. Then again, that might not mean anything at all, since Frank tends to act peculiar, anyway. And getting more peculiar the older he gets."

Dawn laughed a little, then squatted down by the cradle, running her palm over the edge. "You know, if you had an ounce of compassion, you'd let him retire."

"Uh-huh. I asked him if he wanted to retire five years ago and he acted like I'd suggested he cut off a limb. Only thing keeping him alive is working on the farm. Although even he has to admit he can't keep up like he used to…"

"What about Ethel?"

Cal frowned. "I think the world of Ethel, but I don't think she'd be much good at fixing fences—"

"No, goof," Dawn said on a laugh, some of the tension seeming to leave her muscles. "I meant, would Ethel maybe know something about my father?"

"Already asked her. Dead end there, too. But we can keep trying. Somebody's bound to know something."

"Not necessarily," she said on a sigh, then got to her feet and headed toward the kitchen. Cal followed, arriving as she was running water into a mug. "Not if the affair happened someplace else, or maybe before Mama moved to Haven. You want some tea?"

"No, thanks. And I suppose that's true." He leaned against the counter, watching her clunk the mug inside the microwave. "What if you never find out? Can you live with that?"

"Of course I can *live* with that. What do you think I've been doing for the past twenty-nine years? It's not as if I'm going to obsess about this or anything."

"You? Obsessive?" he said on a chuckle, and she swatted at him.

So he grabbed her wrist. Just to fend off the blow.

Except he found himself disinclined to let go right away…

especially when her pulse quickened beneath his fingertips.

A tiny *yee-ha!* went off inside his head as triumph, mixed with a healthy dose of arousal, spurted through him. Which naturally led to his gaze dropping to her mouth, which had fallen open, although apparently only so the word *no* could get out…except she took a step closer as she said it and he thought, *Oh, what the hell,* and touched his lips to hers.

And everything he wanted and needed, everything he'd been afraid to want and need, everything that had been missing in his life since she'd left all those years ago was right there, in that kiss, in the scent and feel and thereness of her—

"No!" he heard, more sharply. And this time she was definitely backing up, cheeks blazing.

"It was just a friendly little kiss, darlin'—"

"That was not just friendly, and you damn well know it!"

"So maybe it wasn't. What the hell are you so damn afraid of, Dawn?"

"Nothing's going to happen between us, Cal! Okay?" He nearly winced at the terror screaming in her eyes. "This is why I can't be alone with you for more than ten minutes, because my brain shuts down and I lose control!"

He frowned. "Pardon me, but I'm still not seein' the problem here. What's wrong with losing a little control now and again?"

"Because *this* is what happens when I lose control!" Her right hand flattened against her slightly curving belly. "Because my entire *life* is out of control! Because—"

"Dawn?"

They both whipped around at the sound of Elijah's voice. His brow creased, the boy looked from one to the other, clearly wishing he was somewhere else right then. "I finished up with those leaves. But I need to get back, Daddy'll be wanting me to help him by now."

"Of course," she said, every shred of her outburst immediately erased from her features, as if it'd never happened. "I'll just get my keys—"

"I'll take him back," Cal started, but Dawn lanced him with her gaze. "No, I'll do it," she said in *that* tone of voice. "Thanks for bringing—" she cleared her throat "—thanks for the cradle. It really is beautiful."

Okay…would somebody please tell him why, out of all the females he could've had over the past ten years, the only one he wanted was a freakin' *crazy woman?*

A crazy woman who—he fought back a grin—wanted him, too. Lord, the heat simmering in her eyes, radiating from skin so soft it made him ache, that sweet little fluttering pulse at the base of her neck….

It was everything Cal could do not to throw back his head and howl.

"You're welcome," he managed to say, then leaned closer and added in a low voice, "This ain't over yet, darlin'. Not by a long shot."

He couldn't quite tell whether that was stupefaction or anger in her eyes before he turned to leave, any more than he could figure out what it was that had blasted to hell whatever had kept him from making a second move all those years ago. Pure cussedness, most likely. The same stubbornness that kept him tied to a business that would never make him rich, which, if he had a lick of sense, he'd walk away from before he lost his shirt, his home and his sanity to boot.

But then, he thought with a grunt as he started up the truck, he hadn't exactly relied on *sense* to get him whatever he wanted ever since he was little, had he? For nearly thirty years, luck and charm had paved his way…except when it came to the only thing he'd ever really wanted, he now realized. The only thing he'd been too scared to go after. Well, brother, his luck had run out, and his charm—not to mention his seductive talent—was worth squat. Which meant he was gonna have to rely on his brains for this one.

God help them all.

Chapter 7

The GTO's engine was way too loud to talk over as Dawn drove Eli back home. But not, unfortunately, too loud to think over.

Man, she was in deep horse pucky now. The only other time she'd seen that look in a man's eyes... Oh, God. Marcus Walsh. The firm's senior litigator. When he had the victim in his sights.

Oh...God.

And she'd never kissed Marcus Walsh. A thought that produced a shudder due equally to revulsion and gratitude.

How could she make Cal understand she simply could not let this so-called life of hers get any more chaotic than it already was? That she didn't dare let herself get sucked into the whirlpool of need she'd seen in his eyes, felt in his kiss.

Felt reciprocated in some place so deep inside she couldn't have found it with a brace of bloodhounds and a Pentagon-generated map—

"Hey! We were supposed to turn back there!" Elijah yelled over the engine's roar. "What's wrong with you?"

"Nothing's wrong with me, you rotten kid," she yelled back, making a U-turn, then backtracking to the weed-choked entrance to the road leading to his house. So she couldn't take on Cal and whatever it was about him that scared her to death and made her want to crawl inside him at the same time, but she *could* take on a smart-ass twelve-year-old boy with kleptomaniacal tendencies.

"So why were you yellin' at Cal, anyway?" the twelve-year-old in question said, loose gravel pinging this way and that as they bumped along.

"Grown-up stuff," she said. "Nothing for you to concern yourself with. Now hush. Trying to talk over this noise is giving me a headache."

The kid crossed his arms and scowled the rest of the way to the house. To her surprise—and apparently to Eli's as well—Jacob Burke was dressed and out in the yard when they pulled up, surveying the drifts of yellow-gold ash leaves smothering what little grass there was. Leaning on a metal cane, he pivoted awkwardly as they pulled up, radiating an almost fetid resentment as the wind whipped his too-long, somewhat curly dark-brown hair. The dog, his leash trailing him, woofed and wriggled up to the car to get at his boy.

Dawn felt him tense in the seat beside her. "It's okay," she said softly. "I won't tell. About the magazine."

"You think I care about that?"

"Yeah. I do. So sue me."

The boy gave her a puzzled look, then banged open the car door and got out. The dog jumped up, nearly knocking him over.

"That the lady you were telling me about?" his father asked.

"Yes, sir. This here's Dawn."

Who was out of the car by now, her hands stuffed in her sweatshirt pockets. Blue eyes, pale as smoke but hard as diamonds, scrutinized her for a long moment from a too-thin but still startlingly handsome face. She was suddenly aware she had on her sorriest jeans—with the zipper undone to accommodate her expanding middle—the sneakers with the mismatched laces because one had broken and she'd been too lazy to go buy a new pair, the leaf bits that still clung to her hair.

"Dawn...Gardner, ain't it? The midwife's gal?"

"That's right. How'd you know that?"

"Your mama delivered my boy." He clutched the cane, his stooped posture camouflaging his true height. An otherwise well-defined mouth stretched into a shapeless grimace. "The wife insisted."

His obvious annoyance regarding his wife's birthing choice rankled. "She was in good hands with my mother," Dawn said, patting the dog when he trotted over to say hey. "The best."

"I s'pose. They tell me you'd gone off to New York City or somesuch."

"That's right," she said, wondering who "they" were, since it was highly doubtful he entertained much.

His eyes narrowed. "Why'd you come back?"

"Personal reasons."

She thought maybe she saw a flicker of a smile, decided it had been a trick of the light. He shifted his weight on the cane. "The boy give you any trouble?"

"Not at all. He's a good worker. Which I suppose you already know."

After several more seconds of subjecting her to that relentlessly unnerving gaze, he said to Elijah, "Go on inside, start peeling those potatoes for supper."

Then, on the heels of the screen door slapping shut, Jacob moved close enough for her to see that, despite his thinness, his shoulders were nothing to sneer at. "I'd appreciate you not lookin' on us as some sort of reclamation project," he said in a low voice. "Elijah and me, we've been gettin' on fine for nearly nine years without anybody's interference. And we sure as hell don't need it from some upstart gal with her big-city ways, out to save the world. So good day to you, but we won't be needin' your 'help' anymore."

With that, he turned and made his slow, obviously painful way back to the house, leaving Dawn feeling as though she'd been dropped into the middle of a bad made-for-TV movie. What, exactly, "big-city ways" would he be referring to? Her designer attire? Her salon coiffure? Or maybe it was her high-toned accent.

Geez. No wonder the kid had problems.

A few weeks later Dawn understood why she'd never been inclined to take vacations before this. Now that she was past the first trimester blahs, with her "project" having been effectively swiped from her, having nothing to do was making her feel more drained than happily rested, like a battery running out of juice.

And the fact that the only time she did feel energized was whenever she came into contact with Cal was doing nothing to assuage her grumpiness. Like this morning, when he'd shown up—unannounced, of course—with Halloween decorations and pumpkins and that damned cocky smile of his, and *zzzzzt*—she'd felt plugged into life again.

Or just plain fried, one.

He hadn't touched her, not even once. Hadn't tried to play cute, either. Instead, they'd spent half the day carving pumpkins and decorating the yard and gabbing their heads off, the way they used to when they were kids, as if they'd never had sex, weren't expecting a baby, weren't on opposite sides of an emotional minefield of unresolved issues. And for a while, as long as they stuck with safe, neutral topics such as her work, what had happened with Jacob, his breeding program—and didn't that make her heart swell, watching the way his eyes caught fire when he talked about what he loved so much—town gossip, things were fine. Only when he started talking about how Maddie and Jenna had wrought such incredible changes in his brothers did things get hairy. For Dawn, anyway.

The wistfulness in his expression had nearly turned her inside out. *It's my turn now,* his eyes said, searing into hers. *My turn for a shot at happily-ever-after.*

And it wasn't as if she didn't wish that happiness for him, or his brothers. God knows, she couldn't think of three people who deserved it more. But Ryan had only been married since May, and Hank hadn't even known Jenna five months ago. How could any of them be certain of *their* happily-ever-afters?

How could anybody?

"Dawn? Have you heard a single word I said?"

Faith's voice jolted her back to Reality Central. She smiled for her friend, pushing the baby's stroller, her bulge disguised as a lasciviously grinning pumpkin. They never had gotten around to having lunch, what with each of Faith's kids, then Faith herself, being sick through most of October. But even though two of the kids still had horrible coughs, everyone had recovered in time for trick-or-treating. And Faith had asked Dawn to come along, since Darryl, she said, had declared he was just too worn-out to go traipsing all over town.

Dawn had kept her mouth shut. Somehow. Although she had to admit, even though Faith moved about as fast as an arthritic snail these days, she seemed none the worse for wear. Woman seemed downright chipper, in fact, prattling away about people Dawn hadn't even thought about in a million years, as jack-o-lanterns flickered on every porch and the wind sent leaves swirling and branches clacking, lending a just-spooky-enough undercurrent to the giggles from all the excited little Ninja Turtles and SpongeBobs and satin-and-glitter bedecked princesses scampering about.

"God. I'd forgotten how much I loved Halloween," Dawn said as the kids all yelled, "Trick or Treat!" in front of Hazel Dinwiddy's door.

"Heck, I still do," Faith said, snitching a miniature Almond Joy from somebody's loot. "Did you know," she said around a full mouth, "that candy eaten while you're trick-or-treating has no calories?"

"No, I did not. I'll have to remember that." She looped an arm through her friend's and squeezed. "This is fun. Thanks for asking me to come along."

"No problem. Guess y'all don't really do this in New York, huh?"

"Not in Manhattan, no." Just like that, she ached. "Kids go

door-to-door in their own buildings, but the atmosphere's not quite the same.''

Faith chewed thoughtfully for a few seconds, then said, ''It would drive me nuts, not being able to let the kids go outside whenever they wanted, or go down the street to a friend's house.'' The urchins cut straight across Hazel's yard to get to the next house, as Heather, Faith's oldest, screamed at her younger siblings to stop running, which set off a coughing jag.

''I guess it's different when you live there,'' Dawn said mildly.

''I suppose. So…'' Faith unwrapped a miniature Kit Kat bar and stuffed it in her mouth. At this rate there wouldn't be anything left for the kids by the time they got back home. ''You haven't yet told me about the baby's father.''

An unpleasant bubbly feeling stirred in the pit of Dawn's stomach, shoving aside the ache. ''I know. I'm…working up to it.''

The blonde stopped short. ''Oooh! That means I know who it is!''

''Faith…''

''Okay, okay, I'll wait. Impatiently, but I'll wait. So. You gettin' excited about the baby yet?''

''About the same way I'd get excited about going down a roller coaster.'' She sighed. ''Unbuckled.''

''Yeah, that sounds about right. At least, that's how I felt with the first one. By now, I'm like, whaaatever.''

''At least you're married!''

Holy crud—where had that come from? Her words echoed over the wind and the kids' thanks-yous and somebody's dog barking. They were up to the next house before Faith said quietly, ''That doesn't necessarily make it any easier.''

''I know that. It's just…'' Realization thumped in Dawn's chest. ''Faith? Is everything okay? Between you and Darryl, I mean?'' She watched as another Kit Kat met its doom. ''And does my mother know how much candy you're putting away?''

''No,'' she said, chewing, ''and don't you dare tell her. And Darryl and me are fine. For the most part. Marriage is just…hard, you know? I mean, we got married so young, on account of me getting pregnant and all, so we've had a lot of adjustments to make to each other along the way. And God knows, there are some days when I want to wring the man's neck. But then he'll do something real sweet, or I'll catch him playin' with the kids…'' On a sigh she said, ''And I figure I'll have my life back one day.'' Then she smacked Dawn softly in the arm. ''And listen to me, gettin' all weird and mopey. I swear, I'm not like this except when I'm pregnant or PMS-ing.''

''But if you're having problems…''

''We are *not* having problems! Not anything worth gettin' worked up over, anyway.'' Dawn reached inside her jacket pocket and ferreted out a clean tissue, which she handed to her friend. Faith dabbed under first one heavily made-up eye, then the other, then blew her nose. ''Every marriage has rough patches, okay? That's normal. So don't you go making more of this than it is.''

Dawn thought of the college buddies she'd kept up with, how many of them had been in and out of marriage already— sometimes twice, for crying out loud—before their thirtieth birthdays.

''So…you're happy?'' she asked her friend.

''Enough.'' Faith dug around in the loot bag until she found a miniature Krackle bar, her brow creased as she unwrapped it. ''I love Darryl. Always have. Mind you, he's no Brad Pitt,'' she said with a shrug as they walked to the next house, which happened to be Ivy's, ''but he's mine. And he's all broken in, just the way I like. Besides, I'm not like you. I didn't have the options you do. I don't regret my choices, I'm not saying that, but if you're looking to me for answers, you're wasting your time…who the heck's that on your porch?''

''Dracula, looks like,'' Dawn said. Assuming Faith would figure it out soon enough, Dawn watched the kids scoot up the sidewalk toward the house, to where Cal, fangs and all, had crouched down and was greeting them in his soft drawl, so as to not scare the smallest kids. Didn't work. One look and the air was filled with ear-piercing screams, until Heather yelled at them to quit being such babies, for heaven's sake, it was just a costume, was all.

"Ohmigod," Faith said in a monotone as the screams became giggles. "Is that Cal Logan?"

"Mmm-hmm," Dawn said, unable to stop the fizzy, fuzzy sensation inside her at the sight of this big man acting all silly with Faith's babies. Instinctively, her hand went to her belly as Faith's gaze zeroed in on the side of her face.

"Cal Logan. Playing Dracula on *your* front porch."

"Mmm-hmm."

"Why on earth…?" Then she made this sound like a vacuum cleaner sucking up a penny. "He's not!"

"He is."

"Ohmigod." The kids came barreling back down the walk. Faith oohed and aahed over their latest acquisitions, then whispered, "What does this mean, exactly?"

"We're still working *exactly* out—"

"Hey there, Faith," Cal yelled out. "Lookin' good!"

"You, too," she yelled back. "Love the widow's peak."

He grinned, totally annihilating the scare factor. "Why, thank you, ma'am! I thought it was rather fetching myself! And just for the record? You are the hottest pumpkin I have ever seen!"

"Flatterer," she said, then waddled on, waiting until two houses later to say, "You could do a lot worse than Cal Logan, you know."

"That's not the point."

Faith looked at her as if she'd lost it for sure. "The hell it's not," she said in an only-for-your-ears voice. "He's adorable, sexy as hell and good with kids. And the man is up there playin' *Dracula,* for pity's sake."

"And what's that got to do with anything?"

"Well, honey, if you can't figure that out, then I'm sure not gonna strain my brain to explain it to you…Maddie! Hey!"

Dawn looked up to see Cal's sister-in-law, also pushing a stroller, coming straight at them. Her boy and girl, about the same ages as two of Faith's, immediately melded with the others. Barely taller than Faith's oldest girl, Maddie grinned as she shoved her feathery hair out of her light eyes.

"I didn't know you two knew each other!" she said over the shrieking and giggling going on around them.

"We were best buddies all the way through school," Faith shouted back. "Although we kinda lost touch after Dawn went away…"

And while kids bounced and chattered around them, the two women fell into a conversation about potty training and pre-school—*What is it, Noah? Well, go on up and ask Miz Chellete if you can use hers if you gotta go that bad*—and what did Maddie think—*Crystal! Give Jake's candy back to him right now!*—of Taylor McIntyre, the new kindergarten teacher, since that's who Jake would get next year—*Katie Grace, no, honey, the baby can't eat a lollipop*—and did Faith want Maddie to bring over those baby clothes yet…?

Dawn tried to force enough oxygen into her suddenly shriveled lungs to keep from passing out. How could she do this? How could she *be* this? And the thing of it was, Faith and Maddie seemed so relaxed about it all. Sure, she'd seen plenty of mothers in action with their kids over the years, but that had all seemed over *there,* somewhere. You know, that special place where mothers lived. A place Dawn had simply never envisioned herself living. Like…Irkutsk. Now here she stood, passport in hand, right at the border.

Somehow, they'd all moved, like a yammering, sixteen-legged, eight-wheeled insect, down to the corner where Cal's brother Ryan lived. All the kids—including the two who lived there—rushed the two-story Queen Anne and clambered up the porch steps while their mothers continued talking: Dawn looked down the street to see Charmaine Chambers and her three heading their way just as all the kids clomped back down the doctor's steps and rejoined them.

"Mama!" Heather said to her mother, hacking away. "Dr. Ryan says to tell you if my cough's—" *hack, hack* "—not better by next week to come an' see him again!"

"Okay, baby…hey, Charmaine!"

Judging from the look on the other woman's face, Dawn's guess was she would've crossed the street if she'd had her druthers. Her three kids, however—all boys, all dark-haired, all wired—fused with the others like melding oil droplets. By now the noise level was beyond belief, especially as every dog in town had decided to pitch in his two cents.

And still the women talked.

"You remember Dawn, right?" Faith yelled to Charmaine.

The brunette, her arms tightly folded over a suede jacket Dawn thought she remembered seeing her wear in high school, gazed at her impassively. "Saw her over at the diner," she said, her voice flat. "Ruby says you're stayin'?"

The coldness in Charmaine's voice arrowed straight to Dawn's already roiling stomach. "For a while, anyway."

"Hey, Charmaine," Faith said, "We missed you at the last PTA meeting."

"Sorry. Guess I forgot," the brunette said, then yelled out to her kids to get a move on, she didn't have all night.

When she'd moved out of earshot, Faith let out a sigh and said, "Brody's leaving her did a real number on her head. Swear to God, I ever catch sight of that scumbag again…"

"I'm right there with you," Maddie added.

Dawn, who was watching Charmaine and her kids fade into the darkness, barely heard Faith's, "You don't even know how I was gonna finish that sentence."

"Does it matter? Hey, y'all," Maddie said, "why don't you come on inside for some cocoa or something? Looks to me like things're winding down anyway, if those chock-full bags are anything to go by. And you," she said to Faith, "look like you seriously need to take a load off—"

"You know," Dawn said over the *Clash of the Titans* number going on inside her head, "that really sounds great, but I'm gonna take a raincheck, okay?"

Faith touched her arm. "Honey? You okay?"

"I…just need to…" Instead of finishing her sentence—which she couldn't have if her life had depended on it—she muttered something lame and probably incomprehensible and headed back for her mother's house.

Where Cal—and that minefield of unresolved issues—waited.

Still sitting on the porch, Cal felt his heart nearly bolt out of his chest at Dawn's shell-shocked expression when she returned.

"Hey," he said, getting to his feet. "What's goin' on?"

She started a little, like she'd forgotten he was there, then shook her head and kept walking. Cal hurried to open the front door for her and followed her inside, the nearly empty candy bowl clutched in his hand. Staring blankly in front of her, she slowly peeled off her jacket, letting it drop to the sofa before continuing to the kitchen. By the time Cal got there she'd made serious inroads into one of Ethel's double-size cinnamon buns. He dumped the candy bowl on the counter, then wordlessly poured her a glass of milk and handed it to her.

"Thanks," she said.

"Talk," he said.

"What good would that do?"

"Damned if I know. But I don't see how it could hurt."

She took another bite of the cinnamon bun, washing it down with half the milk. Then she said, "Okay, but if I start rambling incoherently, you can't complain."

"I live with Ethel, remember? I was fifteen before I realized that incoherent rambling wasn't just the way women talked."

That got a small smile, which did little to ease the torment in her expression. "I must be nuts."

"About what?"

She gestured at her stomach with what was left of the cinnamon bun. "All those kids…at one point, there were…" Her brow knotted as she stopped to count. "*Ten* kids under the age of eleven within a six-foot radius. How do they do it? Maddie and Faith and Charmaine?" Panic sent her voice into the stratosphere. "How do they stand the screaming and the noise and the constant demands for attention?"

"Whoa, honey…" He pried the empty glass out of her fingers and handed her a napkin. "You're not having ten kids. Just one." She frowned at the napkin like she didn't know what to do with it. "You've got icing on your chin," he said, then added, "And you don't have to do it alone, you know."

"What? Wipe off the icing?"

"No." He waited until she finally looked at him. "Raise the kid."

Her face crumpled as two wonker tears popped out and streaked down her cheeks.

"Aw, hell, sweetheart," he said, opening his arms. "C'mere." At her wary, watery look, he added, "Oh, for God's sake—I'm not gonna sling you over my shoulder and haul you back to the farm, okay?"

Another second or so passed before she accepted his invitation. But she wasn't exactly what you'd call relaxed.

"That better?" he asked.

"You must be kidding."

He tightened his hold, just because it felt good, dammit. And *somebody* oughtta be gettin' something out of this, right? "This isn't just about the baby, is it?"

After a moment she shook her head against his chest, then honked into the napkin. "It's about…everything," she said on a wobbly, very un-Dawn-like sigh. "The baby and you and how I'm going crazy here with nothing to do and…and… Oh, Cal, I'm so *homesick!*"

His chin resting on top of her head, Cal shut his eyes against the sensation of being kicked in the gut. "I'm sorry, honey," he said softly, letting his fingers sift through her ponytail. "Although I can see where Darryl and Faith's brood could have that effect…"

"That's not it. Not the homesickness part of it, anyway. I mean…" She pulled away to drop into one of the kitchen chairs, her forehead creasing into that trying-to-figure-things-out frown he remembered from way back. "I was actually enjoying myself for a while, kids and all. Except then Faith started asking me about New York, and this weird feeling came over me…and I suddenly missed the city so much, it hurt.''

Cal dodged another kick, then said, ''I'm sorry you hate it here—''

''But that's just it, I *don't* hate it here! I just want my life back—''

''Honey?'' Ivy said from the doorway. ''What's going on?''

Well. It didn't take a brainiac to figure out where she was going with that thought, did it? And Cal knew if he stayed he'd only end up arguing with her, because that's the kind of mood he was in. Which would be a colossal waste of everyone's time because, for one thing, arguing with Dawn was like trying to order the weather to do what you wanted. And for another, Cal hated fighting more than he hated brussels sprouts, and that was saying a lot. So he said his good-nights and took off.

What he didn't count on was Ivy's going after him.

Chapter 8

Dawn let out a long sigh. See, this was the thing with men. They might say they want you to talk but do they ever really listen? Noooo.

And do mothers ever *really* back off and let you work things out on your own? Noooo, again.

Thinking she should probably try to avoid bloodshed, Dawn hauled herself to her feet, reaching the open front door in time to hear her mother yell at Cal's back, "Where the heck you think you're going?"

The porch light now off, Dawn huddled in the shadows, swiping tentacles of cobweb filament out of her face. Well, hell—if her mother and Cal were fool enough to talk about her, she was fool enough to listen.

"This is your opportunity, boy," Ivy said.

"To do what?" Cal snapped, yanking open his door. "Confuse her more than she already is?"

Ivy slammed her hands onto her hips and lowered her voice. How rude. But the wind still carried snatches of her words: "...you came to me, asking for my help...want her to stay as much as you do...to be happy...blockhead."

"This is your idea of help?" rang out loud and clear. Except then Ivy shushed him, so all she got then was "…somehow get inside that gal's mind…staying here…an option?"

Now Ivy crossed her arms. "…better'n just letting her go…she's begging for help!"

"Help?" Dawn muttered, indignant.

"Help?" Cal said on a dryer-than-dust laugh. Then all she heard was something about "once she set her mind to something, there was no changing it."

Dawn frowned.

The wind shifted, so she heard the next bit clearly.

"So that's it?" Ivy said. "You're just giving up?"

"Didn't say that. But you know, it's a whole lot easier to dig a post hole when you've softened the earth up first. She's homesick, Ivy. And until she gets over that—if she gets over that—I don't have a chance."

"But the baby—"

"Don't you get it? It's like she said, way at the beginning—even if she decided to stay here for the baby's sake, as long as her heart's someplace else, she's never gonna be happy—"

O-kay, time to break up this cozy little chat.

"This is getting to be a bad habit with you two," she said as she approached them, provoking simultaneous guilty jumps, "talking about me behind my back."

She couldn't quite read Cal's expression in the moonlight, but it definitely provoked a shiver or two in a couple of very interesting places. Especially with the widow's peak and the "blood" dribble at the corner of his mouth. "What's gettin' to be a bad habit," he said, "is the way you keep interrupting a private conversation."

"Hey. I'm the one whose life has just gone to hell in a handbasket. I'll interrupt whatever I want." At his why-are-women-like-this? headshake, she said, "Look. I'm a mess, okay? And I'm not going to apologize for that. But it occurred to me while I was ranting and raving in there that one of the reasons I'm such a mess is because I'm bored. So I made a decision. Which I was about to share with the class when you did your affronted-manhood number."

"Hey!"

"I need to go back to work. So...I decided to see if Sherman Mosely *could* use some help while I'm here."

That got a pair of poleaxed reactions. Well, good.

"God knows, this won't solve all my problems—" she looked pointedly at Cal "—but at least it'll keep me occupied."

Cal frowned. "I don't think I much like being thought of as a problem."

"Deal with it," she said, then added, "Besides, maybe Sherman can help me find my father."

Her mother flinched. "Honey, I really don't think you should go gettin' other people involved with this—"

"Then give me my father's name and I won't have to."

Her gaze locked with her mother's, Dawn waited as her heart rammed against her ribs once...twice...three times...

"I can't," Ivy finally said.

"Fine. Then you can't say anything more."

After a moment Ivy closed the gap between them and gave her a wordless hug, then went back inside.

"For God's sake, Dawn..." Cal's voice, harsher than she'd ever heard it, washed over her from behind. "Why the devil you're so determined to find a man who was too much of a coward, or too stupid, or too blind to acknowledge his own daughter is beyond me."

She twisted around to face him. "Probably for the same reason you're determined to win me over."

His brows shot up at that. Silence grated between them for several beats, until a smile slowly worked its way across his jaw. "And if you find your father?"

"What do you mean?"

The grin still in place, he reached out to slip his fingers, warm and rough and insistent, underneath her hair at the back of her neck, and while a million little voices shouted, *No!*, a tiny, very persuasive little one whispered, *Oh, what the hell,* as he gently tugged her to him.

"I don't care what you say, Dawn Gardner," he said, his

breath dancing with hers, his fingertips hypnotically stroking that—oh!—very sensitive little dip at the base of her skull. "We're more alike than you might think. See, both of us thrive on challenge. On doing things the hard way." His lips touched hers, just long enough to tease, to send a wave of little prickles skittering along her skin. "And neither of us can rest until we get what we want."

"And why do you think you want me, Cal?"

He pulled back, frowning into her eyes. "What?"

"Other than the fact that I'm pregnant with your child and that there's enough chemistry between us to blow up every science lab in the state, I'm willing to bet you don't want me nearly as much as you think you do. And I sure as hell doubt you *need* me."

She shivered from the sudden touch of cold air on the back of her neck as Cal's hand fell away. He frowned at her for several seconds, then shook his head, muttering, "Why can't women just take things at face value?" before he got into his truck and drove off.

For a moment that by all rights should have been victorious, she felt remarkably disappointed.

The early-November sun elbowed its way through the partially open miniblinds in Sherman Mosely's waiting room to illuminate, with pinpoint precision, the worn spot in the carpet in front of Marybeth Reese's old walnut desk. Over the secretary's rhythmic keyboarding at the vintage PC, her Dictaphone earplugs smothered by a mountain of spectrum-sucking black hair, Dawn could hear Sherman's animated tenor through the closed door, presumably in a phone conversation. In grating juxtaposition to the hundred-year-old building in which they sat, the slime-green Danish-modern sofa and assorted boxy chairs were unoccupied at present, except for the one Dawn was sitting in.

"I honestly don't know how much longer he'll be," the thirty-something woman tossed out with an apologetic smile as she typed. "You sure you wouldn't rather make an appointment, honey?"

"No, I'm good," Dawn said, tugging at the hem of her half-unzipped black Calvin Klein skirt, not sure whether she was more concerned that somebody might question where she'd gotten her stylishly oversize fur-blend sweater or whether they'd notice the steadily growing mound beneath it. She glanced over at Marybeth, a vision in Jaclyn Smith. It didn't take much to overdress around here. Actually, Dawn couldn't have cared less about designer labels, but working at a Madison Avenue law firm had kinda precluded a discount store wardrobe.

"Dawn! Sorry to keep you waiting!" She looked up to see a smiling Sherman standing in the doorway to his office, his striped tie lolling to one side of the sagging stomach straining against the buttons of his white dress shirt. "Come on in, come on in…Marybeth, hold my calls, wouldja?"

When she'd settled herself into the worn upholstered chair in front of his desk, she looked across to see the older man's warm hazel eyes fixed on hers. As a child, their paths had rarely crossed—his daughter, Brenda Sue, hadn't exactly been one of Dawn's favorite people—and she'd seen him hardly at all since then. Age had leached the color from his thick hair and softened features she remembered as once being keenly defined, but the result wasn't unpleasant. And when he smiled, his whole face went along for the ride.

Just like Cal's, she thought with a start. Quickly reeling her thoughts back in, she said, "Mama told me about your wife's passing. I'm so sorry."

"Thank you," he said with a nod and a slightly sad smile. "Barbara had been sick for a real long time, though. It was hard, watching her suffer like that, you know? And we had a good thirty-five years together. Mostly good, anyway. So, Dawn…" He leaned back, cradling his head in his folded hands, his scrutiny no less shrewd for its avuncular nature. "What can I do for you?"

Dawn assumed her standard "competent professional" pose—spine straight, chin out, hands loosely folded in her lap, feet crossed at the ankles. "Word around here is that you need some time off. Since, as it happens, I need a temporary job, I thought we might be able to work something out for our mutual benefit.''

Thick, still-dark brows hiked up over his glasses. "You sayin' you want to work for me?"

"Work *with* you is probably a better way of putting it. But, yes. I'm already licensed to practice in Oklahoma," she added quickly. "If that's a concern."

"Why?"

"I took the Oklahoma bar as a precaution—"

"No, I mean why would you want to work here? I thought you were working for some highfalutin firm in New York City."

"It's a long story."

"I reckon I got time," he said, removing his hands from behind his head to link them over his protruding belly.

So she explained, about losing the partnership, about the clinic's closing, about the baby…about Cal being the father. "And that's not general knowledge just yet, so—"

One hand shot up. "Say no more, I completely understand."

"Anyway. Since I'm here until at least after the baby's born, I need something to do. And since this is the only thing I know *how* to do…" She spread her hands.

Sherman scratched the side of his nose, then frowned at her. "I don't know…this here's pretty much a one-man—person, excuse me—operation."

"And I know Dr. Logan's been after you to cut back ever since your heart attack last year." She leaned forward. "If I was here, you could go visit Brenda Sue. Where is she? Spokane?"

"Portland, now. She moved a couple years back."

"How is she, by the way?"

"Oh, she's doing okay. I'll be sure and tell her you asked about her." He swiveled slowly from side to side in his chair, studying her. "So how come you didn't get that partnership?"

"Because…" Funny the difference a month makes. It almost didn't hurt to talk about it now. "Because I have this little problem with being more concerned about helping people

NO POSTAGE
NECESSARY
IF MAILED
IN THE
UNITED STATES

BUSINESS REPLY MAIL

FIRST-CLASS MAIL   PERMIT NO. 717-003   BUFFALO, NY

POSTAGE WILL BE PAID BY ADDRESSEE

SILHOUETTE READER SERVICE
3010 WALDEN AVE
PO BOX 1867
BUFFALO NY 14240-9952

Get FREE BOOKS and a FREE GIFT when you play the...

LAS VEGAS
GAME

Just scratch off the gold box with a coin. Then check below to see the gifts you get! →

YES! I have scratched off the gold Box. Please send me my **2 FREE BOOKS** and **gift for which I qualify.** I understand that I am under no obligation to purchase any books as explained on the back of this card.

345 SDL DVEH   245 SDL DVEX

FIRST NAME

LAST NAME

ADDRESS

APT.#

CITY

STATE/PROV.

ZIP/POSTAL CODE

(S-IM-01/04)

7	7	7	Worth TWO FREE BOOKS plus a BONUS Mystery Gift!
🍒	🍒	🍒	Worth TWO FREE BOOKS!
🔔	🔔	♣	TRY AGAIN!

Visit us online at **www.eHarlequin.com**

Offer limited to one per household and not valid to current Silhouette Intimate Moments® subscribers. All orders subject to approval.

who really need it than baby-sitting wealthy, whiny clients who bring half their problems on themselves.''

A half smile touched his lips. ''You think you'd really like it here?''

''For a few months, I could like anything.''

He gave her an assessing look, then stood up. ''Let me think on it, okay?''

Not what she'd hoped to hear, but she supposed she'd be just as cautious if somebody tried to horn in on her practice. ''Sounds fair to me,'' she said, standing, too, as he came around his desk to see her out. But when she went to ask him about her father, the words disintegrated in her mouth. What exactly did she think he could do, if she didn't even know her father's name?

''What is it?'' Sherman asked.

''Nothing. I mean, I was going to ask for your help with something—''

''So ask. If I can't help, I'll tell you.''

''It's about my father,'' she said on a rush of air, watching Sherman's reaction. But there wasn't one, other than a cautious, ''Oh?''

''Yeah. See, I've never known who he was. Or much cared before this, to be honest. But for some reason, now that I'm pregnant, I've got this bee in my bonnet about finding him. Although I have absolutely nothing to go on. Not even his name. But I guess I thought…I don't know, maybe because you were around at the time, you might have some connections or leads or…shoot, I'd settle for hunches at this point. Anything to at least find his trail.''

''I see.'' Sherman shoved his hands in his pockets. ''I assume you asked your mother?''

''I didn't graduate at the top of my law school class for nothing,'' she said, smiling. ''But Mama said she can't tell me who he is.''

The man took a deep breath, then said, ''Dawn, you're what? Twenty-seven, twenty-eight…''

''Twenty-nine. Same age as Brenda Sue. And to answer the question you're about to ask me, because after all the kids I've seen whose fathers abandoned them, I guess I just want to know…*why?*''

His gaze in hers was steady. Too steady. ''You're right, honey. I can't help you. I wish I could.''

Adrenaline spurted through her. ''Oh, my God,'' she said softly. ''You do know who he is, don't you?''

''Dawn…let it go. And that's all I'm gonna say on the subject—''

''If a woman came to you for help finding her kids' father so she could get child support, would you refuse to tell her where he was if you knew? Even if he'd asked you not to?''

''Oh, for the love of Mike,'' he let out on a frustrated breath. ''Of course not! That would be unethical, if nothing else. But you're comparin' apples to oranges—''

''Not if you knowingly aided my father in avoiding his financial obligations!''

''And what in tarnation makes you think I did that? Or that he did, for that matter?''

She jerked. ''What did you say?''

''I'm saying, you got child support. Or rather, Ivy did for you. Your father never shirked his financial responsibility to you, as far as I know. And the only reason I'm sayin' even that much is because I can tell you're gonna drive me up a tree about this otherwise. I remember what my wife was like when she was pregnant, and that's something you don't ever fully recuperate from. Now for God's sake, gal, please do me and everybody else a favor and move on. Seems to me you got more important things to worry about,'' he said, nodding toward her stomach.

''And maybe that's why I'm doing this. Because I don't feel right starting a new life before I've plugged up the holes in my own.''

''You know,'' Sherman said with a bemused expression, ''where'd folks get this notion that life is supposed to be neat and tidy with all the holes *plugged up,* as you put it? Life's full of holes, honey. Always has been. Far as I can tell, you can either let yourself fall in 'em or learn how to avoid 'em.

But which d'you think is gonna get you where you're goin' faster?''

"Mr. Mosely—you're talking to somebody who can't stand to leave a *crossword* puzzle unfinished."

He chuckled. "Okay, okay…I get your point." Then his mouth quirked into something that might have been a smile. "You this tenacious on behalf of your clients?"

"You better believe it."

After another few seconds of that inscrutable gaze, he opened the door.

She lifted one eyebrow.

He let out a huge sigh. "Okay, fine. You're hired. But don't even think about wearing some ridiculous miniskirt like they do on those TV law shows."

By the time Thanksgiving rolled around, pretty much everybody in town not only knew Dawn was pregnant, but that Cal was the daddy. Understandably enough, most people greeted this news with some surprise. An initial reaction, Cal noticed, which subsequently turned into either delight or tight-lipped disapproval, especially when faced with Dawn's smiling response to the inevitable question—did this mean she and Cal were getting married?—that, no, they weren't, but thanks for asking.

Then she had to go and hang her shingle beside Sherman Mosely's. That *really* got the tongues to wagging. Not that Haven's child-bearing women hadn't been going out to work for a good three decades, but he still heard the occasional "Well, I know times have changed, but…"

And did she give a damn what anybody thought? Hell, no. Just look at her, sitting over there on Ryan's sofa talking to Jenna Stanton, her hands going a mile a minute like always, not six inches away from that not-so-little belly sticking out underneath her fuzzy gray sweater. Propping a shoulder against one side of the opened pocket doors between Ryan's living and dining rooms, Cal took a pull from the can of beer in his hand, unable to stop staring at Dawn and not much caring what anybody thought about that.

Hank came up beside him, popping the tab on his own beer, doing a little staring himself at the classy, down-to-earth blonde who'd saved his hide. "Looks like those two sure hit it off."

"Mmm."

In a cloud of giggles, Hank's daughter, Blair, and Maddie's oldest two burst out of the kitchen, rattling the china and glassware on the already set dining table as they pounded across the old floorboards, past the two men and on up the stairs to the second floor. A second later Maddie yelled from behind the closed kitchen door for Ryan to *please* come take the baby before Maddie tripped and broke her neck.

"Haven't seen much of you lately," Hank said to Cal.

"Been busy. Figured I may as well get some repairs done around the farm while the good weather holds." Cal looked over. "What's doing with your place? You hear anything more from that developer?"

"You don't really want to talk about that, do you?"

"No. But it sure beats some other things I *really* don't want to talk about."

Grinning, Hank leaned against the opposite side of the doorway. "Actually, he made me a partnership offer, but I need to have someone look it over, make sure I'm not getting the short end of the stick." He took a slug of his beer, his black hair gleaming softly in the light angling through the sheer living room curtains. "Thought maybe I'd run it by Dawn, see what she thinks. Or is Sherman back yet?"

"No, Dawn says she's holding the fort until the end of January."

"So…you do see her from time to time?"

Yes, he saw her. Not as much as he might like, although probably more than Dawn would prefer. But after what she'd said on Halloween, all that stuff about needing versus wanting, he'd felt like he'd been tossed back in that damn calculus class his senior year of high school, where he didn't even understand enough to know what questions to ask. Smart enough to make it into the class to begin with, too dumb to figure out what the hell was going on.

"We're having a baby together, Hank," he said at last. "So

we have to talk on occasion. And you might want to think about stepping back from this topic of conversation, okay?"

Hank chuckled softly. "She ever find out anything else about her father?"

Cal decided he liked it better when he and his brothers didn't have much to do with each other. "No. She's asked everybody in town who was around then, nobody knows anything. Or aren't telling." He took a sip of his beer. "I think she's given it up as a lost cause."

"You do realize you're staring at her, don't you?"

"You rather I stare at Jenna?"

"Smart-ass. So why don't you just go join the conversation instead of mooning over the woman from halfway across the room?"

"I'm not mooning. I'm…giving her space."

"That what you're callin' it?"

Hooking his thumb in his belt loop, Cal lowered his beer and glared at his brother. "Look, hotshot…it generally works better to let the fish come to the bait instead of clobbering 'em over the head."

"Oh, I don't know. Clobbering seems to work okay for bears."

Cal snorted.

"Besides," Hank continued, "what're you planning on using for bait?"

"That's the part I haven't quite figured out yet."

After some more thoughtful beer guzzling, Hank said, "You really serious about her? Or is this just some possessive thing? Because she's having your baby?"

"You know, I *have* asked myself that."

"And?"

"And I think…hell, Hank," he said on a sigh. "All I know is, I see her sitting there with my baby growin' inside her and I want them both so badly I think I'm gonna lose my mind. And I know that's not enough, not for either one of us. I mean, she came right out and asked me the same thing. Could I tell her why I needed her? And I couldn't answer her. Not in any way that'd make sense to her. I mean, I know I do. I just don't know why. And what's even worse is that I can't offer her anything she can't do for herself. Yet in a bizarre way, it's her *not* needing me that turns me on so much."

"Because of the challenge, you mean?"

"No. Because…because I know if she ever does come to me, it'll be because she wants me, not because she needs me. That make any sense?"

"Yeah," Hank said in a way that made Cal glance over, then follow his line of sight to Jenna. "It sure does."

Cal pushed away from the door to inspect the set table. "But doesn't that mean we're working at cross-purposes?" He fingered one of his mother's silver forks, relishing the feel of the heavy metal in his hand. "Man…I am not used to thinking this hard. Especially about stuff I don't understand worth spit to begin with."

"And here I thought you were the ladies' man."

He thought again of that calc class. "Yeah, well, it's like starting all over. New game, new rules, and nothing I've learned prior to this point is even remotely useful. Dawn no more resembles those other women than—" he held up the fork, angling it in the sunlight "—than real silver does stainless steel. Stainless might be shinier and easier to take care of, but silver's got substance." Setting the fork back down, he added, "And a glow that seems to come from inside, you know what I mean?"

The back of Cal's neck prickled; he turned and met Dawn's gaze, tamping down a sigh when he saw that damned ambivalence in her eyes. That same look that told him if he went up to her right now and kissed her, she'd ignite like dry kindling. Only to burn out just as fast.

"If I were you," Hank said in a low voice beside him, "I'd tell Dawn all that stuff about comparing her to silver. If nothing else, you'd probably stun her long enough to move in for the kill."

"You really think so?"

"Sure. Only thing is," he said, moving out of the line of fire, "you better move fast before she starts laughing her head off."

"And for the last time, Maddie…" Seated next to Dawn at the dinner table, Jenna leaned over to address her soon-to-be sister-in-law. "…no bridal shower! I don't have room in that dinky kitchen—"

"Hey!" Hank said across the table from her.

"—for half the stuff I've already got! And don't get your boxers in a wad, big stuff," Jenna said to him, laughing.

"Yeah," Cal put in with a wink at Dawn that sent heat creeping up her neck, "it's not like she was calling anything else of yours dinky!"

No less than a half dozen people shrieked, "Cal!", but you could hardly hear it over all the laughter.

Hard to believe it had only been a year since she'd last sat at this table, how much all their lives had changed since then. Dawn had been engaged to one man and was now carrying the child of another. There'd been a found daughter, an engagement and two weddings in the group, including—she glanced across the table at the elderly man plopping mashed potatoes on his wife's plate—Maddie's octogenarian great-uncle-by-marriage, Ned, to Mildred Rafferty, the woman he'd loved for more than fifty years. Last year there'd been bitterness and apprehension and doubt; now there was unbridled domestic bliss as far as the eye could see.

It was enough to make a girl barf.

From across the table, Cal caught her eye, his raised brows silently asking, *What's wrong?*

A shiver of awareness, of longing, raced up Dawn's spine. She shook her head and forced a smile. *Nothing.*

He frowned, clearly not believing her.

She should have found his constant scrutiny unnerving at best, irritating at worst. Should have…but didn't. Instead, as always, she found his calm, steady gaze reassuring.

And she felt like dirt.

Dawn shoveled in a bite of yams, mentally smacking herself. This was Thanksgiving, for crying out loud! She had tons to be grateful for! She wasn't engaged to Andrew anymore! She loved her new job! She was going to have a baby, and the pregnancy was progressing normally! Her baby's father wasn't a creep or a nerd or a jerk!

The sweet potatoes stuck in her throat as hot tears burned in her eyes. She blinked them back and kept chewing, jumping slightly when she felt Jenna's touch on her arm.

"You okay?"

Smiling, Dawn forced herself to meet the blonde's concerned smile. "Sorry, just spaced out for a second."

Jenna's pale blue eyes lit up with amusement. "Tell me about it. After three years of it being just Blair and me, hanging around this clan for too long would send anybody scurrying for cover." She laughed. "Spacing out becomes a matter of survival. It's funny, though—" a bite of turkey disappeared into her lightly lipsticked mouth "—I lived my entire life in a major city, but I never really knew what it felt like to be part of something until I moved here."

Dawn thought about that for a second or so, then said, "Do you miss it, though? The solitude?"

Hank's fiancée took a sip of her drink, then shrugged. "Sometimes. It takes some getting used to, having so many people give a damn about you when you're used to being ignored in the name of 'not wanting to interfere.'"

"Oh, Lord," Dawn said. "Around here, interfering is a way of life—"

"…and I'm telling you, woman, you were seein' things!" Ned's raised voice, directed at his wife, caught Dawn's attention. "Kid can't be more'n twelve years old—"

"And I'm telling *you,* old man, I saw him with my own eyes, trying to get into Hootch's truck! In broad daylight, no less!"

Dawn and Cal exchanged a brief glance before he asked, "Who was, Mildred?"

"The Burke boy," the old woman said. "What's his name, Elias?"

"Elijah," Dawn said on a sigh.

"Elijah, that's right. Well. I'd just come out of Luralene's yesterday after I got my hair done, so it'd look nice for today, y'know, and old slowpoke here—" she jabbed Ned in the arm with her bony elbow ''—wasn't done in the hardware store yet, so I decided to do a little window shopping. Not that there's much to see, but still. Anyway, I'd just gotten to the end of the block, which was pretty much deserted, when I caught movement out of the corner of my eye. I looked across the street just in time to see the boy getting ready to open the door to Hootch's truck, so I hollered out, *Hey, boy, what're you doing*—'' everyone at the table flinched at her demonstration ''—and he took off without even botherin' to look around. After he'd gone, I walked over to see Hootch'd left his keys in the ignition. Man doesn't have the good sense God gave a gnat—''

''How did you know it was Elijah?'' Dawn asked.

''Mildred and I drove out there a couple of times in the spring,'' Maddie put in as she wiped yams off the baby's face. ''Just to check how Jacob was doing, take them a pie or something. But Elijah's daddy was so…so…''

''*Ungrateful*'s the word you're lookin' for,'' Mildred said, shoving her glasses back up onto the bridge of her nose. ''Told us to go away and not bother him again. Said he didn't need anybody's charity.''

More than one person stifled a smile as Uncle Ned—who, until Maddie made it her mission to recivilize her uncle-in-law, had been the most irascible, unsociable old coot in the county—obliviously shoveled in another bite of turkey and gravy.

''That sounds familiar,'' Dawn said, then went on to explain about Elijah's shoplifting attempts, Jacob's less-than-enthusiastic reaction when she'd brought him home, how she hadn't seen or heard from the boy since.

''If you ask me,'' Mildred said, ''that man's got no more business being somebody's father than…than the man in the moon.''

''Anybody ready for pie?'' Ivy said, standing and collecting Mildred's and Ned's plates. ''I know you boys have games you want to watch, so we may as well get a move on.''

Except for Mildred and Ned, who were forbidden to lift a finger, and Maddie, who was still trying to convince Amy Rose that mashed potatoes were not intended for use as hair mousse, all the other adults got up to help clear the table. As Dawn backed through the swinging door into the kitchen, her hands full of gravy boat and green-bean casserole, she overheard Hank say, "But if prices keep going down, don't you run the risk of losing the whole thing?"

"Not if I'm careful," Cal said.

Ryan took the casserole from Dawn, thunking it on the counter. "Look, Cal, there's no shame in lettin' go of something that's not working. You gave it your best shot—"

"Where do you get off tellin' me if it's working or not?" Cal said, leaning one hand on the counter, the other jammed in his jeans pocket. "Yeah, things are rough right now, but if you think I'm throwing in the towel, giving up my *home,* at the first sign of trouble, you're nuts."

"I'm just saying—" Ryan swung open the refrigerator to shove in the casserole "—it might be better to get out now while you still have a chance of makin' something from the sale." He let the refrigerator door swing shut. "Then you can start up again sometime down the road when things are better—"

"You can't ask him to do that!"

Every head in the kitchen swiveled in Dawn's direction. Especially Cal's, whose expression was nothing short of flabbergasted.

"That farm was your father's dream!" she said, her cheeks heating, her gaze bouncing from Ryan's startled blue eyes to Hank's nearly black what-the-hell? ones. "And now it's…it's Cal's *life.* You might as well ask him to stop breathing as to give up his horses! And…" Her heart felt as though it was about to pound out of her chest. "And that's all I'm gonna say on the subject, since it's really none of my business, anyway."

The swinging door nearly smacked her in the butt as she scooted back into the dining room, breathing deeply in an attempt to quell the tremors racking her body. An apple pie balanced in one hand, Ivy gave her a one-armed hug.

Dawn grimaced. "I have no idea where that came from."

"Don't you?" her mother whispered back.

By the time dessert was served a few minutes later, the conversation had returned to less controversial topics, most notably Hank's and Jenna's upcoming wedding. Then, when everybody had at least one slice of the pie, or pies, of their choice in front of them, Ryan clinked his fork on his glass until it got quiet, except for Amy Rose who clapped her now pumpkin-pie-slathered hands and squealed, "Daddy!" After the laughter died down, Ryan stood, raising his glass of cider and smiling at Maddie at the other end of the table in a way that made Dawn's breath catch in her throat.

"Since we've got y'all in one spot, I suppose this is as good a time as any to announce, being as this wife of mine and I are clearly out of our minds—" he winked at Maddie "—that come July, there's gonna be another baby in the house!"

Delighted congratulations broke out around the table as Noah, Maddie's six-year-old son, yelled, "An' if it's not a boy this time, I'm sendin' it *back!*" Her ears ringing from the din of laughter that followed, Dawn's gaze bounced from person to person, each rapidly blurring face beaming with more joy than the next, until all the turkey and potatoes and yams threatened a major revolt in her stomach.

In the happy confusion of handshakes and hugs, she fled.

Chapter 9

Cal found her out in the backyard, wedged into the rubber-seated swing Ryan had strung up for the kids from the tallest sycamore. She glanced up at his approach, clumsily catching her sweater coat when he tossed it to her, then pivoted so he couldn't see her face.

"What's going on, honey?"

"Nothing," she said to the tree as she punched her arms through the sleeves. "I just needed some air, that's all."

Cal walked over and grabbed the rope, twisting it back around so she had to look at him. "Ah, hell…you're crying!"

"Of course I'm crying! I'm always crying!" She dug a tissue from the pocket of those stretchy pants she was wearing and honked into it. "I'm a w-walking hormone dump! Yesterday, I got all teary be-because Ruby'd run out of split pea soup by the time I got there. Then she said she'd saved me the last piece of Maddie's lemon meringue pie, at least, and I cried even h-harder—"

"Get out of the swing," Cal said.

She glared up at him. And sniffed. "I don't want t-to."

"Did I ask you if you *wanted* to get out of the swing? So come on."

"Why?"

"Because, Hormone Hannah," he said on a weary sigh, "I can't hold you while you're in the damn swing."

"I don't want—"

He reached over, grabbed her hand and tugged her onto her feet and into his arms.

And what's more, she let him.

"Did you really mean all that back there in the kitchen," he said softly, rubbing her back, "about how I shouldn't give up on the farm?"

Judging from her flinch, this was not what she expected. Frowning, she reared back to look up at him, her eyes huge. "Of course I meant it, doofus. The farm means the world to you!" She sniffed. "And I can't believe Hank and Ryan don't understand that."

"I think the way they see it is, they're just trying to look out for their baby brother. And your eyelash stuff is smearing."

"You're nobody's *baby* anything, Cal Logan!" she said, swiping underneath her eyes. "And they've got no right, none, to give you grief for following your heart. Besides, who the hell are they to talk? Ryan, especially—trying to make a go of it as a country doctor in this day and age?" She gave a sharp laugh. "Yeah, like that makes a whole lotta sense. But I'd like to see anybody try to talk him out of it. So don't you dare let them try to boss you around, you hear me?"

Since she'd missed at least half the smudges, Cal took the tissue from her and gently wiped at them himself. "Wow— look up, wouldja?—I had no idea you felt so strongly."

"Neither did I," she said on a little sigh. "Except I know it's something you've wanted ever since you were little. Did you get it?" she asked when he handed her back the tissue.

"Yeah," he said, and she tucked her hand between her cheek and his chest and said, "Besides, I also know how it feels to have your dreams threatened."

"Well, just for the record, darlin'—" he wrapped his arms

a little more tightly around her ''—my brothers can bluster and blow all they want, but it takes a lot more than a little hot air to blow a Logan off course. Which, if either of them stopped to think about for a minute, they'd figure out.''

''So…you're not listening to them?''

''Oh, I'll listen. Doesn't mean I have to pay attention, though.''

''Good,'' she said.

He rested his cheek in her hair and said, ''Now. You got any idea what's really bugging you?''

She stiffened. ''I told you. Nothing.''

''Right. Honey, in my experience, women don't bolt from a room over nothing.'' He frowned. ''Let me rephrase that. *You* don't bolt from a room over nothing. So my guess is…there was just a bit more happiness going on in that house than you could stomach.''

That got a tiny, muffled laugh. ''How'd you know?''

''Because it was driving me nuts, too.''

She looked up. ''Yeah?''

''Yeah,'' he said, trying not to think about how much he wanted to kiss her.

A small frown marred her forehead. ''Why?''

''Because…everybody else has got their lives figured out but me. Because I *don't* know how I'm gonna keep this business afloat, and I've got a baby on the way and I don't know how to make you happy—''

''Whoa, buster! It's not up to you to make me happy!''

''Doesn't mean I don't want to. Dammit…'' He gathered her close again—as close as her big belly would let him, anyway—because he had to. Because this way, he didn't have to see that damned indignant expression. ''Nothing makes any sense right now. This isn't…it's just not how I ever saw becomin' a father, you know?''

''Well, hell,'' she said, ''it's not like this was exactly my first choice, either! And believe me, things would be a lot easier if I didn't care about you. If I…'' She stopped.

''What?''

"Never mind."

"Oh, no…don't you pull that 'never mind' crap on me. One thing I could always count on with you, and that was you being up-front with me, no matter what. Even when we were kids, you always said exactly what was on your mind. I didn't always like it, and I sure as hell didn't always understand it, but at least I never had to wonder what you were really thinking. So don't go hiding behind those hormones now, you got that?"

After a moment she pulled away, cocooning herself in her sweater. "I always thought I knew what I wanted, what I was going to do with my life, who I was. But now…" She walked back to the swing and wriggled her butt into the seat. "I'm having a blast working in Sherman's office, much to my shock. That should make me happy, right? But does it? Noooo, because if I'm happy here, that means everything I've believed about myself before this has been a sham. It means…I might not even want to leave."

Cal's heart rocketed into his throat. "And the problem with that is…?"

"The problem is, if I stayed here, it would be all too easy to get caught up in what everybody else wants for us. What everybody else in your family has." Her eyes glistened with new tears. "Don't you see? It's not…" The sentence got cut off on a little gasp; he could see her focus inward, like he wasn't even there anymore. Only he was, and she was making him nuts, and no way was she getting away with not finishing that sentence.

"Dawn?" he said, more sharply than he intended.

She glanced up, slightly dazed, then motioned him over. "The baby's moving," she said on a whisper, like it might stop if it heard her.

Cal moved closer and crouched down, letting her guide his hand to a spot low on the outside of those stretchy pants. He glanced up at her face, his heart melting at the look of wonder that had, for the moment at least, erased most of the worry.

"Sorry, honey, but I don't feel—"

"Shh," she said, still whispering. "Think subtle. No hooves.

There!'' She laughed. ''It kind of tickles!'' Her hand over his, she moved it a fraction south. ''Right…there.''

This time he felt it, a tiny ripple against his palm. Emotion dammed up inside him, making him feel like a sap—he was hardly the first man to experience this, for Pete's sake—but he didn't care, they'd work it out somehow, everything would be okay…

''At least, I can give you this,'' Dawn said, blowing his endorphins or whatever they were all to hell. When he met her gaze again, the worry was back. In spades. ''It's very tempting to believe, at moments like this—'' she removed his hand, tugging her sweater back down over her bulge ''—that we could make it work. Because we both love this child. Because we're good in bed together.''

Before he could say anything, she bracketed his face with her hands. ''I don't want a pretend relationship. And I know you don't. And that's all we'd have, no matter how good the sex might be, no matter how devoted we'd both be to this baby. Because I have no idea what it takes to—'' she cut herself off, then finished with ''—to keep a relationship going.''

Cal stood up before his legs cramped permanently in that position. ''Who the hell does? I mean, it's not exactly something you're born knowing, is it?'' At her implacable expression, he blew out a sigh. ''Dammit, Dawn… Okay, so maybe this is one of those things you have to take on faith. Learn from other people's examples or something. Like, I don't know…Faith and Darryl. Or Maddie and Ryan. Seems to me they've got a pretty good handle on things.''

''I think Faith's more resigned than happy, to be honest. And Maddie and Ryan haven't exactly withstood the test of time, have they?''

''Fine. Then how about Ruby and Jordy? Luralene and Coop? Faith's parents?'' He paused. ''*My* parents?''

''And for every example you can give of a couple who has it together,'' she said quietly, ''I can name you two more that started out just fine, but for one reason or another broke up.''

Like he'd said, there was no arguing with the woman once

she'd made up her mind. And with that realization, hopelessness spread through him like frost. He crossed his arms. "And this really doesn't have a damn thing to do with anybody else, does it?"

She frowned. "I don't know what—"

"Dawn, be honest. It all boils down to one simple fact—you don't want to be with me."

"It's more complicated than that—"

"No it's not. Do you or don't you?"

She got up and would have headed back toward the house, but he grabbed her arm, making her face him. "Answer me, dammit."

This time there was none of that aggravating ambivalence in her eyes. This time all he saw was pure, unadulterated fear, so much that he jerked, her arm falling from his grasp.

She blinked, once, then turned and walked away.

Two days before Christmas, the brutal wind practically shoved Dawn into Ruby's, blasting the paper place mats right out of the nearest booth and making the tacky tinsel decorations hanging from each suspended ceiling fixture—could they really be the very same ones Dawn remembered from high school?—shimmy frantically.

"Wondered if you were gonna make it today," Ruby hollered from the kitchen, peering through the serving window. "It's later than usual."

"Sorry," she said, shrugging out of her down coat and snagging it on a hook by the front door. "Is there anything left?"

It was nearly three; Ruby officially stopped serving lunch at two, so the diner was basically deserted. But she always kept a pot of coffee on for anyone who wanted to come in and visit for a few minutes, and she'd told Dawn in no uncertain terms that she could come in for lunch anytime, didn't matter when, but she was not to neglect that baby, was that clear?

"For you, baby," Ruby said, her crepe-soled shoes squeaking on the linoleum as she came into full view, "there's always something left, you know that. Another big storm coming in, according to the weatherman.'' She set a cup of piping-hot mint tea in front of Dawn, who immediately picked it up to warm her frozen fingers, inhaling the sweetly scented steam. ''I suppose it might be nice to have a white Christmas, but after that, it can go someplace else as far as I'm concerned. This'll make, what, the fourth storm we've have since Thanksgiving? So…we're all out of the meat loaf, though I've got more in the oven. But Jordy can make you up a hot roast beef sandwich, how's that sound?''

''Like heaven.''

Ruby yelled out Dawn's order to her husband, then got herself a cup of coffee and settled in on the other side of the booth, as she did most days. ''So. Sherman's practice keeping you busy?''

''To say the least. Who knew a town of this size could generate so much legal work?''

''Think you might stay, then?''

Dawn clunked the thick ceramic cup into the saucer. ''That's called leading the witness, Ruby.''

''Since this ain't a court of law, I'm not worried. Well?''

''I don't know yet,'' she said softly. After that conversation with Cal at Thanksgiving, she'd been more muddled than ever. For the past month, all she could think of was the look on his face when he'd confronted her about whether or not she wanted to be with him…and she'd been unable to answer. Their awkwardness with each other at Jenna's and Hank's wedding. The merciless, taunting yearning in his eyes that she could only withstand by avoiding altogether. Which brought home the fact that, no matter whether she stayed or left, she was going to hurt him, a prospect—an inevitability—that was making her ill.

''But it's an option, at least?'' Ruby said.

Dawn smiled into the hopeful dark eyes. ''We'll see.''

Ruby chuckled, patting her inch-long white 'fro. ''Well, at least you didn't say *hell, no,* so that's something. And maybe you'll have made up your mind for sure by the time this baby comes—''

''Speaking of babies coming…'' They both looked up as

Ivy, who'd popped up out of nowhere, slid into the booth beside Ruby, a cup of coffee in her hand. "Faith just had hers a couple hours ago. A gorgeous baby boy, seven pounds and change! They're callin' him Nicky. For St. Nicholas, 'cause he was born so close to Christmas—!"

"Dammit!" Luralene Hastings yipped as the door slapped her in the butt. Then the sixty-something Lucille Ball redhead scurried across the floor, teeth chattering, her arms strangling her ribs over her violently violet Hair We Are smock. "That wind is downright *mean* today!"

"Well, for heaven's sake, woman," Ivy said, frowning. "Why the hell don't you put on a coat?"

Shaking so badly her already bouffant hairdo looked twice as big—AquaNet and the teasing comb being Luralene's main weapons in her war against bad hair days—she batted away Ivy's concern. "For a thirty-foot walk? Not hardly worth the effort. But I'll tell you what," she said, toting her coffee to the table and wedging herself in beside Dawn, "if this weather keeps up, I may just dig out that fur-lined bra from Frederick's of Hollywood that Coop gave to me for Valentine's day a couple years ago!"

That merited an appropriate pause for reflection, until Jordy shattered the silence by asking was anybody gonna pick up this roast beef sandwich or what?

Since Dawn and Ruby were both trapped, Ivy got up and retrieved Dawn's lunch, chiding her for not having a vegetable to go with it.

She held up her tea. "This is green, right? Close enough."

Ivy shook her head.

Some time later, as Dawn was trying to digest both her second piece of apple pie and the latest gossip, Charmaine came in with her boys, her face pinched with worry.

"I'm sorry, Ruby, but I had to bring 'em again today…"

"And I told you not to concern yourself about that," her boss said, getting up from the booth. "Your mama not feeling well again?"

A furtive look crossed the woman's features. "Yeah," she

said in that leaden way of somebody worn-out from twisting the truth. "I'm thinkin' I really need to get somebody else, one of these days. Is it okay if they go into the office for a bit, get started on their homework?"

"Sure, baby. And tell Jordy I said to give 'em something to eat. Put some meat on those skinny little bones."

After Charmaine and the boys had gone, Dawn asked, "I take it Charmaine's mother gets sick a lot?"

Luralene leaned one elbow on the table. "Honey, I wouldn't leave my *dog* in her care. Woman's drunk as a skunk more days than she's sober. And her hair looks like she took a weed whacker to it."

Sidestepping Luralene's non sequitur, Dawn said, "Which means, since Charmaine can't afford to hire a real sitter or put the kids in day care, she's stuck."

"That's right—"

"You got it—"

"Uh-huh."

"Okay, that's it. Scoot," Dawn said, shooing the redhead out of the booth. "I can't stand this any longer."

She found Charmaine in the ladies' room, jerking a cheap plastic brush through her hair. The brunette had been pretty in high school, still was despite the effects of stress and overwork. Now, however, her eyes sat cowering in their sockets, the harsh lighting in the utilitarian room emphasizing her sallow skin, her thin, pale lips.

"We need to talk," Dawn said.

"Talk?" Her blue-gray eyes flashed in the mirror. "Don't see where you and I have anything to say to each other."

"I'd like to help you find Brody. So you can get child support for the kids."

The brush clattered against the sink, echoing sharply in the tiny room. Charmaine yanked her hair back into a ponytail, her movements jerky as she wrapped a coated band around it. "I don't need your help," she said, dumping the brush in her purse, then turning to leave. Dawn blocked her way out. "Excuse me, but I got work to do. And my kids—"

"—have got four people watching them. They're fine. You're not."

"And how the hell would you know how I am? Now get out of my way—"

"Not until we clear the air about a few things. And until you understand that I'm on your side!"

The waitress backed up slightly; for a second, Dawn wondered if she was going to slug her. God knew she looked mad enough.

"*My* side?" she said on a humorless laugh. "That's a good one. Well, get this, Miss High and Mighty—I don't need you lookin' down on me, or feelin' sorry for me. You're no better'n any of the rest of us, even if you sure did act like it when we were in school. You and Faith Meyerhauser, both." She crossed her arms under breasts too small to fill out the top of her bilious-pink uniform. "Her thinking she was such hot stuff because she was the preacher's kid, and you with all your big plans for what you were gonna do when you finally got out of here. Lord, all anybody could talk about was how you got that scholarship to go to college in New York City—"

"Which nobody heard from me!"

"Oh, yeah? If you didn't tell, who did?"

"How the hell should I know? The stupid guidance counselor, would be my guess. God knows, nobody'd ever be able to accuse Gertie Schultz of taking secrets with her to her grave." At Charmaine's eye roll, Dawn lifted her hands. "Okay, maybe I'm not real proud of the way I acted back then, but I am not about to apologize for something I *earned!* I studied my butt off because, yes, I wanted to do something with my life that I thought I couldn't do here. And since my mother had already scraped together everything she had for my education, getting that scholarship was the only way I could accomplish that. That's not a crime, Charmaine."

"And what good did it do you in the long run?" she said, her colorless mouth tightened into a smirk. "I mean, here you are, aren't you? Right back in Haven, knocked up and unmarried…and thinkin' you're too good to marry your kid's father."

Dawn lost her breath. *"What?"*

Charmaine shrugged, triumph hovering at the edges of her lips.

After two seconds spent regaining her balance, Dawn looked her old classmate straight in the eye. "My reasons for not marrying Cal have nothing to do with…that. And maybe I hadn't planned on coming back to Haven, but here I am. And whatever you might think about my leaving, if I hadn't, I wouldn't be in the position to help you find Brody and make him pay up."

They glared at each other for several seconds. Until Charmaine said, "And how do you plan on doing that if I don't even know where he is?"

Dawn let out a very…tiny…breath. "You got his social security number?"

That got a frown. "Yeah, I guess. From our last tax return."

"That's all I need." At the brunette's skeptical look, she added, "Charmaine, I *live* for these kinds of cases. And you need someone who's not emotionally involved to go after him."

"I can't pay you."

"Neither can most mothers in your situation. Don't worry about it."

Dawn could see the war in her eyes, sense her waffling. So she added, "Hate my guts if you have to, but do this for your boys, okay? My father abandoned me, too, remember? Even if I never knew him, it hurt just the same. I didn't do what I did, or act the way I did, because I thought I was better, but because I decided I *deserved* better. There's a difference."

She left the bathroom, not realizing until she was nearly back to her booth that her knees were shaking.

Between the sleet hammering on the barn roof and the whuffling and crunching from upwards of two dozen horses chowing down their feed, Cal lost five years off his life when he turned around and saw Dawn standing a few feet away, drops of moisture sparkling in her hair. All wrapped up in one of those shawls or whatever they were that Ivy wore, flat black riding boots poking out from underneath the hem of her dark-red skirt, she looked like something straight out of an old novel.

"Sorry, I didn't mean to scare you," she said breathlessly, her eyes on his as he closed the distance between them, the sound of his boots against the cement floor adding a base note to her "When you weren't at the house, I figured I'd find you here."

"Is everything okay—?"

"Are people saying I won't marry you because I think you're not good enough for me?"

Cal stopped dead in his tracks, his insides churning from a mixture of relief and shock. "What?"

"Are people—"

"No, I heard you." Frowning, he shoved his hands into the pockets of his sheepskin coat. "And what the hell do you care what people say?"

"Then it's true?"

His ragged breath misted around his mouth. Somebody whinnied behind him, adding her two cents. "I might've heard it once or twice. Not from anybody whose opinion means squat, though."

"Then have *I* ever done or said anything to make you think that?"

"*No.* For God's sake, Dawn—"

"You're sure?"

"Honey, what's this all about? After us barely exchanging ten words over the last month, you mean to tell me you came all the way out here in this weather to ask me that?" Sudden realization cramped his stomach. "In the *GTO?*"

A smile touched her lips, but it didn't do much for the troubled look in her eyes. "Okay. I won't. Although in my own defense, it was only cloudy when I started out. And I put new tires on the thing."

"I do have a phone, you know."

"I had to see you," she said, taking a step closer. "I had to know…"

"I'm a big boy, honey," he said over the ache in his gut. "I don't break easily."

She nodded, then said, walking over to one of the stalls, "Where's Ethel?"

"Gone to Kansas City to be with her daughter over Christmas."

The mare, a four-year-old dapple gray, reared her head at Dawn's approach, then retreated farther into her stall.

"It's okay, sweetie," Dawn said gently, then frowned. "I don't remember this one. Is she new?"

"Yep. Just bought her last week."

"Poor thing…she looks scared to death. What's wrong with her?"

Cal joined her at the stall, trying to understand how, whether they'd been apart for ten minutes, ten days or ten years, the instant the woman slipped back into his life, it was like she'd never left. "Chronic homesickness, from what I can tell. I bought her cheap off a family who needed to move fast and couldn't take her with them. On paper she looked good. Hell, in person she looked good. Responsive, even-tempered, good stock…but she's taking her sweet time about settling in. What?" he asked at Dawn's bemused expression.

"You really needed another horse?"

He felt his mouth tilt into a grin. "Women don't *need* more than one pair of shoes, either. But a bargain's a bargain."

She laughed. "Yeah, but shoes don't breed in your closet and beget more shoes. Even if it does seem that way sometimes." Folding her arms on top of the stall door, she said, "I can see why you found her irresistible, though. She's beautiful."

Cal beat back the impulse to say something hokey about how irresistible he found Dawn. He might be crazy enough to buy another horse when he already had a barnful, but he wasn't *that* crazy.

"What's her name?" Dawn asked.

"Sunnyside's Blaze of Glory. Blaze to her friends."

At the mention of her name, the mare's ears flicked. Dawn smiled. "You say a family had her before?"

"Yeah. Husband and wife, two kids. She belonged to the oldest girl, who was going to train her to show."

"How old was the girl?"

"Not sure. A teenager."

"She wouldn't hurt me, would she?"

"I don't know. Gal seemed nice enough when I met her—"

Dawn whapped him in the arm. "Not the girl, dweeb," she said over his chuckle, then started talking softly to the mare. Nonsense, mostly, about some case she was working on or something. After a minute or so, Blaze lifted her head, her ears pricking in curiosity as Dawn kept up her soothing, one-sided conversation. Then the mare took a step closer, nodding her massive head and snuffling.

"See if she'll take this," Cal said, cutting a chunk of apple with his pocket knife and handing it to her.

"Treat time," she said to the horse, holding out the apple, flat palmed like Hank, Sr., had taught them so many years ago. "Although if you feel anything like I do right now, you'd probably prefer one of Ruby's ice cream sundaes. And don't you dare tell Mama," she said in an aside to Cal. Bit by bit, the mare got closer, finally wriggling her lips to take the fruit from Dawn's hand.

Only to immediately retreat once more to the back of her stall, eyeing Dawn morosely.

"Don't take it personally, honey," Cal said. "She looks at everybody like that."

On a soft sigh, Dawn said, "I thought maybe she was just missing the sound of a woman's voice. That—I don't know— maybe…she needed someone to talk to who understood how she felt." Her gaze flashed to his, then back to the horse. Smiling, she said, "Somehow it didn't sound stupid while it was still in my head."

Cal leaned one hand on the stall's door frame, close enough to get a whiff of that flowery stuff she used on her hair. "It's not stupid at all. And yes, I'm serious, so you can wipe that look off your face. Animals are a lot more attuned to what's goin' on in our heads than a lot of folks give 'em credit for. But it takes time for 'em to learn to trust somebody, just like it does people. See," he said, when the mare nodded, "she's agreeing with me."

Dawn smiled, but some time passed before she said, "Promise me you'll teach our child how to hear what the horses have to tell us."

Cal waited out the thumping in his chest and said, "I'll do my best," and she sighed, like a great weight had been lifted from her shoulders.

"You can't stand seeing anything unhappy, can you?" he said.

She laughed softly. "I suppose not. Although my drive to fix things is way beyond my ability to fix things."

"Bet the people you've helped don't feel that way."

She shrugged, wrapping the shawl more tightly around her, as a little more vulnerability leaked through those hairline cracks in her tough exterior.

"You had supper yet?" he said. "Ethel left enough stew to feed half the state, I could heat some up for us if you like."

She blinked up at him like somebody just awakened out of a deep sleep. "Oh, no…I need to get back—"

"Like you're going anywhere in *that* car in *this* weather."

Her brow knotted. "I did manage to get here without doing myself in, Cal. And since when do you tell me what I can and cannot do?"

"Since you're carrying my kid, dammit! You wanna take your own life in your hands, you go right ahead…but not as long as that baby's inside you!"

Dawn gawked at him for a moment, then dropped onto a nearby hay bale as if all the fight had drained right out of her. "Oh, God…I'm sorry, that was a totally knee-jerk reaction. I'm just so used to only having myself to think about…" One of the cats jumped up into her lap. "Sorry," she said, stroking the loudly purring tabby's fur. "It's been a long day."

Lord, but the woman was going to be the death of him. "Don't take this the wrong way," he said, "but you got a real problem with letting people look out for you, don't you?"

She batted the cat's tail out of her face to look up at him. "Yeah. I do. With good reason. You lean on somebody, they walk away...*wham!* You fall on your face."

"Who said anything about leaning?" he said, because he figured that was safer than going anywhere near the *walking away* part of that sentence.

Confusion clouded her eyes for a moment. "You did. Didn't you?"

"No, ma'am." He reached out, grasping her hand to pull her to her feet. Then he hung on, just because he felt like it. "I'm talking about caring. Enough to maybe point out dangers the other person might not be able to see. To catch 'em when they stumble, push 'em back up, if need be." He entwined their fingers, feeling his heart rate pick up at the simple skin-to-skin contact. "I'm talking about the kind of relationship," he said carefully, looking deep into her eyes, "that makes each partner stronger, not weaker."

He watched her pupils darken, her throat convulse.

"That offer of stew still stand?" she said.

Cal just grinned.

Since the lights kept flickering as if the power was thinking about going off, the only light came from the haphazardly decorated Christmas tree in the corner and the fire Dawn had made while Cal had gone to take a shower. And he'd put on some seriously sensuous jazz in his handy-dandy, battery-operated CD player—unlike his brothers, his mother's love for classical music hadn't rubbed off on her younger son—that was threatening to turn her inside out. And despite that business in the barn, she was feeling very...relaxed, curled up on the old leather sofa, cozy and safe and warm while a sleet storm raged outside.

She decided not to think about the business in the barn. She decided not to think at all, for a change. Except to complete

her thought, which was that she was stronger than all of it—
the dim lighting and the sultry music and the coziness and the
whatever-that-was in the barn.

That was her story and she was sticking to it.

"You call your mother?" Cal asked as he walked in from
the kitchen, handing her a heavy crockery mug filled with
Ethel's stew.

"Yes. And for the record," she said around her first bite of
tender beef, holding the stew close in an attempt to mask the
sing-it-to-me scent of freshly showered male, "she agrees with
you that I should have my head examined for driving out here
in this weather."

"Always knew I liked that woman," he said with a grin,
easing himself down on the floor across from her with his own
mug, his back propped against the wing chair. Tags jingled as
dogs stirred, intrigued and hopeful.

Dawn snorted. For the next few minutes hunger staved off
conversation. Until Dawn said, "I've come to a conclusion."

"Am I gonna like this?"

"Probably not." She scooped out the last bit of broth, then
said, "I've decided pregnancy makes me weird."

Cal's eyebrows quirked. "*Makes* you weird?"

"Okay, weird*er*."

"That's better…get outta here, mutt!" Cal said, elbowing
one of the Australian shepherds out of his face. He shoveled
in a bite or two, then looked over. "You planning on explain-
ing that, or do I get to draw my own conclusions?"

"I don't know if I can. It's just…scary. I mean, my biggest
thrill these days is lying in bed and watching my stomach
move. What's up with that?"

Cal chewed for several seconds, then said, "And you think
that makes you weird?"

"Well, it sure as hell isn't…*me*."

"Sure it's you," he said with what sounded like gentle exasperation. "It's just you, pregnant. Which you've never been
before."

So, naturally, tears welled up in her eyes. For at least the millionth time in the past five months.

Dawn pushed herself up off the sofa, a task becoming increasingly difficult as the days wore on, and held up her mug. "You said there was more?"

"Sure," Cal said, getting to his feet. "Let me get—"

"No, I can do it…oh!"

One of the dogs got in her way, making her stumble. The empty mug went flying, landing safely on the sofa, as she landed—not so safely—in Cal's arms.

"Whoo-ee," she said, her heart break-dancing inside her chest, "you've got great reflexes."

"One of my many talents," he said, and swooped in for the kiss. And, man-oh-man, kissing him back wasn't even a question. His lips touched down and her own just smashed right up against his. Boy, and she clung to him, to his hot, gentle, possessive mouth, wishing he could somehow suck out her apprehensiveness and confusion as if they were snakebite venom.

She growled, low in her throat. Cal backed up, amusement dancing in his eyes. "Was that a *please stop* or a *please continue?*"

"Damned if I know," she said, and a grin eased itself across his face.

The baby kicked; Cal slipped his hand underneath her sweater, his palm warm and strong against her bare skin, and every nerve ending she had went *Yes!!!* As did the baby, who kicked one over the goalpost.

"Not now, kid," he whispered. "I'm busy."

He kissed her again and again, and some more after that until each and every brain cell she possessed tiptoed quietly out of the room, and her breasts, heavy with desire and pregnancy, begged Pleeease? Although they were being far more polite about it than another, much brattier area of her body which was screaming ME! NOW!

Which is when she snatched back a couple of those brain cells, plugging them in long enough to pull out of Cal's arms and whisper, "Damn."

Except for the fire's crackling, the dog's whine, a slow sax in the background, there was silence. Dawn raised her eyes to Cal's, expecting to see…something. Annoyance? Confusion? Disbelief? But his expression, his body language, were as mute as his vocal chords. Instead, he reached over to pluck her mug from the sofa cushions—assorted dogs had already attended to the clean-up detail—as well as his own from the floor, then calmly walked back to the kitchen.

"You still want more stew?" he said.

She shook her head, which only made her dizzier than she already was, then cleared her throat and said, "No. I changed my mind."

He came back with his own mug, settling into the sofa. "So I noticed," he said mildly, spooning in a bite.

To calm herself, she'd started fiddling with the jigsaw puzzle spread out on a table near the fire. He'd always loved puzzles, as long as she'd known him. But as usual, he'd assembled chunks of the middle before doing the border, which just drove her nuts. She glanced over, catching just enough of his annoyance to send her gaze skittering back to the puzzle. "I'm sorry. That probably wasn't very fair of me—"

"And you can stop that right now," he said, making her look up again. "I was just seeing how far I could get before you did what you did."

She frowned. "You…weren't planning on stopping?"

"Why would I do that?"

"Because…"

"Lemme tell you something," he said, setting the mug on the end table, then leaning back to cup his hands behind his head. "Contrary to popular belief, seduction isn't about getting somebody to do something they don't want to do. It's about knowing when to make your move." His gaze was steady. "You're not inexperienced, Dawn. I know you know what I'm talking about."

She turned toward the fire, hugging herself. "Only too well."

"Then what happened?" Curiosity, not irritation, colored his words. "You were right there with me, I know you were. Until something spooked you."

"Wouldn't do much good to deny it, would it?"

"No. It wouldn't." Then, softly: "What do you want, honey? I mean, really want. Right this minute."

Her fingers tingled when she skimmed them across the mantelpiece, cluttered with framed photos both old and relatively new, of the brothers when they were kids, of Mary and Hank, Sr., of Ryan and Maddie and Hank and Jenna and all their kids.

"Right now?" she asked. "If I could do anything I wanted without any ramifications, any consequences?"

"That's what I'm talking about."

She turned. "To make love with you until my eyes fall out of my head."

Both sets of dimples came out in full force. "So what's the problem?"

"The problem is, my body wants to mess around, but my head is telling me this is a very, very bad idea."

"Why?" he said softly.

"Because it won't change anything. About…us."

A log popped and tumbled; behind the firescreen, sparks danced.

"Who says it has to?"

"Oh, right. You expect me to believe we could go to bed and it wouldn't mean…something?"

The heat in his eyes made her insides flip. "Oh, it'll mean something. Just like it meant something when we made that baby. But if you're afraid I'm gonna expect…well, whatever it is you seem to think I'm gonna expect, you can rest easy on that score." He leaned forward, his hands knotted between his knees, his eyes locked with hers. "Dawn…if you want sex, all you have to do is ask. I'm ready, God knows I'm willing, and unless something drastic's happened in the past few months, I'm more than able."

She faced the fire again, for some reason unable to unglue her tongue from the roof of her mouth.

"And," he added, "if your hesitation has anything to do with some fool notion that I'm gonna be put off by the changes in your body, you can forget about that one right now."

Dawn spun around. "I don't have a problem with my body, either! I've never felt more feminine in my life!" Or, judging from the look in his eyes right then, more powerful.

"You do realize you're killing me, don't you?"

Oh, buster—you don't know from killing.

"From all the way over here?" she said.

"Considering I've been hard since the minute I saw you in the barn, proximity isn't even an issue."

That's not good, some brain cell piped up, only to have another one chime in with, *Like hell it isn't!*

"Tell you what," Cal said, interrupting this fascinating argument. "Why don't you come over here and sit down beside me—" he patted the sofa, one of the dogs jumped up, Cal pushed him back down "—and we can just, I don't know, make out or something, see where that takes us."

She barked out a laugh. "I *know* where that will take us."

He lifted one eyebrow, and she laughed again.

She meant what she'd said, about this not changing anything between them. Not in the long run. But between her hormones and—she swallowed down a sigh—her simply wanting to be close, to somehow connect to this man's confidence and serenity, she could no more resist his offer than she could a fifty-percent off sale at Barney's. Just for a little while, she wanted to feel safe.

Even if that safety was as illusory as holding a magazine over your head to keep the rain off.

With a half smile, as if he knew what she was thinking, he held out his hand. Once again her brain cells left the room.

Unfortunately, she didn't follow them.

Chapter 10

Cal watched Dawn slowly cross the room, his heartbeat in his ears a hundred times louder than the sleet ticking against the windows. She stopped in front of him, her hands clenched at her sides; he looked up, frowning.

"You come over here to fool around or belt me one?"

"I haven't decided yet."

He reached up and grabbed one of those knotted fists, tugging her down onto his lap. "Let me help you with that decision," he whispered, wrapping his arms around where her waist should have been and assaulting her neck.

"Oh, geez, Cal! I must weigh a ton…"

"Not even close," he said, cupping her jaw to draw her mouth down to his. After, oh, a minute or so of some of the hottest kissing of his life, he reached under her sweater.

"I thought we were just going to make out," she murmured against his mouth.

"I lied," he said, snatching another kiss, skating a fingertip along the top of her cotton bra. "And anyway, since we've already determined where this is headed, I didn't exactly think

I needed to ask permission. And I heard that,'' he said in response to her gasp.

"Heard what?"

He dipped under the bra, past breath-stealing softness to sweet hardness. This time her gasp had some real substance to it. "That," he said, thinking, if this is all she would let him give, then this is what he would give her.

"Oh, you ain't heard—'' she swallowed "—nothing yet.''

He smiled. "I take it that means I can keep going?"

"Uh, yeah, I think you're safe with that assumption.''

So he unsnapped the front clasp of her bra and did just that. She tangled her hands in his hair and said, in a Kathleen Turner voice, "Oh, man…you have *no* idea how good that feels,'' and Cal decided this was going to be one of those times a man knows he's going to remember for a long, long time. Then they kissed some more, slow and frantic, gentle and demanding, mouths desperate and tongues eager to get aquainted, her breasts so heavy, so right in his hand.

Then she wriggled her soft little fanny on his anything-but-soft lap and he said, "Whoa, cutie pie…I want to take this nice and slow.''

"Says you and whose army?"

He thought for a moment—which was the biggest challenge he'd faced in quite a while—and said, "Okay, this time fast, next time slow?''

"Whatever,'' she said, standing up long enough to ditch the sweater, then straddling his lap. And, oh, man…there they were, right in front of him, the breasts of his dreams—

"Hey. You down there,'' she said, planting her hands on the back of the sofa. "Quit staring and do something, already.''

—and, glory hallelujah, all his.

It quickly became apparent that, one, while the sofa was fun to get started on, it kinda limited options, and two, they both still had on far too many clothes. Within ten seconds, give or take, they'd remedied both situations to their mutual satisfaction, and were now on the floor in front of the fire, Dawn's skin pale and luminous as he traced her fullness with his tongue, his lips, kissing her belly again and again, loving her, loving the child asleep just underneath her skin, the child he'd put there…

"Touch me," she said.

"I thought I was."

She laughed. "Not there." She lifted her knees, unafraid, unashamed, doing the whole Dawn-going-after-what-she-wanted thing. "Here."

"Any preferences?" he said.

"Whatever floats your boat," she breathed. "Just make it snappy."

Snappy? Cal grinned, shifting to lie on his side so he could see her face. Then, savoring his own ache, his mouth watering with anticipation, he slo-o-owly traced one finger down the inside of her thigh, barely touching.

"Harder," she said.

"No." He leaned over, brushing his lips over one erect nipple, then kissing her on the mouth. "Not yet."

Her breath caught as he did it again, skimming down the other thigh, then pulling back…stroking…retreating…knowing how sensitive the skin was there, knowing she was even more sensitive now—he hadn't forked over a hundred bucks on pregnancy and childbirth books for nothing—each time passing closer to that spot he wanted to touch as much as she wanted him to touch it.

"Cal!"

"Shhh…see, your problem is, you're far too goal oriented." He brushed his fingers closer, closer…finally touching, but so lightly, so gently… "Bet you're one of those people who skips ahead to find out how the book ends, too."

"So what if I…*am!*" Her breathing hitched. Among other, very unladylike things, she muttered something about him making her crazy.

He smiled, thinking this was more fun than he'd had in a dog's age. "That's the idea," he said, his breath teasing the hair at her temple as he staked his claim in the only way he knew how, by making her want him badly enough to beg. He hadn't lied—he kissed her again, enjoying the hell out of the desperation in her response—when he'd told her he didn't expect this to change anything...

"And now I'm going to...do...this."

...because he couldn't be more in love with her than he already was.

It was as if all his previous experience had only been practice for this moment, when nothing else mattered but giving her the time of her life. His own breathing grew ragged as he stroked and teased and spread and dipped inside, watching her...wanting her...wishing harder than he'd ever wished for anything in his life, loving this woman who was so afraid of being loved. He paused, just for a moment, then applied exactly the right pressure at exactly the right spot, whispering, "Now," in her ear...and with a cry, she spasmed, and a vicious *Yessss!* hissed inside him, and he felt like he wanted to beat his chest or do one of those dumb victory dances or something.

"How was that?" he asked when her breathing slowed. Her eyes popped open, followed by a very wicked, very dangerous smile.

"Oooh, I'll show you—" like a turtle on its back, it took her a couple of tries to right herself "—how that was!" Her breasts and belly arrogant and proud and more beautiful than anything he'd ever seen, she pinned his shoulders to the floor and straddled him, surrounded him, and he nearly lost it right then at how it felt like this, with nothing between them. Her darkened nipples peeking through her long hair, the ends teasing his chest, she leaned over and whispered, "Move a single muscle before I tell you it's okay and I'm outta here."

Panic sliced through him. "I'm not sure I can—"

"Try," she said, sitting erect. Grinning. Then, without any movement on her part that he could tell, she did...something.

"What was that?"

She smiled. And did it again. "You mean this?"

"Yes!" he got out on a strangled breath.

"Oh—" she flipped her hair back over one shoulder, completely exposing one breast. "I'm just doing my Kegel exercises. To keep my pelvic floor toned. I'm supposed to do them whenever I think about it." She traced circles around his nipples with her fingertips. "And I'd read this was a good way to practice—" he sucked in another breath as she did it again "—but this is the first chance I've had to see if it works. It does, I take it?"

He sucked in a painful breath. And tried to buck his hips to meet her.

"Uh, uh, uh," she said, pushing him back down. Damn, she was strong for such a skinny thing. "You didn't say 'may I?'"

Cal tried to laugh, but he was in too much agony. Especially as she then decided to adjust her position.

She clicked her tongue against the roof of her mouth. "My, my…such *language.*"

"I'm gonna lose my mind here!"

"Good," she said, grinning, sliding up…so…damn…*slowly*… then down…then up…then—

He roared. And thrust. And thrust again and again and again until, with a shout that originated somewhere around the soles of his feet, he climaxed so hard he thought he was gonna pass out.

When he recovered enough to open one eye—he half expected to see his brains splattered all over the room—he saw victory flashing in hers.

"What…the hell," he panted, "was that…all about?"

"Rule Number One…" Dawn leaned as close she could, her nipples brushing his chest, her breath soft and warm in his ear. "Don't mess with the pregnant lady."

Dawn had no idea what time it was when the phone jerked her awake. Reality rushed in much more quickly than either full consciousness or coordination: her attempt to bolt from the bed at the same time Cal lunged across her to answer the phone resulted in a brief but fierce tangle with a large, naked man and a wily phone cord.

"Ho-hold on," she heard him mumble into the phone as she

finally broke free. "Hey," he whispered, "where the hell you think you're going?"

"If I leave right now," she said, yanking the blanket off the bed and awkwardly wrapping it around her, "I might just make the last train back to Sanity."

"Hold *on,* dammit!" she heard again, followed by the click—and subsequent glare—of the bedside lamp being turned on. "That means you, too," Cal said, now grabbing a pair of discarded jeans off a nearby chair and trying to put them on with one hand. "You're not going anywhere!"

"Like hell!"

"Stay!"

Dawn froze—though more at the sight of the wild-haired idiot gawking numbly back at her from Cal's mirror than his bellow—as the evening's sexual euphoria collapsed like a soufflé. Fear billowed up inside her, thick and acrid and suffocating, buoying along the horrible truth she could no longer ignore: She'd fallen in love. With every hormone-drenched atom she had in her.

A realization that any normal person would have greeted with joy. Or at least equanimity. Not this choking, brain-sucking terror that made her feel like tossing her cookies.

Why am I so screwed up? she thought wearily. *Why, why, why?*

Cal's sudden *"What?"* into the phone startled her out of her pityfest. She turned, her stomach free-falling at the expression on Cal's face. *"Dam*mit…is he okay?"

"What is it?" she mouthed, clutching the blanket to her breasts. He held up one hand, focused on the call.

"Yeah. Yeah," he repeated on a sigh, glancing over at her. "Yeah, I think she'll want to know, too. I'll be sure and tell her. Thanks." He hung up the phone, then dragged a hand through his rumpled hair. "That was Ryan. Seems Elijah decided to take his daddy's truck for a joyride. Hit a patch of ice and ended up in a ditch—"

"Oh, God, no…"

"It's okay, he's more shaken up than anything else. Least,

that's what Ryan said the sheriff told him." A wry smile twisted his mouth. "And scared spitless. Since Ryan'd get there before the paramedics, he's on his way to the accident, but the plan's to take him over to the hospital in Claremore."

Her eyes stung. "We have to go."

Cal's mouth curved, just enough. "I'm one step ahead of you, darlin'."

"I still can't believe Eli'd do something that stupid," Cal said for probably the twentieth time in the past half hour. It had stopped sleeting, leaving the sky deep and clear and sprinkled with stars and the roads treacherous as hell.

"He's twelve," Dawn said in an oddly calm voice beside him. "Among other things."

He didn't need to see her expression to know what it was.

"You wanna say 'I told you so' so bad you're about to pop, aren't you?"

Her sigh filled the cab. "Not hardly. After all, I was the one who thought buying the kid a magazine and spending a few hours with him raking leaves would somehow…"

"Fix him?"

"Focus him, maybe. I should've followed up, checked on him, instead of letting his father creep me out."

Cal frowned. "You never said that before."

"I don't think I fully realized it until a moment ago. Something about the way he looked at me, though, made my skin crawl."

"But you didn't feel Eli was in any danger, either?"

"No, much as it pains me to admit that. Or believe me, I *would* have called Family Services. But I guess I felt Jacob's animosity stemmed more from his simply not wanting anybody to interfere. And Eli wasn't showing any signs of abuse…" Out of the corner of his eye, he saw her rub her belly. "And anyway, it's not as if I don't have problems of my own to deal with."

The regret in her voice arrowed through him. One hand on the wheel, Cal reached over to squeeze her hand. "He's gonna be fine, honey. Ryan didn't think it looked too serious, remember?''

"It's not that. Well, not completely that. It's just…" She sighed. "God, it's scary, thinking about all the things that could happen. To your own kid, I mean."

Cal let go of her hand to get a better grip on the wheel, trying to do the same with his thoughts. "Okay, obviously I can't guarantee that nothing bad's ever gonna happen, but I sure as hell can promise you that no twelve-year-old of mine is gonna be out in a sleetstorm, going for a joyride." He paused, then said, "Now, when he gets to fifteen, that's something else again."

She gave a weak laugh. "Gee, thanks. That makes me feel *so* much better."

"Boys do dumb things, no doubt about it."

Her laugh was stronger this time. "And you think girls don't?"

"Oh, no, not the way boys do. Not even close. But…there's dumb, and then there's insane. I always knew the difference."

"Now, see, that's where your theory falls short. Because I don't."

Cal waited a couple of seconds, then said, "I take it you're talking about tonight?"

"Yep."

His stomach torqued into about five hundred knots. "You wish it never happened?"

Now it was her turn to pause. "I wish…" Her sigh was sharp. "I wish I was more like you."

"Well, I sure as hell don't," he said, then added before she could respond, "Just so you know…I have *never* had sex like that before."

"Cal…"

"Don't worry, I'm not going back on my promise. But I sure as hell am not gonna pretend that it was just average, okay? At least, it wasn't for me." He waited, holding his breath.

''Me, neither,'' she said after far too long a pause, and he let the breath out. ''But that doesn't mean—''

''—anything other than we're good in the sack together, I know.'' He slowed down for what looked like a slippery spot, easing the truck over it before saying, ''Okay, this is probably gonna tick you off, but what the hell. I don't know what's got you so scared of falling in love, or being loved, or whatever it is that's holding you back. Then again, maybe it's me, that I'm fine for a toss in the hay when you're feeling down or insecure or whatever, but that's it. But dammit, Dawn, you've got more love to give than any woman I've ever known, only it's like you're afraid to…to use it or something, the way my mother used to horde the fancy perfume Daddy'd given her, only wearing it for special occasions. Like she was afraid if she used it up, she'd never have any more.'' Suddenly unsure of where this line of thought was headed, he flexed his hands on the steering wheel. ''Anyway. It just doesn't seem right, is what I'm saying, keeping it bottled up like that. And that's all I've got to say.''

They drove for probably another mile or so before she said, looking straight ahead, ''And all *I* have to say is, if I ever hear you say again that I think you're only good for a toss in the hay, I will make your life so miserable you'll wish you'd never been born.''

''Oh, yeah?''

''Yeah.''

Figuring it was too dark for her to see anyway, he didn't even bother to hold back the grin.

Cal heard Dawn's sharp intake of breath at the sight of the boy, all banged up and bandaged and bruised. Didn't do much for Cal's insides, either, seeing the kid looking so helpless. And puny. His eyes still sparked with defiance, however, even though he couldn't help but wince when he tried to talk.

''What're you two doin' here? And where's Daddy?''

''I'm sure your father will be here any minute,'' Dawn said

gently. "And Dr. Ryan told us what happened. We were worried about you."

"Well, you don't have to worry no more, since you c'n see I'm fine."

"You're not fine, Eli," Cal said, standing at the foot of the bed with his arms crossed. "But you are damn lucky. What on earth possessed you to do a fool thing like that?"

"It's not like I don't know how to drive! Daddy lets me drive the truck all the time!"

"But not on the open road in the middle of a freakin' ice storm! Besides which, you're *twelve,* for the love of Mike—"

"Cal, please," Dawn said, laying her hand on his arm.

Eli shouted, "Go away! It's none of your business! Go *away!*"

"Eli—"

"Come on, Cal," Dawn said in a voice that reminded him a lot of his mother's when he knew he'd pushed a quarter inch too far. Then she said to Eli, "We'll come see you tomorrow, when you're feeling more like company."

"What if I don't want you to?"

"Tough," she said, then tugged Cal out of the room. "Honestly," she said when they got back out in the hall, "the two of you were like a pair of cats scrapping over their territory."

"I was not—"

"Yes, you were," she said, sagging against the wall. "And thank God for it. It's about time the poor kid has somebody in his life who cares enough about him *to* scrap with him, instead of just…whatever it is that Jacob's done to him to make him that way."

"If he needs somebody to care about him so much, how come he told us to go away?"

"Because he was testing us," she said. "See, our leaving showed we cared enough to listen, to give him some control over his life, a life that's obviously totally *out* of control. But telling him we were coming back, no matter what, reassured him that he couldn't scare us off. I mean, for God's sake, where *is* his father? And where the hell was he tonight when his son almost got killed?''

''Beats me. Ryan said he'd called him right before he called us.''

''Things can't go on this way, Cal. Something's got to be done before Eli does something even more stupid.''

Cal propped himself against the wall beside her, slipping an arm behind her neck and clamping his hand onto her shoulder so she couldn't wriggle free. ''You know, another man might feel threatened by a woman like you.''

''What do you mean, 'a woman like me'? And think very carefully before you answer.''

He chuckled. ''A woman as smart as you. Giving as you. Gutsy as you.''

''Oh,'' she said, softening. A little. ''But not you?''

Leaning closer, he whispered, ''Why else do you think I get so turned on when I'm around you?''

She seemed to think about that for a moment, only to announce she had to visit the little girls' room, right as Ryan came around the corner. By mutual, if unspoken, consent, the brothers gravitated toward the coffee machine in the waiting room across the hall.

''So…you picked her up on your way, huh?'' Ryan said, retrieving his coffee. Not looking at him.

''Once she heard,'' Cal said, sidestepping both the question and the issue, ''nothing would've kept her from being here.''

Coffee in hand, Ryan gave him one of those looks that said he knew exactly what was going on. But all he said was, ''I don't imagine so,'' then sank into one of the waiting room chairs. ''Some way to spend Christmas Eve, huh?''

Cal frowned, plopping his butt into the chair next to Ryan's. ''Isn't that tomorrow? Or did I miss a day somewhere?''

''Technically it started about ten minutes ago.'' His brother took a sip of his coffee and said, ''I'm supposed to be putting together a doll house right now.''

A brief image of Cal maybe doing the same thing in a couple

of years made his skin tingle. Then he said, "Any reason you have to stick around?"

Ryan slouched further in the chair, crossing his stretched-out legs at the ankles. "Two, actually. Jacob Burke being the first, since there's no way I'm leaving until I hear his side of the story." He took another slug of the coffee and looked at Cal. "You being the other."

"Lord almighty," Cal said, glaring at his coffee, "what'd they brew this with? Bilge water?"

"Cal—"

"Save your breath, Ry." He got up, tossing the sludge into a nearby garbage can and refusing to look at his brother. "This is between Dawn and me—"

"Where is he? Where's my boy? Is he okay?"

They both looked up to see Jacob lurching toward them as fast as he could manage with the cane. Wearing a worn Navy pea coat over stained jeans and a wrinkled plaid shirt, his shaggy hair looked like it hadn't been anywhere near a comb in days, anymore than his face had a razor. But those ice-blue eyes blazed bright with fear and shock. And annoyance, Cal thought with a jab of his own.

"He's right in there," Ryan said. "And yes, he'll be fine. They're gonna keep him overnight to make sure nothing goes haywire, but that's just a precaution." He frowned. "Kid's been asking for you for the past hour."

"Blasted truck wouldn't start," Jacob said, his hand darting in and out of the pea coat's pockets like he was looking for something. "Had to call out Darryl Andrews to jumpstart it, he charged me nearly thirty bucks, can you believe it?"

"How'd this happen, Jacob?" Cal asked.

Jacob glared at them for a moment, then seemed to shrink into himself. "Damn painkillers, something new they gave me, must've knocked me out...." His gaze flickered to Cal. "That gas tank was dry as a bone, far as I knew, I swear it. Kid must've put siphoned gas off the other truck or something. Had the keys to the good truck in my pocket when I fell asleep, the other ones were hanging on the peg in the kitchen where they always were…''

His customary bravado disintegrating by the second, the man looked up at Ryan, leaning heavily on his cane. ''Can I see him now?''

Ryan nodded; Dawn reappeared just as Jacob slipped through the door.

''I heard,'' she said, but whatever she was thinking, she kept to herself. For a change. Then her brows lifted. ''What?'' she said, looking at Ryan. Over Dawn's head, Cal shot his brother a don't-go-there look.

''Nothing,'' Ryan said. ''Just wondering how you were holding up. You look…worn-out.''

''I'm fine,'' she said, and Ryan got that damned look on his face again. Fortunately for everybody, since he'd talked to Jacob, he decided to go on home. But not before extracting a promise from Dawn that she'd do the same in the very near future. Naturally, as soon as Ryan left, Dawn planted herself in one of the waiting room chairs, obviously settling in for the duration.

''I want to talk to Jacob, too,'' she said before Cal could even think *Why?*

On a weary sigh, Cal sank into the chair beside her. ''You do realize he's liable to tell you this is none of your business?''

''I ran into the sheriff on my way back from the ladies' room. This is really serious, Cal. Especially as Eli's been shop-lifting again. From people not inclined to overlook it this time.'' Her mouth thinned. ''Roy said he was sorry, but he's got to report this to Family Services. And he's right,'' she added on a rush of air. ''Not only was Eli endangering his own life tonight, but what if he'd run into somebody else? If the social worker thinks Jacob really can't handle him, a judge could very well rule that he'd be better off living with some-body else.''

Cal leaned forward, thinking evil thoughts about the coffee machine. ''Would that be so bad?'' he asked after a moment, then twisted around to find her giving him a look like he'd grown fangs. "At least he'd be supervised."

She pushed a stray hair behind her ear, then crossed her arms. "I've done a lot of work with juvies. And sure, some of them are so hardened nothing short of a brain transplant would change their attitude. But for the ones who are still reachable, ones like Eli who maybe haven't completely gone over to the other side, I'm not sure taking him away from the only security he has, no matter how shaky it is, is the best way to go. It's not Eli who needs to be fixed, it's his relationship with his father—"

"What're *you* doing here?"

They looked up to see Jacob looming over them, vibrating with anger.

"I'm here because I care about your son," Dawn said, her voice a lot steadier than her move to get to her feet. "And because I might be able to help."

"I don't need your help—"

"Jacob, for God's sake! The sheriff has to report this to the county! What do you think's going to happen then?"

"'S'got nothing to do with anybody but me and the boy! Kids get into trouble, everybody knows that! And it's like I told your boyfriend here, he took off after I'd fallen asleep! Who the hell knew he'd do a fool thing like that with the weather the way it was? So what do you expect me to do, lock the kid up?"

"He could have been killed," Dawn said, her voice ominously soft. "Or he could've killed somebody else. You can't ignore this, Jacob."

Cal jerked at the sudden, blazing intensity in the man's eyes when he focused on Dawn. "And maybe you should wait until the one in your belly's out in the world before you go judgin' other people's parentin' skills!"

"And maybe it's because of this one I can't just stand by and watch a child's life go down the tubes because his father's too damn stubborn to do something about it!"

Atta girl, Cal thought as he stood there, transfixed. Amazed. Proud.

Hot.

Jacob, on the other hand, looked—justifiably enough—like he'd just had the wind knocked out of him. After a moment he limped over to a chair, falling heavily into it.

"Do something about it?" he said on a dry laugh. "Like what?"

"That's where I come in," Dawn said. "If you'd let me."

On a sigh, he leaned back, shaking his head. "I'd never figured on havin' kids, y'know? Or even settling down. Me and Justine, both, we liked movin' from place to place, meetin' new people. Didn't need any kids to mess that up. Except then…"

He shook his head, like he was trying to clear it. "To this day I remember the look on her face when she told me she was pregnant, her eyes all big like she was petrified I'd ask her to get rid of it. Totally blindsided me, her wanting the kid. Think it did her, too. But once I saw how she really felt…well. Guess sometimes, you just gotta roll with the punches. Even though I knew it meant we couldn't go gallivantin' all over creation like we'd been doing."

"How'd you end up back here?" Dawn asked.

"My mama died, left me the house. My first thought was to maybe sell it, you know, use the money to buy a place somewhere else, since I had no love for Haven. Or the house, frankly. But Justine, she took to the town right off, in a way I ain't never seen her do with any other place we'd lived.

"So we stayed, and she had the baby, and for a while things were okay. She was crazy about the kid, and real good with him, too. And she was young. Who would've figured on her dyin' before Eli was even out of diapers?"

The man looked up at Cal, helplessness burning in his eyes. "I remember seeing your daddy with your older brothers, when they'd come into town, the way he'd talk and laugh with 'em, how they all got on. I never had that with my own father, never knew firsthand what a father was supposed to do with a son.

But after Justine died and it was just me and Eli, I guess I thought it'd get better, somehow. That eventually I'd catch on, figure out what I was doing. Besides, it wasn't so bad when I was working, I left him at the Methodist church's day care, and they'd have him fed and what-all by the time I picked him up. Then I hurt my back on the job, wasn't pulling enough on disability to put him in day care no more, couldn't really take care of him right myself…'' He shrugged, then offered an almost apologetic smile. ''I do love the boy. You gotta believe that. But having a kid, or even lovin' him, don't automatically make you a good parent.''

Dawn sat beside him, laying a hand on his arm. ''But if you couldn't take proper care of him,'' she asked gently, ''why didn't you place him up for adoption? Or at least put him out to foster care?''

Again Jacob looked like he was trying to see inside Dawn's brain. And way deep inside Cal's, a faint alarm went off. ''Because he was all I had left,'' he said.

''Then…you really don't want to lose him now, do you?''

Jacob shook his head.

Dawn glanced up at Cal, then back at Eli's father. ''Jacob, listen to me. I'm not judging you, even if that's what it sounds like. But I'm afraid for Eli. And I can tell you if you don't take some preemptive measures to make things better before this comes before a judge—which I'm sure it will—the county may decide to remove Eli from your care whether you want it or not. Do you understand what I'm saying?''

A beat or two passed before he pushed out, ''Yeah. You're sayin' I'm supposed to let some strangers tell me how to raise my kid.''

''Some counseling, is all I'm suggesting. Maybe a parenting skills class—''

''Forget it.''

''Jacob,'' Cal said, figuring he may as well throw in his two cents. ''Listen to the woman. I know she's pushy and all—'' Dawn glared at him ''—but she knows what she's talking about. There's no shame in asking for help. In fact,'' he said with one of those why-don't-we-just-humor-the-lady shrugs, "it seems to me you agreeing to go to those classes might offer Eli some reassurances. You know, show him how you really feel about him and all."

Jacob grunted.

"Not only that," Cal said, figuring he might as well keep going, "maybe we could, I don't know, find something to keep Eli from gettin' bored, to give him a sense of purpose. Keep him out of trouble, y'know? Kids need their fathers," he said with another, and yes, pointed, glance at the glowering pregnant woman at Jacob's side, "so we need to do whatever's necessary to keep you and Eli together. Right?"

Jacob shot a wary glance at Dawn, who nodded her agreement, then focused again on Cal.

"I take it you got something in mind?"

"As it happens," Cal said, "I do."

"I've been thinking," Dawn said, her eyes closed over there on the other side of the truck.

Cal chuckled. Woman hadn't said word one since they'd left Claremore more than a half hour before. "Looked more to me like you were sleeping."

"Goes to show how much you know," she said, but she didn't open her eyes. "Anyway, I was thinking about Jacob and what he said about how having a kid doesn't automatically make you a good parent."

He gripped the steering wheel harder, his heart thudding against his ribs. The clouds had returned while they'd been at the hospital; about halfway back to Haven it had started to snow, big feathery flakes darting in and out of the truck's headlight beams like moths.

"Please tell me you're not starting up again about what kind of mother you're gonna make."

"This isn't about me, doofus," she said, finally opening her eyes. "Not like that, anyway. I mean—" he sensed her twisting to look at him "—do you think Eli's any better off because his father *did* keep him?"

Cal glanced over, then back out at the road. The snow was getting heavier. "What are you getting at?"

"I'm not sure. Except…if my father was anything like Jacob, maybe it was just as well he wasn't part of my life."

Over the tug to his heart, Cal said, "Even though you think he's fixable?"

"I think if he really wants it, it's possible. But only because we're going to bat for him. An awful lot of struggling parents don't have anybody in their camp, you know. And he certainly didn't before this."

"He wouldn't *let* anybody in, remember?"

"Good point." Then, a moment or two later: "Thanks, by the way."

"For what?"

"For jumping into the mouth of the volcano right along with me. Andrew…never understood why I bothered with 'those people,' as he put it. Why I wasted my energy and talent—his words—on them."

"I'm not Andrew," Cal said quietly.

A good thirty seconds passed before she said, "I know." Then she added, "Suggesting Eli come work on the farm was a stroke of brilliance."

"Only if it takes."

"It will," she said, tugging her shawl more closely around her. "Oh. We're here already?"

Cal smiled. "Time flies when you're sawing logs."

"I told you, I wasn't asleep."

His smile faded, however, as he pulled in front of Ivy's house, cutting the engine. "What if you did find your father? Only he *wasn't* the kind of man you hoped he'd be. How would you feel?"

"Cal, the man wanted nothing to do with me. My expectations aren't exactly high, here. Besides, I'm not looking for a father, I'm looking for answers. And why's this suddenly so important to you, anyway?"

"Hey, you brought it up, cute stuff." And it was probably a safer topic of conversation than the one they were both avoiding. Silence, thick and soft and heavy, filled the truck as they both sat there, watching the snow twirling in the light from the street lamp.

"So," he said, "Maddie says you and Ivy aren't comin' over for Christmas?"

Dawn shook her head. "No. We thought we'd celebrate by ourselves. It's been a long time since we've done that. And a long time before we'll get a chance to do it again. Once the baby comes, I mean." A pause. "I'll have Mama drive me out to get the car sometime tomorrow, I guess."

"Oh. Sure. Maybe we could go see Eli then."

"There's no reason why we have to visit him together, is there?"

He looked at her for a long moment, then muttered a cuss word under his breath. "I hope to hell this Jekyll and Hyde number of yours has something to do with you bein' pregnant."

"What on earth are you talking about? I just said—"

"It's not what you said, Dawn. It's why you're sayin' it."

"Great," she muttered. "Leave it to me to find the only male on the planet who reads between the lines."

"Maybe that's because you leave enough space between them to drive a freakin' convoy through."

"Cal, we're not really a couple. So I don't see any reason for us to act like one, doing everything together, being with each other at every holiday. Once the baby comes, that's something else. And now you're mad at me."

"I'm not mad at you," he said, realizing that's exactly what he was. "I just don't understand you, is all."

She sat quietly for a long time, then said, "That makes two of us, then."

Cal banged his palm on the steering wheel. "Dammit, Dawn—are you deliberately trying to drive me away?"

"Is it working?"

"Hell, no. But honest to God—what do you *want?* For me to pretend like we never laid eyes on each other? That you're not carrying my kid? That we can't get within twenty feet of each other without settin' off alarms in five counties?''

''No!'' In the odd, pinky light from the snow, he saw her grimace. Then she looked back out the windshield. ''That's just it, Cal...I don't want us to *pretend* anything.''

''You think we were pretending tonight?''

She didn't answer.

He laughed. ''Honey, if you think for one minute I can be in the same room with you without wanting to touch you, you're crazier than I thought. And that's going some. Take now, for instance.'' He reached over to brush her hair away from her face, smiling at her involuntary shudder. ''My head may be on your words, but my mouth's thinking how much it wants to kiss you. As for other parts of me—'' his smile broadened ''—let's just say you can forget everything you've heard about men not being able to multitask....''

''Cal!'' She smacked at his hand, then cleared her throat. ''Could you *please* be serious?''

''Trust me, darlin'. I am.''

Her head whipped back around. But she was still in the car, wasn't she? ''You don't play fair,'' she said.

''Never said I did.''

She mumbled something probably best left indecipherable. Cal propped his elbow on the back of his seat to rest his head on his fist. ''You wanna know what I think?''

''Do I have a choice?''

''No, as a matter of fact. Now...seems to me if we deny what sure as hell feels to me like a very *real* attraction, eventually we'll get so we won't be able to stand the sight of each other. All that pent-up frustration, you know.''

That got a sideways glance. ''I don't suppose you ever heard of, let's see...what's that word again? Oh, right—*control.*''

''Sure I've heard of it. Don't have a whole helluva lot of use for it, though.'' He started fiddling with her hair again. God, he loved her hair. ''Especially when it comes to you.'' When her eyes shot to his, he smiled. ''Oh, now, that doesn't mean I'd ever try to force you when you weren't in the mood,

I don't mean that. But these feelings are far too powerful to ignore.'' He gently tugged her hair, like he used to when they were kids. ''Aren't they, darlin'?''

''You should really get going before the snow gets any worse—''

''Aren't they?''

She looked down at her hands. But she stayed quiet. She stayed, period. Cal leaned close enough to smell her fear. And her desire, mingling with his. Sweetness to his musk, intoxicating as Ethel's blackberry wine.

''Wantin' to make love to you's as impossible to resist as breathing,'' he whispered, trailing one knuckle down her cheek, across her jaw. ''Friendship's fine as far as it goes, don't get me wrong. But the two of us living in the same town and not being lovers—''

She groaned. He grinned.

''Yeah, you heard me right. *Lovers*. As in, getting naked and sweaty on a regular basis. Anyway—'' he tilted her face to his and stole a kiss ''—it seems to me our *not* doin' that…well, now. That's what seems like *pretendin'*. Besides—'' another kiss ''—you need to keep up those exercises.''

A second or two passed before a short, sharp laugh burst from her mouth. ''I can do those alone, you know.''

''No doubt. But exercising's a lot more fun when you have a partner.''

She slugged him in the arm and finally got out of the truck, although with about as much grace as a drunk elephant, her head bowed against the now rapidly falling snow as she made her way up the walk.

Cal lunged across the seat and cranked down the passenger side window, getting a barrage of snow in his face for his efforts. ''Well?'' he yelled out.

She turned. ''I'll think about it,'' she said.

He sang at the top of his lungs all the way home.

Chapter 11

"You always come in this early?"

With a start, Dawn looked up from the real estate contract she was reading over, breaking into a grin at the sight of her boss standing in the doorway.

"Sherman! I thought you said you weren't coming back until February!"

Dressed in a navy suit that hadn't been new—or top of the line—twenty years ago, the big man drifted into his office, sinking into the chair in front of his desk. "All that resting about drove me crazy. And Brenda Sue wouldn't let me do a blessed thing. It was either cut my vacation short or lose my mind."

It occurred to Dawn that maybe losing *her* mind would be the solution to her problems. Some of them, at least. If her old one were to go missing, maybe she could put in for a nice, uncluttered new one.

The past three weeks had been challenging, to put it mildly. Jacob had finally agreed to go to his parenting classes, but only if Dawn went with him. And then, every time, he argued with her for a hour afterward about what the instructor had said. Then there was Eli, who hadn't been exactly thrilled with the idea of mucking out stalls. Or, worse, of returning to regular school. Which naturally provoked regular yelling matches between father and son, which Dawn found herself refereeing far more often than she might have liked.

And then there was Cal. Mr. So-What's-Wrong-with-Naked-and-Sweaty?

Damned if she knew.

Okay, so she was a wimp. Because Cal was right. Hoo-boy, was he right. Between the man's powers of persuasion and her double-crossing hormones, she was doomed. Oh, she'd tried staying away from him. She had. Only to discover that despite her best intentions, vicious, insatiable need gnawed at her day and night like some ravenous little beast, sabotaging her sleep even more than the army-booted critter doing calisthenics inside her.

For her health's sake, she told herself, she'd given in.

Of course, finding the time, and a place, to fool around without anyone knowing—her one nonnegotiable demand—hadn't been easy. Lord, she'd never look at a tack room the same way again. Or that old mattress up in his attic. Thank God Ivy had that midwifery conference in Chicago this weekend—

"Dawn?"

Sherman's voice reined her back in. "Sorry. Guess I'm not as awake as I thought. I was going to say, though, that the time away must've done you some good. You look great!"

"For an old fool, right?"

"You're not old, and I know you're not a fool. In any case, I refuse to believe it wasn't nice, getting to spend so much time with your daughter. I don't imagine you get to see her all that much these days."

"No," he said softly. "That's certainly true. But—" he slapped his thighs

"—I'm glad to be back. And you haven't answered my question. About coming in so early. It's not even eight o'clock, for crying out loud."

"It's a habit I got into in school. Getting a jump on the day while it's still quiet." Not to mention getting up with the chickens was the only way she could get her work done and still have time to baby-sit the Burkes. "Marybeth tells me you're just as bad," she added.

Sherman chuckled. "Makes her madder'n hell that she can't ever sneak in late, since I'm always here. Must've fried her clams to find out you were the same way. So fill me in on what's been going on in my absence."

Twenty minutes and a cup of coffee later, she'd brought Sherman up to date on all the current cases, including her work with the Burkes. Which, as of last week, was in an official capacity as the family's court-appointed attorney.

"Boy always was on the loose, like a stray dog," Sherman said, slouching back in the chair. "You really think he should stay with Jacob?"

"Not without intervention, certainly. But I don't think removing him would solve the problem. Especially as they're all each other has."

Sherman gazed at her steadily for a moment. "Sounds to me like you've got a personal stake in this."

"I like the kid," she said. "And for some bizarre reason, something about Jacob gets to me." She shrugged. "Nothing more to it than that."

"I assume you're not neglecting the income-producing cases?"

"Of course not." One brow lifted. "But I don't take cases based on the size of the checkbook being waved in front of my nose. You got a problem with that?"

"No," he said on a chuckle. "But I guess that means you're no better at money-grubbing than I am."

"If I were, I'd be sitting in a spiffy Manhattan office right now. Not here."

He smiled, then tented his fingers in front of his lips.

"What?" she said.

"Oh, nothing. Just tryin' to remember what it felt like to be so idealistic."

"Please. That was dead and buried by my last year of law school. I might fight to the death to make sure somebody gets as fair a shake as possible, but I'm well aware that reality often sucks." Her mouth flattened. "And that good intentions don't put food on the table."

Sherman studied her intently from behind his glasses, a half smile playing around his mouth. "When's the hearing?"

"Next week."

He set his mug down on the edge of the desk and folded his hands over his stomach. "What the boy did was serious, Dawn. Not to mention dangerous. Maybe gettin' him off the hook's not in his best interest."

"I have no intention of getting him off the hook. But I think he deserves somebody to help him find the right track, not steer him even further away from it, don't you?"

Instead of replying, Sherman got up and walked over to the window, hands in pockets as usual. "And Jacob? You think he deserves another chance?"

"He does love his son," she said. "Even if he doesn't know what to do with him. Speaking of somebody who got off the track somewhere along the way."

"From what I remember," Sherman said, looking out over Main Street, "he never even came near it. Had an abusive father who wasn't around much, a weak mother who basically let him run wild, too…it's no surprise he wouldn't exactly win any parenting awards. Likable enough kid, as I recall, but not real big on responsibility." He turned, his brow furrowed. "I know you want what's best for both of 'em, but it's Eli you should be most concerned with. Don't forget that."

"I don't intend to," she said, wondering why she was getting the feeling there was more behind his words than he was letting on. But before she could think any more about it, he'd gone on to another topic.

"Now," he said, "since I'm back, looks like we need to do something about an office for you. If you're planning on staying for a while, that is."

Ah, yes. The Question That Refused to Go Away.

"If you're still okay with taking it month to month, sure."

Another odd look—this was getting worrisome—then he said, "How about that other office across the hall, the one that looks out over the backyard? Might be better for the baby, if you're planning on bringing him or her to work. Not so noisy. Hasn't been used in years, though, not since Jesse Morris moved to Enid in 1984. Last time I had a partner," he said, more or less to himself, then looked at her. "You can do it up any way you like and send me the bills."

"Oh, no—"

"Let me do this, Dawn," he said, adding, when she frowned at him, "As a way of…saying thanks for letting Brenda Sue torment me for the past six weeks. Not to mention I'm not above bribery." He pushed his lips out into something like a pout. "I want you to stay."

She sighed. "Which I just said I can't promise."

Sherman dropped into the chair, doing that pensive tenting thing with his fingers again. "So tell me what's goin' on between you and Cal."

Her laugh sounded tinny in her own ears. "Is this your courtroom technique? Switching the line of questioning every half second to keep the witness off guard?"

His mouth twitched. "Works like a charm, doesn't it?"

"Only if there's something to tell."

"You're forgettin' this is a small town, honey. We don't have to hear news. We can smell it."

Yeah, well, what everybody could probably smell was the scent of a perpetually horny, pregnant woman who couldn't go for five lousy minutes without aching for a certain man's touch. But no matter how often Cal assured her he was more than okay with things the way they were…

Dawn looked across the desk at her boss. "Have you ever been torn between what you wanted to do and what you felt you had to do?"

He looked slightly startled, then said quietly, "More times than I care to admit."

"How did you make a decision?"

That got a weighty sigh. "Oh, Lord…I'm not the one to ask this."

"No, really…say somebody came to you with a case that wasn't cut-and-dried, that you could see where both the defendant and the plaintiff had equally valid points. What would you do?"

After a second or two, he said, "Analyze the facts as best I understood them, then choose whichever way won't make things worse than they already are." He tapped his index fingers together. "Not much help, am I?"

Dawn got up, looking out the window as she massaged the base of her spine. If she stayed too long in any one position these days, she started to ossify. "What's weird," she said, almost more to herself than Sherman, "is that I can't ever remember waffling like this. Even as a kid, once I set my mind on something, I simply figured out what I needed to do to and did it. If staying up half the night was the only way to get straight As, and straight As was the only way to get that scholarship, and that scholarship was the only way to get out of here, then that's what I did."

"Why?" Sherman asked quietly behind her. "Why was it so important to you to succeed?"

She turned around. "To prove I was more than just Ivy Gardner's bastard," she said softly. "That having 'father unknown' on my birth certificate wasn't a prescription for failure."

He frowned. "You really think people were judging you that hard?"

"Oh, for heaven's sake, Sherman—there were mothers who wouldn't let me play with their kids, as if my illegitimacy was contagious." She didn't think it prudent to point out that Sherman's own wife was one of them. "Of course," she went on, "these were the same people who were convinced my mother smoked dope, never bathed and probably practiced Satanism. And I don't mean to say everybody felt that way, even then. But still."

He was quiet for a moment, then said, "Funny how you can

live in a place all your life and not see certain things. Things you don't want to see, I guess."

"If it makes you feel any better, this isn't the same town I left. Or maybe I'm not the same person," she added with a smile. "Not that this—" she gestured toward her belly "—doesn't provoke the occasional raised eyebrow, but attitudes seem much more relaxed than I remember growing up. To a kid who could only hear the one or two kids razzing her, not the ten who weren't, Haven sure didn't seem like much of one back then. Not unless you fit certain prescribed parameters. Everybody else had to earn their acceptance."

"So you didn't feel you were allowed a single misstep."

"Something like that."

"And with Cal?"

Dawn backed up to perch on the windowsill, her arms crossed over her bulge. "I've only got two facts to work with. That I want to do whatever's best for this baby. And that I don't want to hurt his or her father." She blinked back the stinging sensation behind her eyelids. "But I can't seem to come up with a solution that accomplishes both of those goals."

"You think your staying won't be in the child's best interests?"

"No. In Cal's."

His brows floated up over his glasses. "I see." Then he frowned. "What about what *you* want?"

"Oh, Lord, Sherman," she said on a breathy laugh, "if I throw that into the mix, my brain will melt!"

"An unhappy mama isn't gonna make for a happy child, you know."

"Yes, I do. But this particular mama's entire belief system has just been shot to hell. It's not only that I can't make a decision, I can't trust the ones I *do* make—"

A knock on the door shattered her thoughts. Sherman got up to answer it, slipping out to the waiting room as Charmaine stormed into the office and straight for Dawn, a slash of bilious pink glowing beneath her open car coat.

"I only got a few minutes before the next rush," the brunette said, out of breath and thrusting a piece of paper at Dawn with a number written on it. "It's Brody's social security number. You sure this is enough? To find him?"

"Unless he's gone into the witness protection program, probably so." Dawn took the number from Charmaine, who spun around and headed right back for the door.

"Why?" Dawn said to her back.

Charmaine turned around, her mouth pulled into a grimace of pure exasperation. "'Cause the school said Adam's gonna need glasses an' the stove's broke and all the boys need new shoes and my car's on its last legs. And even with food stamps, there's only so far the money goes, you know? And Ruby and Luralene've been bugging the living daylights out of me, sayin' just what you did, about how it's dumb to let either my pride or my personal feelings about you stand in the way of helping my kids. Because you're right. This is something Brody owes them. An' it's way past time I went after his sorry-assed hide."

"Good for you, Charmaine—"

"No, wait, there's more. A lot of folks've been talking, about what all you're doing for Jacob and Eli Burke. About how instead of sittin' around waiting to see how things'll turn out, you take action to *make* 'em turn out." She glanced down at her white athletic shoes, then back up at Dawn. "So I'm thinkin' maybe I could learn a thing or two from you."

"Oh, God, Char! I'm the last person to use as an example right now!"

The brunette's mouth pulled into a wry smile. "Yeah, well, this is one of those 'make do' situations, y'know?"

Dawn burst out laughing. "This mean maybe you and I could be friends?"

"Don't push it," Charmaine said.

But damned if she wasn't smiling.

"You should feel good about her comin' around at last," Cal said, rhythmically stroking Dawn's naked belly underneath the down comforter, her tight, smooth skin like silk against his roughened fingertips.

She rolled over to lie on her side—it was getting so she couldn't breathe if she lay on her back too long, she said—her hands tucked underneath her cheek. In the light from that puny little lamp on her old dresser, those big brown eyes looked bottomless. "Yeah, but am I feeling good for Charmaine? Or me?"

"Honest to Pete, woman," he said, smiling into her eyes as he moved his hand to her hip, "only you could get so balled up about this. Nothing says you can't both get something out of it, you know."

"I suppose," she said.

Cal leaned his head in his hand, his other one back on her tummy. "One of these days, we've really got to think about naming this critter."

"I know," she said, then fell silent.

Sometimes the silences were okay. Comfortable. Like maybe she was finally getting used to the idea of them being together. Other times, like tonight, he knew she was quiet because she was thinking. And when Dawn thought for more than three or four seconds at a stretch, Cal worried.

It had been her idea, him coming over tonight while Ivy was out of town. And she'd been as eager to get down to things as him, no more timid about going after what she wanted in bed than she was about anything else. Still, no matter how often he told her he was okay with their arrangement, he knew she wasn't. In fact, it was almost like the more often they made love, the more scared she got. And it was killing him, not knowing what to do to erase that fear in her eyes, what to say that wouldn't make things worse than they already were.

"Hey…" He reached over to sweep her hair back from her face. "Guess what? I sold two of the weanlings today."

"You did?" she said, her eyes lighting up.

"Yep. Some guy looking for a good young horse he could train from the get-go."

"But I thought you said you sold two?"

Cal chuckled. "Guess he couldn't resist my powers of persuasion."

She laughed, then palmed his cheek, her eyes locked with his. "You know something?" she whispered, her fingers rasping across his cheek. "I am so proud of you, I could just about pop. And I bet your father would be, too."

Emotion clogging his throat, Cal pulled her close and kissed her for a long, long time, showing her what he didn't dare say. When he stopped, though, he noticed her cheeks were wet.

"Hey, darlin'," he whispered, brushing away the moisture with the pad of his thumb. "What is it?"

"Nothing," she said. "Just me being…whatever it is I am these days."

"You want me to go home?"

She shook her head.

So he wrapped himself around them both, the woman he loved and the child they'd made, holding them as close as he could. As close as she'd let him. The baby kicked him, and his heart bled. "Everything's gonna be okay, honey," he said, because at least one of them had to believe it. And it looked like the honor had fallen to him.

By the first week of March, Dawn was convinced she'd been consigned to limbo. The winter, her unresolved relationship with Cal, the pregnancy—all seemed to trudge on, relentless and interminable and seriously undermining her determination not to be a pain in the butt.

Not that there weren't bright spots. For one, she'd hunted Charmaine's ex down in Reno and sicced the appropriate authorities on him, who were now extracting child support out of the creep's sorry hide. And the family court judge had, as Dawn had hoped, taken Jacob's parenting classes and Eli's working with Cal as positive signs that the pair were making strides toward repairing the cracks in their family life, and had thus decided there was no need to remove Eli from his father's care.

Fixing other people's problems? Piece of cake. Her own, however…

"Whatever you're thinkin' about," Ivy said beside her, frowning at the blood pressure valve as Dawn lay on the bed for her now weekly prenatal exam, "cut it out. I am not liking these numbers, young lady."

One order of men in white jackets to go, please.

After all—she hiked up her sweatshirt so Ivy could measure the beachball where her flat tummy had once been—only someone with a seriously diminished mental capacity would be running from a man whose face lit up the way Cal's did whenever he saw her. A man who gave the best foot rubs in the world. A man who didn't think a burp was effective unless it could be heard three counties over. A man who *put the toilet seat down,* for the love of Mike.

A man whose worries and joys and triumphs had become hers. But for all that Dawn loved Cal, worried about him, wanted him—and as much as she really would like to believe they could have a future—what she couldn't give him back was his own certainty that they could.

Could her life *get* any more complicated?

"Except for that blood pressure," Ivy said, bracing an arm behind Dawn's shoulders to heave her to a sitting position, "everything's lookin' good. Head's down, baby's nice and big, heartbeat's strong…." She grinned, packing her stethoscope and tape measure back into her bag. "Only four weeks to go."

"*Only,* she says," Dawn muttered, swinging her legs over the side of the bed and glaring at her frighteningly huge middle. At least she could see progress in her life on this front. Literally. "You're *sure* there's only one kid in here?"

"Honey, you'd have to go back a whole bunch of generations to find anybody petite on either side of this baby's family. Frankly, I'd be worried if I thought you were carrying a five-pounder."

Dawn looked at the cradle beside her bed, already outfitted and waiting for its newest inhabitant. "At this rate," she pushed through her tight throat, "I just hope the kid fits."

Following Dawn's gaze, Ivy said, "That's a Logan cradle. The baby'll fit, don't you worry."

"Which has nothing to do—" Dawn pushed herself to her feet "—with the eighteen appendages beating the tar out of my kidneys. And quit laughing, dammit. Look at me!" She pulled a face at her reflection in the mirror over the dresser. "I'm morphing into the Pillsbury Dough Boy!"

"Yeah, you're retaining a bit more water than I'd like—"

"A bit? I slosh when I walk!"

"—but nothing to worry about yet. Why don't you go see if anybody left a message while I finish updating your chart?"

The phone had rung during the exam; since Ivy's patients generally only used her pager, they'd let the machine pick up. Grumbling, Dawn twisted her belly around until she found her slippers, took it on faith she was putting them on the right feet and went shuffling down the hall.

"This is Kyle Fischer, looking for Dawn Gardner?" spewed forth from the machine. "Gloria Menendez gave me your name…"

She listened numbly to the message, her mouth falling farther open with each sentence.

Oh, boy. About that question as to whether her life could get any more complicated?

Guess what?

"Don't let him get away with it, Eli," Cal said over the stall gate when the weanling shied away from the boy's attempts to rub him with the saddle blanket. "Get right back in there and do it again, that's right, like that. And keep on talkin' to him, just like you've been doing. Show him he's got nothing to be afraid of, that he can trust you."

Eli shot him a look. Cal chuckled. "I'm serious. Horses learn real fast if a certain action on their part gets a certain response on yours. And the last thing you want 'em to think is that if they aren't in the mood to be messed with, all they have to do is put up a fuss and you'll back off."

The boy huffed out a breath, set his mouth in a way Cal'd

learned meant determination and took the blanket to the colt again. And for the next minute or so, demonstrating both the intuition and patience that had impressed Cal to no end these past six weeks, Eli and the horse did their little tango until eventually the colt gave up. Well, he kept giving Eli these wide-eyed glances over his shoulder, like he wasn't too sure about what was going on, but at least he stood still.

And the kid favored Cal with a grin of triumph that warmed him to the soles of his boots.

Boy'd taken to the horses like a retriever to water, and—for the most part—they to him. Hell, he'd even won Blaze over, right about the time Cal'd begun to think the mare was a lost cause. Oh, the kid griped about cleaning out the stalls, but Cal couldn't blame him for that, seeing as he didn't seem to remember being any too thrilled about that particular chore when he was Eli's age, either. But he showed up like clockwork every day after school—which he griped about, too, but between Cal and Dawn nagging him about it, he was doing okay in his classes—and on Saturdays. No more getting in trouble. And the only joyriding the boy did these days was when Cal let him ride one of the mares when the weather wasn't being a pain in the butt—

"Hey, you guys."

Speaking of pains in the butt. Cal whipped around to see the woman who was going to take him under for sure waddling down the center of the barn in what looked like layers of sacks, her hair loose and gleaming in the overhead lights, so full of herself and her womanhood it made his mouth dry.

While she stopped to chew the fat with Eli, Cal mused—for the umpteenth time—that this was, bar none, the craziest relationship he'd ever had. Not just with a woman, with another human being, period. But every time she came to him, made love with him, smiled for him, was a point on his scorecard. Now if only he had a clue how many points he needed in order to win, he'd be cookin' with gas.

"Is it my imagination," she said, scanning the full-up barn, "or have you still got a *lot* of horses?"

"It would look that way," he said mildly. Yeah, the idea was to sell off most of the weanlings before winter set in so he didn't have to feed 'em over the winter. But other than that double sale a bit ago, things hadn't gone as well as he might have liked. With a shrug he added, "No matter. They'll be even bigger and prettier come spring."

"Meanwhile," she said softly, "your bills are piling up."

Cal called to Eli to take the blanket to Abby, the filly in the next stall, then led Dawn back outside. "I don't want you worrying about this, okay? I'm getting some nibbles from a new round of ads I placed a couple weeks back. And once the stud fees for Twister start coming in, I should be okay."

"I'm not criticizing you, Cal, you know that." She dodged a patch of mud-streaked, slushy snow left over from the last storm. "I'm just concerned. *For* you."

He fished his gloves out of his coat pockets and shoved his hands into them. "Well, don't be. It's like you said—this is my life. I'll figure something out." He tried to smile away the worry in her eyes. "I always do."

"God, Cal...how do you do it? How do you stay so calm even when—"

"It looks like everything's fallin' apart? Because gettin' all worked up about what I can't fix tends to take the fun out of life. This is where I belong, what I do. If I have to scale back in order to survive, I will. If I have to go work at Wal-Mart in order to keep the farm," he added with a grin, "then that's what I'll do."

She actually laughed, but it quickly died out. And instead of looking at him, she wrapped her arms around herself inside the outermost sack and squinted out toward the pasture. "I'd kill to have your confidence, you know that? To be so sure about what you're supposed to be doing. Who you are."

"And who the hell do you think I learned that from?"

Her eyes flashed to his. Then she made a sound that was equal parts laugh and snort. "Yeah, I guess I used to be a little...dogged. When your priorities change, however—"

Jacob pulled up in the drive, cutting off her sentence.

"Afternoon," Eli's father called out from the window, his gaze settling on Dawn in that unnerving, intense way he had that made Cal's insides squirm, before it shifted to Cal. "I need to take the boy into Claremore, get him some new shoes, if that's okay with you."

"Sure, no problem. He's in the barn—you want me to get him for you?"

"No, no…" Moving with a freedom Cal knew was a direct result of his new, and less drug-dependent, treatment program for the bad back, Jacob climbed out of the truck, the icy breeze ruffling his now-shorter hair, a grin crawling across freshly shaved cheeks. "I'll get him myself," he said, plopping what looked like a new cowboy hat on his head. "And how are you this morning?" he said to Dawn.

"Still pregnant," she said with a grimace, and Jacob actually chuckled. But was there something…odd about his laugh? Or was Cal looking for ghosts where there weren't any?

"Won't be long now, though," Jacob said, then said, "By the way—I forgot to tell you…I signed up for a mail-order course to learn how to be an insurance claims adjuster." He grinned. "Figured that'd be something to bring in some extra cash and get me out of the house more at the same time."

"Jacob! Good for you!" Dawn swung an arm around his neck and gave him a quick peck on the cheek; the man blushed, then touched the brim of his hat and strode off toward the barn. Cal watched him, torn, as his suspicions refused to gel into conviction; as the justification for keeping those suspicions under wraps until he figured out what to do, and how to do it, crumbled more with each passing day. And God knows it had been shaky to begin with. Lord, Dawn would skin him alive if she thought he'd been trying to *protect* her.

But even though the nasty, embittered man Cal had wanted to shield Dawn from in the beginning no longer existed, he still had nothing to go on except a gut feeling. A gut feeling obviously not shared by the extremely pregnant woman at his side, who he figured wouldn't have the slightest compunction about saying, "Hey! You wouldn't happen to be my father, would you?"

"Can we go in the house?" she said. "I'm freezing."

He glanced over, frowning at the look in her eyes. And once inside, Cal didn't think the chill in his gut had anything to do with the temperature as he set about making Dawn a cup of tea—Ethel having gone off shopping—while she went to the bathroom. When she didn't return within a reasonable time, he went on a search mission, finding her in the living room, fingering the piano keys. She tapped a key, but not hard enough to make any sound. "Why do you hang on to this if you don't play?"

"Because it was my mother's," he said, handing her the tea. "And because maybe one day it'll get played again. By a niece or nephew. Or my own kid."

Sipping her tea, she scanned the room, that little crease settling between her brows. And something prompted him to say, "You know, I only kept everything the way it was because there didn't seem to be any reason to change. Not because I'm trying to keep a museum to my parents or anything. I mean, I always figured, if I ever got married, there'd be changes—"

"I got a job offer today," she said quietly, her gaze fixed on the keyboard again. "Back in New York."

"Oh," he said, but the word sounded like somebody else was saying it. "I didn't know you'd applied for anything."

"I hadn't. My old boss at the free clinic put in a good word and…things happened."

He watched her take another sip, noticed her hands were shaking. Not that that helped his own quaking, but still.

"This your dream job?" he said.

"Financially?" One side of her mouth tilted up. "It's to run a Legal Aid clinic in Brooklyn. So for most people, no. It wouldn't be."

"I'm not asking about other people, Dawn. I'm asking about you."

She set her cup on the windowsill, then pressed one of the

keys, sending a sad, lonely note floating out into the room. "It comes damn close."

"So…you gonna take it?"

She lifted her eyes to his. "I can't make that decision by myself, Cal."

"Since when? You always said this is what you'd probably do, go back to New York if you could find a good job. Well, now you have. So I guess I just have to deal with it, don't I?"

"But the question is, could you? For real? Settle for being a part-time father, I mean."

He waited out the punch to his gut, then said, "I'll cope."

"But you wouldn't be happy about it."

"That's got nothing to do with it."

"Of *course* it has something to do with it! If you don't want me to take this job, just say so, dammit!"

"Oooh, no…you are *not* putting this on me—"

She slammed the keyboard cover back down over the keys, startling the old instrument into an off-pitch groan. "Do you care if I take the job or not?"

"What the hell do you think?" he bellowed. "My priorities *haven't* changed, sweetheart! I still want you, and my baby, right here where the three of us can be part of each other's lives on a full-time basis. But damned if I'm gonna let you make me the heavy in this. Damned if I'm gonna be the reason you turned down the opportunity of a lifetime." His throat convulsed. "Damned if I'm gonna give you a reason to hate me."

She regarded him steadily for several seconds, then pushed past him. And Ethel, who was just coming in. Two seconds later the house shook with the force of the front door banging shut.

With an R-rated curse, Cal dropped onto the sofa, ramming his hands through his hair.

"Okay, doody-for-brains," the housekeeper said, shucking off her old Pendleton coat and dumping it on a chair. "Which foot did you ram in your craw this time?"

"Don't start, Ethel. I am not in the mood."

Undaunted, she made a beeline for him anyway. "Like I give a damn what kind of mood you're in. You've got no idea what the woman was really asking, do you?"

Cal assumed a scowl guaranteed to shave five years off Hannibal Lecter's life. "I got every idea what she was asking. She wanted me to let her off the hook so she could take that job with a clear conscience."

"Wrong. She was looking for an excuse *not* to take it. Only for some harebrained reason I can't even begin to comprehend, you wouldn't give her one. One without about a thousand strings attached, anyway."

Cal's head started to pound. He collapsed back against the sofa cushions, pressing the heels of his hands into his temples. "Okay, so maybe I didn't handle that too well," he said, glaring at Ethel when she snorted her obvious agreement. His hands dropped to his thighs. "Well, she caught me off guard, for cripe's sake. And anyway, I meant what I said. Baby or no baby, I don't want her making a decision about her life based on what I want."

"Which came across to her as *stay or go, it doesn't make the least bit of difference to me.*"

"That's nuts! How could she possibly get that from what I said?"

"Because the one thing that little girl needs is for somebody—let's say you, just for the hell of it—to put his big dumb butt on the line and say what you really feel. Not what you think she wants to hear."

"I *did* say what I really felt—"

"Only to immediately qualify it by makin' it impossible for her to make an unbiased decision! Now you've made things twice as hard for her!"

Cal opened his mouth to protest, but let out another curse instead. Ethel was right. Instead of getting out of Dawn's way, he'd inadvertently stuck his big dumb butt, as she called it, right smack in the middle. If she took the job, would it be because she really wanted it, or because he'd made her afraid to stay?

With a groan, he leaned forward, burying his face in his hands. "I'm an idiot."

"You're not an idiot," he heard Ethel say on a rush of air. He looked up to see her sitting on the coffee table in front of him, her skinny mouth pulled so tight her lips were all but gone. She grabbed one of his hands, wrapping it in both of hers. "You're just scared."

"Scared? Of what, for God's sake?"

"The truth. You forget I've known you from the day you were born. And you were, without a doubt, the most easygoing little kid I ever saw. But after losing both your parents so close together, you changed. Oh, I doubt most folks saw it, but I sure did. On the surface, you might be the same happy-go-lucky goofball who lets troubles roll off his back you always were—" she squeezed his hand "—but I see a hurtin' young man determined to shove troubles away before they can take root. You didn't push Dawn away for her own good," she said gently. "You pushed her away because you're afraid of gettin' hurt."

"That's bull, Ethel," he said, even as the truth of her words—not to mention her don't-give-me-that expression—slashed through him. He sighed. "Okay, maybe I had some trouble at first coming to terms with how I really felt, but I got past it. And all I'm trying to do now is give her all her options."

"Then *give* her all the options, for crying out loud, instead of doing this fool dance around the subject! Honey, you keep paying lip service to how much you want that gal, but until you're willing to risk everything for her, you've got no business expecting her to. So here—"

She turned his hand over and slammed the truck keys into his palm. He stared at them glumly, then said, "She doesn't love me, Ethel."

"What in tarnation makes you think that?"

Frowning, he looked up. "Because she hasn't said she does?"

"Oh, Lord," Ethel said on a sigh, then added, "And have you told her you do?"

"I don't want to scare her off—ow!" he said when she cuffed his head.

"You haven't heard one single word I've said, have you?"

They stared each other down for several seconds. Then Cal did some more hair plowing and some more swearing, until he'd gotten both out of his system enough to say, "Okay, suppose you're right," which he knew was dangerous but he was already screwed, anyway, so it wasn't like he had anything to lose. "How'm I supposed to take back everything I just said and not look like an idiot for sure?"

Ethel shrugged. "Sometimes, that's the chance you gotta take."

"Gee, thanks," he said.

She ruffled his hair, like he was ten, for God's sake. "Anytime."

Chapter 12

"Well," Ivy said, after a good ten minutes spent listening to her daughter rant and rave about the stupidity of men in general and Cal in particular, "he does have a point. If you stay because of him instead of because you really want to, you *will* end up resenting him. And your child'll end up payin' for it, one way or the other. Besides," Ivy said calmly, lifting up the lid on the Dutch oven to check on the pot roast, "it's not him you're mad at right now."

"Ah, but I think it is."

"Well, you're wrong." She turned to meet her daughter's annoyed expression. "Oh, you're hot 'cause he wouldn't make your decision for you—"

"I didn't want him to make the decision for me! I only wanted his input!"

"Well, sounds to me like you got it. And now you're mad at yourself because the ball's back in your court and you don't know what to do with it."

On a strangled groan, Dawn yanked back a kitchen chair and lowered herself onto it. But wonder of wonders, she didn't have a comeback. Ivy sat down across from her, looking into the same confused, angry eyes that used to confront Ivy all those years ago, after some kid had taunted her or she'd overhead ignorant whisperings in the supermarket.

"Poor baby," Ivy said softly, brushing Dawn's hair back over her shoulder. "Everything's come crashing down around you, hasn't it?"

"To say the least." Her mouth flattened. "I don't get it. I mean, things have never been simple, or easy, but at least they used to be clear."

Ivy smiled, even though her heart was splintering into about a thousand pieces inside her. "I've been dreading this from the time you were a little girl."

"What? That I'd make a total mess of my life?"

"Oh, for God's sake, Dawn! You really don't get it, do you? *You* haven't made a mess of anything! Stuff *happens,* honey. Stuff none of us—not even you—can control. And I knew it was only a matter of time before you had to learn that the hard way. Sometimes we gotta trust things'll work out even if we can't see how…."

The doorbell rang. "If it's Cal," Dawn said as Ivy got up, "I do not want to talk to him."

"Now there's a mature response," Ivy said, chuckling when she heard Dawn blow raspberries at her back.

Yep. It was Cal, all right, standing there on her doorstep with hat in hand, his hair more of a mess than usual, his mouth pulled down at the corners and his eyes full of something she sure had never seen in a man's eyes for her.

"Dawn here?"

"She's in the kitchen, she said she doesn't want to see you, and if it's any consolation, she looks as bad as you do."

Cal frowned at her. "That mean I can see her or not?"

"Honey, I'm just a messenger, not a guard dog. Just make sure to clean up the blood when you're done, since I am not mopping that floor twice in one day."

"So much for tellin' Mama I didn't want to see you."

"You were outvoted," Cal said with a helluva lot more composure than he felt, dragging out a chair and settling in across from her. He took a deep breath, inhaling what should have been the mouthwatering scent of simmering pot roast or stew or something on the stove. That his stomach didn't leap to attention only went to show how bad off he was.

"Why are you here?" Dawn said, crossing her arms over her belly.

"To apologize."

Her brows crashed. "For what?"

Cal leaned back in his chair, messing with his hat for a bit, then looked over at her. Lord, he hadn't felt this shaky since that time a few years back when he'd gotten on a horse far greener than he'd realized. The question hadn't been *if* he'd get thrown, but when. And how hard he'd land. "After you left, I got to thinking—"

No point in mentioning Ethel's kick in the pants, he didn't think.

"—and it occurred to me that, for all this discussion about what you should do, what would be best for the baby, we're still avoiding the real issue. Which is how we feel about each other." He watched those big, brown eyes, sure at any moment his heart was going to pound clean out of his chest. "Right now. Not how we may have felt ten years ago. You with me so far?"

He could see her pulse hammering in the base of her throat, but since she nodded, he leaned forward again to take her hand, which was freezing; he covered it in both of his to warm it. To keep it, even if only for a moment.

"Honey, believe me, what I feel for you is as real as it gets. It's not about sex, it's not about the baby, it's about me and you. It's about me wanting to marry you." The bucking got worse; he swallowed and hung on even tighter. "Even if you decide to take that job."

There. That should give her all the options.

Shouldn't it?

He'd never seen Dawn's eyes that huge, and that was going

some. "I…ohmigod, Cal…I…" She snapped shut her mouth. Opened it again. "I honestly don't know what to say. That you'd be willing to settle for that kind of arrangement…"

"The question is, would you?"

She struggled to her feet, waddling over to the refrigerator to pull out a bottle of juice. Cal stood as well, his stomach giving him five fits even as he closed the distance between them to pull her into his arms, juice and all.

"You wanna think about it?" he said. But she lifted her eyes to his, followed by her hand to his cheek.

"I can't marry you, Cal," she whispered. "It just wouldn't be fair. To either one of us."

Past the cold, hard knot lodged in his chest, he pushed out, "You've made up your mind, haven't you? About the job?"

Tears glittered in her eyes. "The job's got nothing to do with it."

Well. Time to pick himself up, wipe the dust off his sorry butt and get the hell out of there before he got trampled but good.

An hour later Cal stomped into his kitchen, flashing only a cursory glance at the woman responsible for him making a total ass of himself.

"You were gone longer'n I expected," Ethel said behind him as he yanked a beer out of the refrigerator.

He shrugged.

"Frank put up the horses. And supper's ready."

"I'm not hungry."

She clunked a plate on the table for him, anyway. He ignored it.

"So what'd she say?"

"What the hell do you think she said? She said no."

"No? To what?"

"I asked her to marry me, even if she takes the job—which it looks like she is—and she said no. You satisfied now?" He took a swig of the beer, adding, "What?" at the stymied look on her face.

"Who the hell said anything about askin' her to *marry* you?"

"You did! All that stuff about comin' right out and letting her know how serious I was—"

"Oh, of all the damn fool things…" The housekeeper let out a huff, then shook her head. "Honestly, boy—for someone as smart as you are, you have got the lousiest sense of timing of anybody I have ever seen. You don't spring something like that on a woman, for cryin' out loud! 'Specially not one with abandonment issues."

"Abandonment issues? Which dumb talk show you get that from?"

"I do not watch those things! Leastwise, not on a regular basis. And anyway, I don't need anything but my own two eyes and ears to figure out what she's afraid of. Her engagement fell apart, the man she thought was gonna be her father walked away, her own father never wanted anything to do with her… Lord above, no wonder the gal has a problem with lettin' anybody get close, if it looks like all they're gonna do is leave, anyway."

"Except I'm not the one leaving. She is."

"Only so you can't!"

Her words twanged between them, until she batted at the air in front of her and said, "Oh, well…don't suppose there's anything to be done for it now. You may as well sit down and eat your supper before it gets cold."

Cal gawked at her. "I've just shot myself in the foot and all you've got to say is 'sit down and eat your supper'?"

Ethel gave him one of her looks. "The gal's not leaving tomorrow, so I doubt twenty minutes one way or t'other's gonna make much difference. Besides, nothin' says she can't change her mind."

"This is Dawn we're talking about, here," he said, sitting down.

"Precisely," Ethel said, only God knew what she meant by that. "But for heaven's sake," she added, pouring him a glass of iced tea, ''don't be asking me for any more advice! My poor old heart just can't take it!''

He swore around a mouthful of country-fried steak.

Seated on the sofa in Faith's tiny living room the next Sunday afternoon, wearing a gift-bow-studded paper-plate hat and surrounded by boxes and tissue paper and more onesies and sleepers and rattles than ten babies could use, Dawn watched her friend nurse her two-and-a-half-month-old son with a mixture of fascination and dread.

The blonde looked up and chuckled, then said over yet another dramatized labor story a few feet away, ''You should see the look on your face. Like you just found out we're serving grubs for lunch.''

''In a nice lemon butter, I'm sure they'd be fine,'' Dawn said, and Faith laughed again.

''Here.'' She detached her son, grabbed a cloth diaper off her shoulder and thrust both out toward Dawn. ''You need practice.''

''Oh! No! I can't—''

''Faith's right,'' Maddie said beside Dawn, her own tummy nicely rounded underneath a knit jersey tunic. ''Nothin' like a little hands-on experience to prepare you for your own. Which should be here in, what?'' She shoved in what must've been her twentieth pig-in-a-blanket, finishing her question around a full mouth. ''Three weeks?''

But Dawn was too busy trying to adjust the tiny, wriggling, amazingly solid person on her shoulder to answer, trying to fathom that holding a tiny, wriggling, amazingly solid little person would be part of her normal, everyday experience in a matter of weeks.

''Rub his back,'' Faith was saying as she buttoned up her blouse. ''Yeah, like that. You wanna push the burp out—''

Little Nicky let out a belch loud enough to rattle windows, every woman in the room went, ''Awwww,'' and Dawn was stunned at the strange sensation of accomplishment that swept through her.

"Good job, guy!" she said, tilting the baby back to smile for him. Not recognizing her at first, the infant scrunched up his face; then his mouth twitched into a goofy little grin, followed by the funniest burbling sound Dawn had ever heard. Dawn imitated the sound, making the baby smile even more.

"Hey," she said. "This might be fun, after all."

"Don't get too excited. He could just as easily have erpped up all over you. And at least this one's not colicky. Lord, I thought Crystal'd take us all under for sure. How something that little could cry for five and six hours straight was beyond me."

Dawn sighed. "You could have at least let me wallow in my illusions until after the baby was born."

"And where's the fun in that?" the blonde said with a laugh as Hank's daughter, who at the rate she was going would be able to buy a small country from her baby-sitting earnings, swooped down and took Nicky to change him.

Dawn straightened her chapeau and scarfed down another one of Luralene's pimento-cheese-spread-slathered Triscuits. She'd been sure, when Faith and Maddie had insisted on throwing the shower, this would be one of those grin-and-bear-it things. Not because of the shower itself, but simply because, since that disastrous conversation with Cal the week before—and her agonizing over that job offer ever since—she hadn't exactly been in a partying mood. But being around all these people who cared about her, whom she'd grown to care so much about in the past months, had gone a long way toward bolstering her sagging, and seriously addlepated, spirits.

Most of the women had disappeared into the kitchen, leaving Faith and Dawn alone. "In a way it's kinda sad," Faith said, "knowing he's my last."

Dawn tried, with no success whatsoever, to find a more comfortable spot on the sofa. "You sure about that?"

"I guess I never told you, huh?" Her curls bobbing, the blonde moved to sit beside Dawn, whispering, "Darryl gave me a vasectomy for my birthday. Well, he didn't give it to *me*, but you know what I mean. And I didn't even have to bring up the subject, he did.''

''Now there's a keeper for sure.'' Dawn tried to pull herself forward to reach Arliss Potts's chicken salad sandwiches, smiling her thanks when Faith handed her the whole tray. ''So things are better between you two, huh?''

''What do you mean?''

''I just thought, from what you'd said in the fall…'' At the look on her friend's face, she decided to concentrate on the bite in her mouth instead. Hmm. Horseradish in chicken salad. ''Forget it. I must have misinterpreted…''

That got a sigh. ''No, you didn't misinterpret. Let me tell you something, if we make it to our fiftieth anniversary without one of us killin' the other, it'll only be because we're both too damn stubborn to give up.''

An explosion of laughter went up from the kitchen.

''That doesn't sound very romantic.''

Faith shrugged. ''It is what it is, that's all. Sometimes I think Darryl and me stay together more because the alternative's even scarier. Lord, who wants to be stuck alone with five kids? But it could be worse. I mean—'' she glanced around to make sure Charmaine wasn't in earshot ''—at least I know Darryl's not gonna take off on me. Or beat me or the kids. And there's a lot to be said for that, y'know? And as long as the sex is still good—oh, for heaven's sake, don't look so appalled—I'm fine. So. Tell me what's going on with you and Cal.''

Dawn decided to blame the twinge in her chest to the horseradish. ''We still can't decide on names.''

''I am not talking about names.''

No, of course she wasn't.

''Something happened between the two of you, didn't it?''

Dawn leaned back, thinking maybe she'd just stay there until she gave birth. ''Tell me something—when Darryl asked you to marry him, how'd you feel?''

''Relieved, frankly,'' Faith said. ''Which is probably not the answer you're looking for…ohmigod! Cal asked you to *marry* him?''

She nodded. "But I turned him down."

"*Why?*" Faith practically shrieked, bringing Ruby's head out of the kitchen door to ask if everything was all right. Dawn assured her it was and she popped back inside, like a prairie dog into its hole.

"Because…oh, God, if you could've seen the look on his face when he asked me…" She rubbed her belly where a little foot was determined to break through. "I've never had anybody look at me like that. As if I meant the world to him."

"Excuse me? Am I missin' something here?"

"Faith, I have no idea what to do with that kind of love. Especially from Cal. I keep thinking, what if something goes wrong? What if—" She stopped.

Her friend's mouth thinned. "What if you two turn out like Darryl and me?"

"I didn't say that."

"You didn't have to. God," she said on an exasperated breath. "When am I gonna learn to keep my big mouth shut? See, what you're not understanding is, Darryl and me didn't start out that way. He never looked at me like that. Like he couldn't wait to get me into bed, yeah, but not like I was the center of the universe. I mean, have you noticed the way Cal's brothers look at their wives? It's genetic, I'm telling you. Havin' a Logan man love you…well. Let's just say there's not a woman in Mayes County who wouldn't kill to be in your shoes."

"Whichever ones these are. I haven't seen my feet in a month."

Faith chuckled, then sighed. "Honey, don't take this the wrong way, but you're bein' dumb as a brick."

"I don't doubt it. But there it is. I mean, Cal and me…" She sighed. "It would be like building a dream house on the San Andreas fault. No matter how perfect the house, what's the point if you're always worrying about the earth opening and swallowing it up?"

"Good Lord," Faith said. "Is this what happens to everybody who moves to New York? They become totally neurotic?''

Dawn grimaced. "In my case, New York had nothing to do with it."

"And Cal loves you, anyway. Maybe you should think about that."

As if she'd been able to think about anything else.

Yanking on a pair of leather work gloves as he stood in the front yard, Cal glowered at the tangle of deadwood that had been his mother's prized rose garden, once upon a time. Talk about perseverance—even though it had been more than twenty years since anyone had given the bushes any real attention, damned if the things didn't bloom every spring anyway. Tried to, at least. This year, Cal thought he might give the things a fighting chance.

Especially as they were giving him the perfect excuse to be out front right now. And not just to avoid Ethel's infernal yammering about Dawn's baby shower yesterday.

"Okay, y'all," he said, flexing his dad's old pruners, "I'm goin' in."

For the first day or two after Dawn turned him down, Cal had done a lot of stomping around, cussing and slamming things. It hurt like holy hell, that he'd taken that risk and lost, that he'd been dumb enough to listen to Ethel instead of following his own instincts. That clearly she didn't return his feelings.

But along about the third day or so, he started seeing things a little differently. That maybe, like Ethel said, Dawn just needed time to get used to the idea. That maybe she did love him, but hitting her with a marriage proposal when her brain was flooded with pregnancy hormones probably hadn't been the smartest move on his part.

Of course, there was that whole job issue snarling between them, too. A week later—he yanked out a particularly nasty dead branch and tossed it aside—and he still hadn't heard whether she'd accepted it or not. He told himself it didn't make any difference, he wanted whatever was best for her, but the not knowing was about to kill him.

But not nearly as much as not doing anything.

Oh, he knew he needed to take a different tack entirely, one that would give her time to get used to the idea that he really loved her, while reassuring her—like they'd done with Eli when he'd been in the hospital—that he had no intention of giving up on them. Not that he'd quite figured out the details yet, but he had a few weeks yet before the baby came. And he doubted she'd be going anywhere for at least another month after that.

Of course, this was Dawn he was talking about.

Frank toodled by on the tractor, stopping to frown.

"Wouldn't it make more sense to dig 'em up and start over?" the old man yelled over the tractor's engine.

"Probably," Cal yelled back. Another clump of branches landed in the wheelbarrow. "But that would be too easy."

He couldn't hear Frank's reply; he figured that was just as well.

One thing Cal had finally decided, though: that it wasn't his imagination, the wistful look he saw in Jacob's eyes whenever Cal saw him and Dawn together, like he'd lost something and didn't know how to get it back. And how many times had he thought Jacob was about to say something, only to suck the thought back inside him? Not that Cal blamed him, in a way; as reticent as Cal'd been to broach the subject before he was sure, he could just imagine how Jacob must feel. At least now Jacob got to see and talk with her on a regular basis. Once she discovered the truth, though, who knew what her reaction might be?

And whether her finding out the truth really would affect how she felt about Haven, and Cal, he had no idea. But it was sure as hell worth a shot.

Hence his being out front that afternoon, to make sure he didn't miss Jacob when he came to pick up Eli.

The older man arrived, right on time. Cal looked up and grinned, his stomach cramping. How he was going to bring up the subject, he had no idea. And if he was wrong, he was going to look like a fool for sure. Again.

"Hey, Pop!" Eli yelled from the barn. "Come see the new foal! I got to watch her being born!"

Not sure whether he was more irked or relieved by the reprieve, Cal followed Jacob into the warm, hay-scented barn, thankfully a little less populated than it had been a month before, now that folks were beginning to buy again. He was getting fairly decent prices, too. And to think his brothers had tried to talk him into selling.

Dawn never had, though. Not once.

Jacob's chuckle stirred Cal from his musings. Cinnamon's newest looked like she was trying to figure out whether those spindly things poking out from her body were really meant to support her or not . But if she wanted what her mama was offering, she had to get to her. Once she did, though, Cindy swung her head around to nuzzle her newborn, encouraging her to eat.

"No wonder the boy can't wait to get here every day," Jacob said after Cal sent Eli off to fill feedbuckets. "I'll tell you what, he's too blamed done in when he gets home to do anything but eat and go to bed. Well, after he tells me about his day. Says he'd like to work with horses as a career, now."

"He'd be terrific at it, that's for sure. He's got a real way with 'em."

Jacob got quiet for a moment, then said, "I've got some apologizing to do to you. And Dawn. For being so muleheaded about acceptin' your help. Or anybody else's. I swear, all that damn pain medicine I was on turned my brains to mush." He paused, then said, "Guess it takes some getting used to, letting other people in. And I just wanted to say…thanks."

"Nothing to thank me for…" Cal glanced back toward the feed room: if he didn't get on with it, the kid would be back and who knows when his next chance would come.

"Cal? Somethin' on your mind?"

He looked at Jacob, thinking tussling with those brambles earlier was nothing compared with this. "Yeah, actually. Trouble is—'' he glanced at the mare and her filly, then back at Jacob ''—I have no idea how to go about it.'' At the older man's frown, Cal said quietly, ''I need to ask you something. About Dawn.''

Jacob's eyes narrowed. Then his mouth pulled into a taut smile. ''I've seen the way you've been looking at me these past weeks, all those questions in your eyes. And I kept thinking, I should just come right out and say something…but I could never figure out how, either.''

''She's your daughter, isn't she?'' Cal asked.

Jacob nodded, then scrubbed a hand over his chin. ''You know, there's a lot of things about my life I'm not proud of. Least of all the way I've raised that boy. But for all the mistakes I've made with him, none of 'em even come close to the one I made that cost me something I'll never get back.''

''Ivy said you made her keep your identity a secret.''

''Well, hell, what else would she say? You honestly think she's gonna admit the father of her kid's some sorry-assed loser who took off on her? Who never even bothered writing or calling or nothing? Then I show up again with a pregnant wife…''

''That why you never said anything, either?''

Jacob turned away, his jaw tight. ''I remember that first time I saw Dawn with Ivy, realized she was Ivy's kid, did some quick math and figured out she had to be mine. Then things got even more complicated when Justine wanted to hire Ivy so she could have the baby at home. After one of Justine's appointments, I finally cornered Ivy, asked her about Dawn…but she denied it, with a look on her face I won't forget until my dyin' day. Like the idea of me being the father of her girl—a girl who was about to go off to college in New York City— completely disgusted her. Wasn't much I could do, especially as I didn't want to upset Justine for one thing. And I wouldn't't've hurt Dawn for the world, y'know? And anyway, Dawn left maybe a month or so after that.'' He shrugged. ''It was too late, y'know? Then Justine died and I had my hands full with Elijah, and I don't know, at some point I took a good, hard look at myself and thought, well, hell—Dawn did just fine without me all the years she was growing up. Why on earth would she need me now?''

''Maybe that's something you should ask her.''

For several seconds Jacob stared at one of the barn cats rooting for something underneath a loosened hay bale. Then he said, ''Is she gonna stay, do you think? After the baby comes?''

''She got a good job offer back East,'' Cal said, wondering when the words would stop tasting like poison. He shrugged. ''I don't know.''

''Funny how much alike we are,'' Jacob said. ''Her and me, both, needing to get away from here, to see what else was out there. Difference is, I left behind a kid I didn't know about. She'd be taking one you *do*.''

Cal thought that over for a minute, then said, ''And maybe it would be harder for her to go if she knew she'd be leaving her baby's grandfather, too.''

Hope tangling with panic in those ice-blue eyes, Jacob hauled in a breath, then let it out on a long, shaky sigh. ''I don't suppose…you'd consider doin' the ground work for me? Give her a chance to get used to the idea before I see her again?''

Cal's initial reaction was, ''Hell, no!'' until he realized it wasn't up to him to define courage for anybody else. Especially since he was having a hard enough time defining it for himself.

''I'll go see if she's home,'' he said.

Her back had been giving her fits off and on all day. No surprise, considering her navel reached her destination five minutes before the rest of her did these days. She'd finally left work early—although Sherman had been fussing at her to stay home for the past week, at least—and now, her sole maternity ''grown-up'' suit ditched in favor of a pair of man's extralarge sweats, Dawn stood in her mother's living room, trying to figure out how to simply sit down without doing herself mischief. Feeling like she was about to lay an egg, she grabbed behind her for the chair arm, then slowly lowered herself into it with a grunt befitting a rhinoceros.

"I've just made two decisions," she said when Ivy handed her a cup of tea and commanded her to get her feet up on the ottoman she shoved in front of her.

"And what's that?"

Dawn craned her neck to frown at her now-propped-up puffy ankles, way on the other end of her body. "One, I'm suing that condom manufacturer. And two, there is no way I'm going through another three weeks of this."

"Could be longer, you know," Ivy said with a maddeningly smug look on her face. "First-timers often go beyond their due date."

"Oh, God. If that happens, I may kill somebody." A certain dimpled smile came to mind. A smile she'd missed this past week more than she wanted to admit. "Probably Cal."

"Like you could move fast enough to be a threat." Dawn stuck her tongue out at her mother, who ignored her and went on, "So when are you supposed to let these people know about that job?"

Her mother would bring that up. "Tomorrow," she said.

"You made up your mind?"

"Yes. And no, I'm not telling you, or anybody else, because sure as I do, somebody's gonna come up with a dozen reasons why I'm making the wrong choice. When it's a done deal, I'll let you know—who's out there?" she said when Ivy made a face out the front window.

"That man you're gonna kill," she said, then turned. "Do I dare let him in?"

Soon as I talk my heart back down off the ledge, Dawn thought, then decided, hell, at this point, maybe he'd at least distract her from the pain in her lower back. "Might as well. He'll only batter the door down if you don't."

And there he was, tall and handsome and frowning, looking as good as she remembered—better—all the reasons why she should leave coming out from their hiding places with their hands up.

"Good God, Dawn—you okay? You look like hell!"

Dawn looked at her mother. "He's never gonna make the three weeks."

"I don't suppose it occurred to you," Ivy said, "that telling a grossly pregnant woman—"

"Hey!"

"—she looks like hell isn't exactly the way to earn points with her?"

"Sorry," Cal said, looking so contrite Dawn made a mental note to forgive him some day. Maybe—she shifted in the chair—after she killed him. He frowned. "Horses don't tend to look like…that."

Definitely after she killed him.

"So what you're saying is, I'm bigger than one of your mares?"

"No, of course not!" he said as Ivy trooped off to the kitchen. "What I meant was, they don't look miserable right before they're about to foal. Which you do. And I feel bad about that, okay?"

"As well you should," she muttered, wriggling a fist behind her to massage the base of her spine, thinking, you know, any other couple would be awkward and stilted with each other right now. Not that everything was copasetic between Cal and her at the moment. Not by any means. But it never ceased to amaze her that, no matter how long they'd been apart, or why, they always seemed to be able to pick up where they left off without even needing a refresher course. And that she could always count on him.

She met that steady green gaze and sucked in a breath.

On *them.*

The thought zinged through her like an electric shock, jerking her into realizing exactly how much she stood to lose.

"What's up?" she said softly.

The pulse hammering in her temples kept time with his boots' thudding against the wooden floor as he came closer. He sat on the sofa, moving her swollen feet to his lap, and she cursed him for being everything she'd ever wanted.

He skimmed his fingertips over her instep, then said, "I know who your father is, honey." When her eyes widened, he added, "It's Jacob."

"*Jacob…?*"

"Oh, for the love of God," Ivy huffed from the kitchen door. "After all these years…I thought we had this settled. Why'd he have to go and bring this up now?"

"Because maybe he was tired of it bein' a secret, Ivy," Cal said, while Dawn sat there feeling as though somebody'd hit her upside the head with her mother's cast-iron skillet. "Because maybe he wants to try to fix a mistake."

"Which might be all well and good except it's not his mistake to fix!"

"He told me about the affair, Ivy," Cal said, setting Dawn's foot on the table and getting to his feet. "About how he'd left you, not knowing you were pregnant, and that he never bothered to let you know where he was so you *could* tell him. That he didn't know about Dawn until he came back, right before she graduated from high school. You telling me none of that's true? That he just made it up?"

"Oh, Lord…yes," she said on a stream of air. "Jacob and I had an affair, although we didn't exactly advertise it. And, no, he never bothered to tell me where he was after he left. Since nobody'd made any promises, that wasn't surprising. So that part of his story's true. But the rest isn't."

"And maybe if you didn't want anybody to know you two had something goin'," Cal said, "you wouldn't want anybody to know he was Dawn's father, either."

Meanwhile, Dawn was still back on *Jacob?*

Ivy barked out a laugh. "I didn't want anybody to know about us because, one, it wasn't anybody's business but ours, and two, he was six years younger'n me—"

"Wait a minute," Dawn said, finally catching up. "Sherman said my father met his financial obligations to me all through my childhood." She looked at her mother. "And I got the feeling from you my father *did* know you were pregnant. But if Jacob told Cal he didn't know about me until I was seventeen…'' She sucked in a breath as, way down deep, something…happened. ''Uh-oh,'' she said, staring at her belly.

''Dawn?'' Cal said. ''You okay?''

''I don't know. I think I need to pee…but I can't get up out of this damn chair!''

Her mother and Cal were instantly on either side of her to heave her to her feet…not two seconds before her waters broke.

She let out a shriek of laughter. ''*Told* you I wasn't going to hold out for three more weeks—ohmigod!'' Just like that, she started shaking so hard she could hardly stand. ''I'm gonna have a baby!''

Cal wrapped an arm around her shoulders, whispering a constant string of ''It's gonna be all rights'' in her hair. But when she lifted her eyes to his, she saw not love or concern or even fear but an anger so fierce, so bitterly cold, it scared her half to death.

Even as she knew it wasn't directed at her.

Chapter 13

Since Dawn's first contractions didn't have a lot of punch to them, Ivy assured Cal he wouldn't be missed for an hour or so. Plenty of time to zip back to the farm and check up on the herd.

Maybe tend to one or two other pressing matters.

The front door to the old Victorian was still unlocked, even though it was getting on to seven o'clock. Cal removed his hat, the carpeting muffling his footsteps as he crossed the waiting room toward the unenthusiastic glow coming through the office door. The man sat at his desk, forehead braced in palm, the room in shadows except for the solitary shaft of light illuminating the papers spread in front of him.

Why hadn't Cal seen the resemblance before? Then again, maybe he had, choosing to shove the impossible to the back of his mind rather than believe somebody so generally, and genuinely, respected, a man Cal's father had admired to the nth degree, could harbor a secret of such magnitude.

Sherman looked up at Cal's light knock on his doorframe.

"Cal!" he said with a smile, removing his glasses. "What on earth are you doing here so late—?"

"Just thought you might like to know," he said mildly, "that your daughter's gone into labor."

For a moment, confusion crumpled Sherman's features. "My daughter? But Brenda's not even preg—" Realization bloomed in his eyes as he sagged back against his chair. It had started to rain. Outside, a car whooshed by, windshield wipers squeaking. "How did you know?" Sherman said at last.

"I was always real good at puzzles," Cal said, forcing his voice to stay even. "Even when I didn't have all the pieces."

"Does…Dawn know?"

"She's a little preoccupied right now, but I don't think it'll take her too long to put two and two together now. I haven't said anything. And Ivy's kept her promise. Heaven knows why, but she has." With that, his calm shattered. "For God's sake, Sherman! Dawn was *working* for you! And you knew she was looking for her father! What harm could it have done now to tell her the truth? Your wife can't be hurt anymore, Brenda Sue hasn't lived here for years—"

"And who'd trust a lawyer who didn't have the guts to acknowledge his own child?"

Cal refused to be derailed, either by Sherman's muleheadedness or this blasted sympathy determined to worm past Cal's anger. "Well, now's your chance to own up to your mistakes. And I don't know anybody around here who wouldn't respect that."

"And how can I do that without screwing things up even more than they already are?"

"I'm not sure you have much choice. In spite of Ivy's denial, Jacob's convinced *he's* her father. And he's likely to keep believing it until you tell the truth."

Sherman stayed silent for a long time, then said, "Until Dawn and I talked a little while back, I had no idea what she'd been through as a kid. Because of me, I mean. Which I know is stupid," he said on a rush of air. "I've lived in this town all my life, I should've known what it would've been like for her.'' He looked at Cal. ''To tell her now… She'll hate me, Cal. And with good reason.''

''And maybe this isn't about *you,* y'know?'' Cal got out through a tight jaw. ''Maybe it's about a little girl who always said it didn't bother her, not knowing who her daddy was, because she was too proud or too stubborn to let anybody know that deep down, she felt abandoned. Like she wasn't good enough for her own father to claim her as his own.''

Sherman's face fell. ''I swear, I was only trying to protect—''

''Your own butt.'' His chest tight, Cal took two steps closer. ''God knows, I'm no psychologist. I couldn't begin to figure out the connection between you refusin' to let her know who you really are and why she's so driven to succeed, or why the idea of staying in Haven gave her the heebie-jeebies. Or most important, why she's so scared to trust a man. To trust *me.* I just know there is one. Just as I know—'' he punched the space between them with his hat ''—that until you show her she's more important to you than saving your own hide, there is no way in hell I'm gonna be able to keep her, or my kid, here.''

''Now hold on here!'' Sherman got to his feet, his expression thunderous. ''God knows, I didn't do right by her, but you have no right to blame all your problems with her on me!''

''That's true,'' Cal said calmly. ''So let's say…seventy-five percent and call it square, okay?'' He crammed his hat back on his head. ''Now, if you'll excuse me, your daughter's about to have my baby, and *I* don't intend to miss it.''

Then he walked out, figuring the old man could just chew that over for a while.

''Here's one,'' Cal said, squinting at page 500 of the baby name book as he sat up beside Dawn on the bed where little whosits had made his appearance barely two hours before. Par for the course, she'd pushed the baby out as she'd always done everything, with a determined efficiency that stole his breath. Didn't even break a sweat. And right at this moment, he thought he'd never seen anything more beautiful than his baby nursing at his mother's breast. Except perhaps the expression on Dawn's face as she did. "It means 'born on a Friday,' but we could ignore that part."

"I see. In what language?"

He squinted at the book. "Akan."

"Oh, this oughtta be good." Outside, about a million birds greeted the new morning. "Okay…" She shut her eyes. "I'm ready."

"Yoofi," he said.

Her laugh startled the baby. "And here I thought you'd hit bottom with Orestes. Could you please be serious about this?"

"Okay, okay, I'm serious," he said, putting on his "serious" face. "How about…Oswald?"

"No."

"Romeo?"

"*Hell*, no."

He flipped through a few more pages. "Goliath."

Dawn chuckled. Even three weeks early, the baby had weighed nearly nine pounds. Any bigger, she'd said, and they would have needed the Jaws of Life to pry him out. "While reasonably appropriate…uh-uh."

"Erskine?"

"Are you deliberately trying to give our child a complex or what?"

"Fine." He slammed shut the book hard enough to make the baby's hands fly out. "Then you name him."

"I tried. You didn't like it."

"Dawn, honey?" Cal leaned over to grasp the baby's chubby, dimpled hand, emotion making his chest tight. When he'd first held him moments after his birth and looked into those alert, curious dark eyes… He swallowed and said, "Can you honestly see calling this bruiser Wesley?"

"Sure as heck beats Yoofi."

"Okay, tell you what—how's about I shut my eyes and just…stab at the page and see what we get."

"Oh, God," she said, laughing, as he made a great show of waving his hand, then zooming in to land on…

"Max," he said, his eyebrows shooting up. He looked at Dawn, who amazingly enough wasn't recoiling in horror. "It means 'the greatest.'"

"That…could work," Dawn said, then stroked a finger down the baby's fat cheek. "Hey, Max." She giggled when the baby's mouth twitched into what a generous person might call a smile. "Looks like we've got a winner," she said.

"Max Logan," Cal said. "I like it."

Silence jittered between them.

"Gardner," Dawn said, softly, looking at the baby.

Cal silently swore. But for once he kept his mouth shut. Now wasn't the time to get into it with her. Any more than it was the right time to tell her about his meeting with Sherman. Far as he was concerned, that ball was firmly in the older man's court now. If and when he decided to out himself was totally up to him. So Cal leaned over to kiss the mother of his son on the forehead, the scent of new birth stirring feelings of protectiveness and pride inside him. Then he palmed the baby's head, so close to his mother's breast, stroking his thumb over the pulse beating strongly beneath a thatch of fine, red hair before getting up to shrug into his denim jacket. "You need to get some rest. And I got me twenty-two large mouths to feed. I'll be back later—"

"I swear, Cal," she said, "if there was any way to make this work, I would. But making a baby isn't the same as making a marriage."

He hooked his thumbs in his front pockets, half wanting to storm out, half wanting to throttle some sense into her. Instead, all the things he'd sworn could wait came roaring out.

"Okay, maybe you don't feel like my brothers and their wives have enough of a track record to prove they can go the distance, but my folks sure as hell did. And if this is about our being too different to make it work, all I have to say is you couldn't find two people with less in common on the surface than my parents. Or more devoted to each other. It's not how much in common a couple has, it's how well they understand their differences."

"I know that," she said. "And you're right."

Cal frowned. Then sighed. "It's about the job, then."

"No." She slipped her index finger inside Max's fist. "I'm turning it down."

"You're *what?* Why?"

"Because it doesn't feel right. Leaving here doesn't feel right. Deal with it."

By rights this conversation should be resolving their problems. That it wasn't was confusing the hell out of him. If she was staying in Haven, and their differences were no longer an issue...

"Just answer me one thing," he said, his lungs so paralyzed he could barely get any air. "Do you love me?"

When she at last lifted her eyes to his, they were filled with tears. "What do you think?"

Cal took a step closer to the bed, bending down to cup her face in his hand. "I think I want to hear you say the words. Out loud. So we can both hear them."

"Fine," she said, clearly mad that he'd boxed her into a corner. "I love you, Cal Logan. I love you so much I can't look at you, or hear your voice, without getting the shakes. I love you so much that not five minutes goes by that I don't think about you in some way. But—" a tear escaped, trickling in slow motion down her cheek "—I'm...so...damn... *scared.*"

"Of *what?*" he said, catching the tear with his thumb, his heartbeat pounding in his head. "Why can't we just reach out and take what's right here in front of us?"

"Because almost everything I've touched recently has turned to dust! Because wanting something and making it work are two different things!" She blinked, sending a second tear slaloming down the trail left by the first. "And I don't think I could bear it if I failed at this. Losing a job is one thing. Losing you..." She shook her head.

He slipped one finger underneath her chin, gently tilted her head so she had to look at him. "You still afraid of being a mother?"

She started. And frowned. "Since I have no choice about that, how I feel's beside the point."

"No, it's not," he said, refusing to let her off the hook. "If you really didn't want to do this, you could let me have full custody and walk away."

"Cal! What a horrible thing—" She awkwardly shifted the baby, clutching him to her chest in the classic it's-okay-I've-got-you pose. "I could never do that! I could never leave my baby!"

"Why?"

"Because I love him too much, why else?"

"Cal," Ivy said from the doorway behind him. He straightened, then turned to see censure, and worry, in her eyes. "She doesn't need this right now."

"Then she shouldn't have brought it up!"

He started for the door, only to pivot back, frustration and what felt damned close to heartbreak vicing his words. "You know, watching how bad my father grieved for my mother scared the crap out of me, too, made me think for a long time I didn't want to ever love that hard. To need somebody that much…" The words got all jammed up at the base of his throat for a second, until he pushed out, "Until I fell in love with you and understood what was goin' on inside his head."

He took a single step closer, not sure which was worse, the agony he felt or the agony he saw. "I could no more leave you than you could leave Max, and for the same reason—because I love you too damn much. No matter how much it scares me. So why on earth would I do *anything* to let the only woman I've ever loved slip through my fingers?" When her mouth dropped open on a soft gasp, he added, "I know…nuts, isn't it? To hold out hope for something I always knew wasn't anything more than a stupid, pointless dream?"

He held her gaze for another second or two, just to make sure she got the message, then said to Ivy on his way out the door, "By the way, your grandson's name is Max." He glanced back at Dawn. "Last name to be decided at a future date."

* * *

On a ragged sigh, Dawn sank back against the pillows, as if Cal's exit had taken all her energy with him. In fact, when Ivy took Max away, she didn't even protest. Which, considering she hadn't wanted to let go of him from the moment Cal laid their son in her arms, only showed how fried she was.

Their son, she thought on another sigh as she watched her mother change his diaper and settle the now-snoozing baby in the cradle.

The cradle his own daddy had slept in.

Her heart cramped.

"You're going to spoil me," she said, feeling downright boneless. "Shouldn't I be doing that?"

"Honey, trust me. By the time you get him housebroken, you'll be so sick of changing diapers you won't be able to see straight. So enjoy it while you can."

"You think I'm out of my mind, don't you?"

Ivy looked at her, then came and sat beside her on the bed, brushing her hair off her forehead. "I think this isn't the time for you to be thinking about any of this, not until those hormones of yours have settled down a bit. You've been up all night birthing that baby. Time you got some sleep."

"After everything Cal just said? You must be kidding." Tears pooled in her eyes. "What's wrong with me, Mama? Why can't I trust my feelings?"

Ivy bent over and kissed her on the cheek. "Get some rest," she said. "Plenty of time for answers later."

"I'm sorry, Jacob," Cal said into the phone, backing up slightly as Ethel put a plate of scrambled eggs and bacon on the table in front of him. "I know that wasn't what you wanted to hear."

The minute Cal had climbed into the truck and started for home, whatever had been keeping him from keeling over had chosen up sides and left for parts unknown. That he'd made it back in one piece was a miracle in itself. Frank had taken one look at him and refused to let him help with the morning chores; Ethel had taken one look at him and forcibly sat him down at the table to feed him, never mind that Ivy already had, or that, at that point all Cal wanted to do was go to bed and sleep for about three days. But that wasn't gonna happen until he'd filled Ethel in on all the details, and filled Jacob in on those details that pertained directly to him.

"And you say you talked to the man who *is* her father?"

"Uh-huh," Cal said on a yawn, even as irritation clawed at him that by the time Cal had left Ivy's, there'd been no sign that Sherman was planning on coming clean. "Jacob?" he said when the silence had gone on longer than he liked. "You okay?"

He heard a sigh, then, "Yeah, I will be. It's just…all those years, thinkin' she was mine… And then gettin' to be around her these last few weeks, you know." Another sigh. "I mean, I'm glad the truth is finally out and all, but…"

"I know, Jacob," Cal said, the food blurring in front of him. "It's gonna take some time. But you know, nothing says what you and Dawn have between you has to change. She's not gonna like you any less because you're *not* her father."

"Huh. I guess you're right at that. Still…I can't believe Ivy'd go and do a thing like that, take up with somebody else so soon after I left."

Someday, maybe Cal'd see the irony, not to mention the humor, in Jacob's indignation, but right now all he wanted was his second breakfast and his bed and for that scene with Dawn to be nothing but a bad dream. So he mumbled something sufficient to disentangle himself from a conversation he didn't even want to be having and handed Ethel the phone to hang back up on the wall.

"Ivy and Jacob Burke," she said, shaking her head. "I had no idea. Talk about truth being stranger than fiction."

Oh, wait. If you think that's *strange…*

"So it was an easy birth, I take it?"

"Ivy said it was." Cal shoveled in a bite of eggs, forcing his eyes to stay open far enough to make sure they landed in his mouth. He flexed his hand where Dawn had nearly broken the bones during one of those last contractions. "Dawn might have a different opinion, though."

"I shouldn't wonder. Nine pounds," Ethel said, shaking her head. "And her first, no less. Of course, you were a shade over that yourself." Then she laughed. "Not bad for the runt of the litter."

After pouring him another cup of coffee, she joined him at the table with her own mug, questions—or at least one particular question—buzzing around her like a persistent fly. Finally she said, "Since you didn't announce anything other than the baby when you came in, I take it she's still sayin' no."

Cal swallowed past that tightness still there in the back of his throat, then took a long swallow of coffee, knowing his thoughts and emotions were far too shredded to say anything even remotely coherent. Ethel laid a hand on his wrist.

"Did you know your mama turned down your daddy four times before she finally said yes?"

His brow pinched, Cal met her gaze. "No. I didn't." He bit off half a slice of bacon and chewed, still frowning. "How'd you know that?"

"Oh, Lord…every time they'd get teed off with each other, your daddy'd say something like 'I should've quit while I was ahead,' and your mama'd say back, 'Well, nobody told you to ask me to marry you four times!' Then they'd get to laughing and that would be the end of it. Until the next time."

Cal leaned back in his chair. "You got any idea what held up the works so long?"

"I asked Mary about it one day, not too long after you were born. She told me she'd had her heart broken, that year she'd spent back East, and she wasn't any too interested in repeating the experience. Said she just wanted to be sure your daddy really wanted her. That she figured," she added with a sly grin, "if she didn't make him fight for her, he wouldn't really appreciate what he was getting. You want more coffee?"

"What? Oh…no, I'm fine. I…need to get some…sleep…" In a daze he stood up, watching Ethel clear his dishes. Then he asked, "Is that a true story? Or just something you made up to make me feel better?"

"Of course it's true, you think I got time to go making stuff up? But tell me something—would it make any difference whether it was or not?"

"No," he said after a moment. "I guess not."

"Well, there you are," she said, then called out to Cal as he lumbered out of the kitchen and toward his bed, "Your daddy was one patient man, that's for sure. And I don't figure you for anything less."

"Whatever," he said on a yawn, barely making it to the bed before he passed out.

Ivy plucked the phone off the receiver on the first ring, answering in a whisper. There was a pause on the other end, like it was one of those solicitors.

"Hello?" she said again, just in case it wasn't, and this time, somebody cleared his throat and said, "Did she have it yet? Our grandchild?"

She nearly wet her pants. "Sherman?"

"Well, who the hell else do you think it is?" he said like they'd been having regular conversations every day for the past thirty years. "So did she?"

"She had a boy. Nine pounds exactly. They're calling him Max."

Sherman laughed softly. "Max. Sounds like something Dawn'd come up with."

"She didn't. Cal did." Perturbed, Ivy smoothed a stray hair off her face. "And how'd you know she was even in labor?"

Another silence. "Cal didn't tell you he came to see me last night?"

Now she had to sit down. She dragged over one of the kitchen chairs and more or less fell into it. "No, he sure didn't."

"You think he told Dawn?"

Ivy glanced down the hall, not that she expected to hear anything. Last time she'd looked, mama and baby both were out like lights. "I doubt it. I think she'd've said something if she'd known."

She heard Sherman take a deep breath. "I…already called Brenda and told her the truth."

Ivy decided it was a good thing she was already sitting down, otherwise that would have knocked her over for sure. "What did she say?"

"The first time? Or when she called me back after she'd calmed down?"

"Oh, Sherman…I'm sorry," Ivy said, because amazingly enough, she really was. By the time a person reaches sixty-five, garbage like this should be behind him, shouldn't it?

"Don't be. I had it coming. Although I gathered she wasn't mad at me so much because of what happened, but because I hadn't told her—"

"Who's that?" Dawn said behind Ivy, scaring the bejesus out of her.

"What are you doing up?" she said, slamming the receiver against her bosom.

"Had to pee." She held out her hand. "Let's get this over with, okay?"

Wordlessly, Ivy handed over the phone.

Chapter 14

She'd figured it out already, but going into labor had kind of shifted her priorities. Then, after the baby's arrival there'd been all that craziness with Cal, and then she'd been too worn-out…but now seemed as good a time as any to deal with this particular loose end. Especially since the loose end had initiated the call.

"Hey, Sherman, it's Dawn."

Nervous laughter. "Hey, yourself. Your mama told me you had that baby last night."

"This morning, actually. So I guess I won't be in to work today."

"No, no…I wouldn't think so."

Then Dawn said, since at this rate her son would be graduating from college before anybody else brought this all to a head, "But you know…something tells me Max would really like to meet his grandfather."

Silence. Then: "I think Max's grandfather would really like that, too."

* * *

After using up every drop of hot water in the tank, Dawn slipped into a pretty white cotton nightgown Luralene had given her and threw open the bedroom window. A warm breeze scrambled inside, stirring her damp hair and filling her lungs with the scent of childhood. She might have almost felt at peace, if it hadn't been for the squirming mass of unresolved issues inside her. On a sigh, she gingerly settled on the floor beside the cradle to stare at her baby, an obsession about which she had no ambivalence whatsoever.

From the doorway, Ivy laughed.

"You be quiet," Dawn said, her cheek resting on her forearm as she stroked Max's hair. "This is embarrassing enough as it is."

"Why?" Ivy said, plopping into the armchair in the corner of the room. "Because you've discovered you're just like any other woman?"

"Like I said." Max's eyelids fluttered in his sleep, and joy and wonder and fear all knotted together in the center of her chest, and she thought of Cal and the love in his eyes, not to mention the understandable anger, and those wedged themselves into the knot, too. "When I look at him, everything else just…goes away. As if nothing is even remotely important except my baby."

"That's the way nature planned it, honey. To make sure babies get taken care of."

"So I'm not weird?"

Ivy chuckled. "Didn't say that." Then she added, "You hungry?"

Dawn shook her head, her cheek rubbing against her arm, then tore her gaze away from her son to look at her mother.

"Tell me about…all of it. You, Jacob, Sherman. Everything."

Ivy tilted her head at her. "What difference would it make?"

"Because maybe knowing the truth might help me finally figure out who the hell I am, okay? Why I do what I do and feel what I feel. So I don't screw up my life any more than I already have. Or my kid, if I can help it."

This resulted in a staring match. For, oh, at least a minute. Then, on a gust of air, her mother said, "I suppose it's hard to see how I could ever have been madly in love with Jacob Burke."

"No arguments there," Dawn said.

Ivy grimaced. "First off, at nineteen, he was one fine, sexy young man. And secondly, at twenty-five, 'in the moment' was the only place I ever wanted to live. So when this fine, sexy young man crossed my path, all I was expecting was a good time, for as long at it lasted. You could have knocked me over with a feather when I realized how devastated I was after he took off. Then I got mad at myself for being devastated. And looking to…I don't know. Get even? Restore my ego?"

"Like I did with Cal," Dawn said with a wry smile.

"On the surface, maybe. But only on the surface. Jacob and I are no more like you and Cal than melons are like marshmallows." She paused. "You sure you want to hear the rest of this?"

"Hey. I just pushed a nine-pound baby out of my body. I can take anything."

"Wait until you've heard the story before you say that," Ivy said dryly. She crossed her legs underneath her loose skirt and said, "Somewhere around two weeks after Jacob left, I fell apart. I was missing him like nobody's business, clients weren't exactly beating down my door, and all in all, I was feeling pretty damn sorry for myself. So I decided to get out, ended up in some honky-tonk out near Bushyhead, God knows why. And while I was sitting at the bar, nursing a beer I didn't even want, this tall, well-dressed man who looked even more out of place than I was hauled himself up on the stool beside me.

"We got to talking. And I swear, that's all I'd figured was going to happen. But if you think Jacob was different thirty years ago, you should've seen Sherman. Big. Handsome. Smart. Oh, Lord…I'd just about forgotten what it was like to talk to somebody who not only could talk politics—" she laughed "—but who didn't turn tail and run when the discussion didn't go his way. Anyway, his wife had filed for divorce a couple of days before, he hadn't seen it coming, even though they'd been having problems, he hadn't thought it was *that* bad...you get the picture."

"Unfortunately, yes," Dawn said, making a face.

"Hey. I warned you. So, we fell into bed. Once. Which is all it took for this cloud that had sabotaged my brain to clear and I thought, *What the hell am I doing with this man?* We had nothing in common, for one thing, and we were only using each other to numb our pain. And frankly—" she leaned over, lowering her voice "—the sex wasn't even that good, if you wanna know the truth."

Frankly, Dawn thought, she didn't.

"Anyway," her mother continued, "we both agreed there was nothing to pursue, and that was that. A week later, I found out Barbara'd changed her mind about the divorce, mainly because she was pregnant. A week after that, I realized I was. And yes, we were being careful—"

Dawn held up a hand. Ivy nodded and went on. "At first I thought about not telling him, letting him think, maybe, that it was Jacob's child—since I didn't figure on ever seeing *him* again. But then my conscience got the better of me and I thought I at least owed him the truth. What he did with it was his business.

"With the possibility of fixing his marriage so close, my news flattened him. He was sure if Barbara found out, she'd leave him again. For good, this time. Whether she would have or not, nobody'll ever know. But Sherman wasn't about to take that chance. And I don't guess I can blame him, really. I mean, Barbara might have been the most clueless woman I'd ever met, but I couldn't find it in myself to hurt her, either. Especially as I didn't have anybody but myself to blame for what happened."

Dawn frowned. "You didn't get pregnant by yourself, Mama."

"I know that. And maybe I would've handled things differently today than I felt I could then. But I decided I'd rather be labeled a loose-moraled hippie than a homewrecker." Ivy got up and went over to the bed, tugging at the covers so hard she nearly yanked them out. "Or having people think I 'tricked' Sherman into getting me pregnant so I'd have a meal ticket. And once the lid was sealed on the secret, there was no openin' it."

"Then why'd you stay in Haven?"

She swiped a stray hair off her forehead with the back of her hand. "Because some folks in this town have a way of putting out tentacles and hanging on to anybody who comes through. Especially people like Ruby and Luralene and Mary Logan, who made a far greater impression on me than the few around here with bugs up their butts. Besides, stayin' here was the only way Sherman would've gotten to see you grow up. And before you say I didn't owe him that, let me remind you that he did indeed provide for you from the day you were born, despite the constant risk that Barbara might find out."

"How did he do that?"

Ivy shrugged and picked up a pillow to fluff it. "All I know is I got a money order every week, in a plain white envelope with a Tulsa postmark." Shaking her head, she replaced the pillow, smoothing out the case with her palm. "He never missed a single week. And there'd always be more for your birthday and Christmas, too. I stashed away at least half of it for your college fund." She laughed. "Of course, you would decide to go to one of the priciest schools in the country. If you hadn't gotten that scholarship, we'd've never made it."

"Does it bother you that I might not ever be able to pay you back?"

Ivy frowned. "Would you expect Max to pay you back for something you gave him out of love?"

"Of course not."

"There you are, then."

Right on cue, the baby started to make little hungry squeaks; Dawn hauled herself to her feet, then scooped him up and carried him over to the chair Ivy had just vacated, her breasts tingling in anticipation. The baby's first tug on her nipple brought a gasp. And an unexpected image of Cal's dimpled grin.

"It hurt?" Ivy asked.

"No. It's…" She blushed. And cleared her throat. "Not at all what I expected."

Ivy continued fluffing and yanking for another few seconds, then said, "Got news for you, honey—the hormones that get all fired up from loving are the same ones that make us feel good when we feed our babies." She arched a brow in Dawn's direction. "And many women say they feel even more bonded to their babies' fathers right after giving birth."

Great. Now she was blushing clear down to her…

Never mind.

"That's called leading the witness," she said.

"Whatever works."

"You know," Dawn said, annoyance making her even warmer, "you've got some nerve pushing Cal and me together when you never got married yourself. I mean, okay, so obviously Sherman was nothing more than a sperm waiting to happen, but what about Charley? What happened there?"

Ivy plucked another pillow off the bed and punched it into shape. "To tell you the truth, I never really knew. I thought things were going as well as you did. Then one day he up and announced he didn't think it was working after all—" she tossed the pillow back on the bed "—and he left. And I decided then and there I obviously had no talent when it came to picking men, and I no longer had the energy to keep trying." She looked at Dawn. "And damned if I was going to let you get hurt again like that if I could help it."

Somehow Dawn figured there was more. So she waited. And sure enough, Ivy looked at her and said, "But you want to hear the irony of the whole thing?" She came around and dropped onto the edge of the mattress. "I'd always felt that marriage depleted a woman, robbing her of her identity, if not her soul. And it certainly robbed her of her freedom to make her own choices, as far as I could tell. And yet, as you got older, there were times I was so lonely I thought I'd lose my mind."

She glanced down at her hands, strong, sturdy hands that had brought hundreds of babies into the world and cooked thousands of meals and stroked away Dawn's fears when she was little. "And those were the times I would have given my eye-teeth to have a man look at me the way Hank, Sr., looked at Mary, or Jordy at Ruby. Or even Coop at Luralene," she added on a chuckle. "Like they couldn't quite believe how they'd lucked out." She paused. "Which happens to be exactly the way Cal looks at you. But what I bet you don't realize—" she got up and laid one hand on her head "—is that's the way you look at him, too."

Dawn shut her eyes, then opened one enough to see her mother's insufferable grin. "Oh, hell," was all she said, and Ivy chuckled.

The doorbell rang. Ivy went over to peer out the window. "It's Sherman," she said. "You ready?"

"As I'll ever be, I suppose." Ivy took Max so Dawn could propel herself out of the chair, only to draw her into a hug when she was on her feet. "Tell me something," Dawn said into her mother's hair, then pulled back to see into her eyes. "If the opportunity to fall in love, maybe even get married, came along…would you take it?"

"In a heartbeat," Ivy said, then gave her another quick hug, whispering, "God gave me a precious gift when he sent you to me. But He's given you *two*. So don't blow it, you hear me?"

"Can I hold him?" Sherman said, his customary self-assurance nowhere to be seen. All around them, a boatload of baby gifts attested to both the man's guilt, she surmised, as well as his desperate need to atone for the past. A small shard of bitterness, that he'd never asked to hold *her* as a baby, worked loose from her heart and kept on going, far less painfully than she might have expected.

"Sure." Sherman leaned over to take Max from her, then settled back in the corner of the sofa, grinning down at his sleeping grandson. A minute or so later he looked up, asked Dawn if she was okay.

She wasn't sure how he meant the question; she was even less sure if she wanted to find out. "Much better than I thought I would be," she replied, deciding that pretty much covered all the bases.

"I don't suppose you'll ever understand why I did what I did," Sherman said after a while.

Dawn glanced out the window, her fingers worrying the button on her cotton robe. "I know that no matter what you'd done, you would've been screwed. Which means I've got no right to sit here, thirty years after the fact, and judge the decision you and Mama made. A decision based on what boils down to nothing more than extraordinarily bad luck." She shifted her gaze to his. "But that doesn't stop the hurt."

His forehead creased, Sherman stared down into his grandson's face for another several seconds, then said, "Secrets are like acorns, you know? Always taking root someplace you don't want 'em to." He looked up at her. "For a long time, the seedling's easy enough to overlook. You keep meaning to yank it out, but you never seem to get around to it, and before you know it you've got a big old oak tree that just seems easier to leave be than to dig up. Until you realize the damn roots've worked their way into your pipes and are about to destroy your foundation. And it's not like you can blame the tree, when it's your fault for letting it grow to begin with."

His smile was sad. "When you walked into my office that day, looking for a job, I suddenly realized that I'd cheated on my wife a hundred times more by not tellin' her the truth than I ever had by sleeping with your mother."

Dawn picked up a stuffed frog he'd brought, wiggling its legs for a second before asking, "If you'd intended on keeping your secret, why did you hire me?"

He let out a long sigh. "Because at that point I figured it was only temporary, for one thing. And that it would've looked suspicious if I hadn't." He smiled. "But if you notice, I went away right after."

"Because you couldn't stand being with me?"

"Because I wasn't sure I could keep my mouth shut. Although, even if it hadn't've been for Jacob, I'd like to believe what little good sense I have left would've eventually worked its way to the surface. But I don't know." Sherman paused, then shook his head. "The stupid thing is, whether or not your Mama and I should've fooled around that night, I was separated at the time. Barbara'd even filed for divorce, for God's sake. Why I thought I had to act like a little kid hiding the broken pieces of his mama's favorite vase, I do not know."

His gaze shot to hers, so intense she started. "I have always loved you, honey. And I couldn't be more proud of the fine young woman you've turned out to be." A grin stretched across his mouth. "Not to mention you're one damn fine attorney. *Damn* fine. In fact…I'm thinking of retiring for good in a few months. Maybe trying my hand at writing that legal thriller I've always dreamed about. And…before all this, I'd been thinking about asking you if you'd be interested in taking over the practice for good."

Not exactly what she'd ever thought she'd be doing. Or want to do. And God knows, it wouldn't be easy on many fronts— making any real money at it, raising a kid and working fulltime….

"And now?" she said.

He shrugged. "I suppose that'd be up to you."

"Yes," she said after a moment. "I'd be very interested."

She could see the tension dissolve from his face, his shoulders. "Well. That's fine, then. When you're feeling up to it, we can hash out the details, how's that? But now—" he pushed himself up off the sofa "—I'm gonna let you get some rest while this pollywog gives you a chance."

Dawn stood, as well; Sherman kissed the baby's head and handed him back to her, then shoved his hands in the pockets of his Matlockesque linen suit.

"You think you can ever forgive me?"

"I think…I'd like to move beyond the past. That's all I can promise at the moment."

"Fair enough," he said with a nod. Then he added, "I've known the Logans my entire life, honey. Watched all those boys grow up. Cal, especially, being as he and you and Brenda Sue were all around the same age. Boy's got integrity and honor in his veins where most people have blood. And if you could see the way he looked at me last night in my office…" Sherman shook his head, then laid a hand on her shoulder. "Just don't let fear make your decisions for you, okay? Fear's like that itty-bitty acorn. And if we don't kick it out of the way…"

"I get it," she said.

"Make sure you do," Sherman said.

Nearly three hours later Dawn awoke from a nap she hadn't even intended on taking. Her heart knocking in her chest, she rolled over to check on Max in the cradle….

But he wasn't there.

Alarm spiked through her, propelling her from the bed so fast she nearly blacked out. Then—as she sat on the edge of the bed waiting for the woozies to pass—she heard Cal's laughter from the backyard. Which did nothing for the alarm factor, that was for sure.

Except…something else began to come into focus, no more than a faint shimmer at first. But as Dawn stood up—more slowly this time—slipping on her robe as she went over to the bedroom window, as she saw Cal sitting in the old canopied glider in her mother's backyard, chattering to the bundle of blankets in his arms that was their son, the shimmer grew brighter and brighter still, until at last it burned off the fading remnants of her fear like the morning sun the dew.

Sometimes, she thought, it wasn't about choosing.

Sometimes, it was simply about *accepting*.

The first thing Cal noticed was that the crease between her brows had vanished.

The second thing was that the rest of her face was equally

noncommittal. Which meant she wasn't giving him a single thing to work with here.

Great.

But he was a patient man. Ethel had said so. And now that he was awake, he decided he agreed with her. So he'd best be about demonstrating that, hadn't he?

"Max and I have been having quite the political discussion," he said, the glider groaning as he rocked.

"Oh, yeah?" she said.

"Yeah. Figured I'd better get him early before *somebody* fills him full of liberal claptrap."

She crossed her arms underneath her breasts, the late-afternoon sun igniting sparks of amber in her brown eyes, streaking copper through her hair. "Whatever happened to the concept of exposing the child to all the sides of an issue and letting him make his own choice?"

Cal stopped the glider, pretending to think this over for a minute, then cocked his head at her. Saw something in her eyes that rocked him to the core. And for once, something that didn't make him feel like yelling in frustration.

"Sounds good to me," he said. "But you know, I'm thinking…"

"Yes?"

"Never mind," he said, pushing off again. "You'd never go for it, anyway."

The glider stopped suddenly, nearly sending both him and Max flying; the feel of her curling up beside him, leaning her full weight against his arm with her head on his shoulder, sent him soaring.

"Try me," she whispered.

No guts, no glory.

"Well…it just seems to me, if you're really gung-ho about making sure Max is exposed to all sides of an issue…"

"Oh, I am. Absolutely."

"…then the most efficient way to do that, it would seem to me, would be to have him live with two people who never see anything the same way."

"I see," she said. "Well, I suppose that makes sense. In a convoluted kind of way. Especially if…those two people happened to be his parents?"

Cal's heart stopped. Only to start up again like a bass drum. "Then…you wanna live together or what? Ow!" he added when she slugged him.

"In your dreams, buster! If you think I put myself and everybody else through all that hell just to *live* with you—"

He stopped her tirade with a kiss. Which she made good and sure didn't end too soon by clamping her hand on the back of his head and holding on for dear life. Cal damn near thought he'd need CPR by the time the kiss ended, but that was just fine with him.

"Well, hell," he said, their foreheads touching, "I guess that means we'll have to get married."

"I guess it does at that," she said, snuggling against his shoulder again.

They rocked for a while, Cal more or less afraid to blink. Finally, though, he said, "You do realize you just did a total about-face, right?"

"Yeah, I know." She skootched closer. "Somehow I didn't think you'd mind too much."

"You can't come back later and blame it on hormones."

"Not to worry. Hormones have nothing to do with this."

"So…you're not scared anymore?"

"Never said that."

"I don't understand."

She started fiddling with his shirt buttons, which probably wasn't the smartest thing she could have done, considering she'd just given birth and button-fiddling was as far as they were going to get. "It's like you said. About the love being stronger that the fear. Or at least—" she removed her hand from his button to scratch her nose "—the fear of what life would be like without you is finally stronger than the fear of being with you. And I got to thinking about how I've never let something as dumb as fear get in the way of going after what I want…" She shrugged against him.

"You want me?"

"Mmm. Since I was five years old, actually."

"Whoa," he said. "Well," he said. "Nobody can ever accuse you of being impetuous, that's for sure."

She laughed, then got quiet again, reaching over his arm to play with Max's hand. "Sherman was here."

"Oh?"

"Yeah. So, you read him the riot act or what?"

"It was the least I could do. So…that's all out in the open now?"

"Yes, thank God. Although I'd figured it out, too, so I would've confronted him eventually, even if you hadn't. But I have to admit, I kinda got off on the knight-in-shining-armor routine. It made me feel…loved." She angled her head to smile into his eyes. "It's a nice feeling. Especially since you're the only man I've ever really loved, too. Which is one of the reasons I left Haven."

He frowned. "At the risk of spoiling the moment, that doesn't make a lick of sense."

"Hey. If you want logic, I'm not your woman. Besides, I said *one* of the reasons. Even now, I don't really understand why I felt suffocated here. Because I was illegitimate? Because I never knew my father? Because that's just the way I am?" She shrugged against him. "I honestly don't know. But I did know that you and I were very different, that we could be friends but that's as far as it could go. The girls you went out with…"

"I did ask you out, Dawn. You turned me down. Remember?"

"I thought you were being…kind."

"You're not serious?"

"I was at fourteen. I was serious about *everything*. Even worse than now. In any case, you can't deny we kept growing apart as we got older. And even though I was convinced we'd never be right for each other, there was this itty-bitty jealous spot that was just as glad I'd already decided to leave. Because

I couldn't stand the thought of watching you hook up with somebody else.''

Cal sighed. ''And I didn't go after you because I didn't want to get in the way of your dreams. Dreams that didn't include staying home and marrying a farmer.'' He rocked some more. ''So basically this whole thing was nothing but a huge misunderstanding?''

''No!'' Dawn sat up straight, practically vibrating with emotion. ''Oh, God, Cal…if we'd gotten together back then, if we'd gotten married, it would have ended in disaster! I had to get out of here, don't you see? Otherwise I'd've been miserable, always wondering what might've been, if I'd sacrificed my soul for my heart.''

''Which leads us back to my question,'' he said, his gaze steady in hers. ''What's different about now?''

Max started to fuss; Dawn took the baby from him, calmly putting him to breast like she'd been doing it all her life. And Max latched on like he'd been doing *that* all his life, too. Which, come to think of it, he had.

''This is going to sound corny as hell,'' she said over the baby's noisy sucking, ''but I really feel our lives are divided into seasons. I had to leave in order to appreciate what I had here. I went to New York because that's what I was meant to do then, where I was supposed to learn whatever I had to learn during that time. The problem was…''

She got quiet for a moment, then said, ''When I came back after Andrew and I fell apart, and we…fooled around, and then I got pregnant… It totally threw me into a tailspin. I mean…'' She blew out a sigh. ''Sex with you was supposed to be a fantasy fulfillment, okay? And that was it—''

''You fantasized about me?''

She actually rolled her eyes.

''Oh. Me, too. Never thought it would happen, though.''

''Neither did I. And that's my point. It did—''

''And it was great.''

''—and it was great—'' he noticed she was blushing. ''But afterward, especially when I realized I was pregnant, my brain

exploded, because suddenly nothing made sense anymore and
my life had spiraled completely out of control.'' She blinked.
''Loving you had nothing to do with it. Trusting you didn't
even have anything to do with it. And the more everything else
seemed to fall into place, like with me working with Sherman—'' she took a breath ''—with my *father,* when I realized
I could actually get into living here far more than I ever thought
I could, I finally had to face the one thing I least wanted to
face.'' She looked at him. ''That you'd eventually wear me
down and get me to marry you, only, then the day would come
when you'd look at the big-mouthed, bossy, uptight, snotty
woman you'd married and go, 'What the hell was I *thinking?*' ''

With a smile Cal stretched an arm around her shoulders and
tugged her against him again. ''Honey, something tells me I'm
gonna wonder that every day of our lives. And then I'll remember exactly what I was thinking and feel like the luckiest
damn man on the planet. Because I need you, darlin'. To keep
me grounded, to make me see and think about things I wouldn't
see or think about without you prodding me. I need you because...'' Smiling, he looked deep in her eyes. ''Because
you're silver and every other woman I've ever known has been
stainless steel.''

''Wow,'' Dawn said. ''I had no idea you were so...''

''Full of it?''

She laughed. ''Poetic.''

''Yeah, well, I think I just shot my wad for the next twenty
years, so don't go expecting stuff like that on a regular basis.''

After a moment she said, ''Yeah, well, I think after that, I'm
good for at least twenty years, so you're off the hook.''

''We'll be fifty,'' he said, then kissed her forehead. ''And
you'll have gray in your hair and all these great laugh lines—''

''And my boobs will be very well acquainted with my navel,'' she added on a sigh.

''That's okay, 'cause I'll be right there to hold 'em up for
you.''

''That a promise?'' she said, grinning.

He held her even closer. ''Absolutely. Because, see, Logan

men are real good at making promises.'' He tilted her face to his and kissed her, finally, *finally* getting his fill of that sweet-tangy essence that was uniquely Dawn's, as his dream sharpened into reality, a reality far too full of joy and laughter for life's sorrows to even make a dent. ''But they're even better at keeping them.''

Then he kissed her again, just to prove his point.

Epilogue

They had the wedding at Cal's the first weekend in June, on the very spot and the same day where Hank, Sr., had taken Mary Louise Brown to be his wife nearly fifty-five years before. Ivy thought that was fitting, that Cal's and Dawn's finally acknowledged love should bring healing to a house where grief had all but drowned out so many years of happiness.

Although Dawn had opted for a simple white dress that floated around her ankles and a few white rosebuds tucked into her French-braided hair, some of the guests, Ivy thought on a chuckle, seemed to be under the illusion this was Mardi Gras. Lord, she'd never seen so many outlandish hats in her life. Ethel's, in fact, was big as a beach umbrella, and nearly as bright. Not as bright as her smile, though.

Speaking of smiles…Jacob and Sherman were both grinning their heads off. For all intents and purposes, Dawn had gone from having no father to having two, though it was hard for Ivy to fathom how she'd ever been involved with either of them. And at the same time, looking at the pair of them decked out in their summer suits, she found it easy to see why. Easier, anyway. Not enough to resurrect that past with either of them, though. Oh, Lord, no.

Mary's beloved Steinway had been tuned, although you couldn't really tell from Luralene's butchered rendition of "The Wedding March." But nobody cared. Especially the bride and groom, who, judging from the goony looks on their faces, probably didn't even hear it. They were going to New York for their honeymoon—with Max, of course—to close up her apartment and for Dawn to show Cal the city she would always love.

Actually, what with all the babies in here, Ivy thought on a chuckle, nobody could hear much of anything. Poor Pastor Meyerhauser had to stop three times during the service to wait out this one's wail or that one's shriek of laughter. He didn't seem to mind, though. Nor did anybody else. Just like they didn't mind that it was hotter'n blazes in here, even with all the windows open. This is what life was all about, after all— weddings and babies and falling in love. It had taken the Logan boys a long time to figure that out. But—she glanced over at Hank, sitting with his arm resting on Jenna's shoulders, holding hands with his daughter; then to Maddie, near to popping with Ryan's baby, near to popping with love as she grinned at her husband, standing up with Cal as his best man—figure it out, they had.

It's okay, Mary, she thought, thinking of the boys' mama. *You can rest easy now.*

And from the piano—even though Luralene was now sitting clear over on the other side of the room—came a single, soft, peaceful note in return.

* * * * *

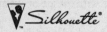

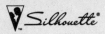

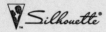

If you enjoyed what you just read,
then we've got an offer you can't resist!

Take 2 bestselling love stories FREE!

Plus get a FREE surprise gift!

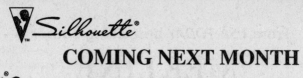

COMING NEXT MONTH

SIMCNM0104